That was how I didn't feel the blow coming.

First he pulls me into the air. Then he turns my bones liquid, so I'm easy to move. Then I hang, like a suicide. My feet kick together. I can see the carpet below them. My head hangs down. Once, I try to fight, but he's too much for me.

He buzzes like flies and flocks like bats—

My bones are liquid—

For one minute a glimpse: silent countryside, a man bleeding to death on the ground, quietly.

They are legion, and they knock to get in—

Fighting's a big mistake. What he does hurts all of me at once.

My bones are liquid, and they hurt, they hurt, like bones in an unquiet grave—

I *am* the grave.

Also by

KAT BEYER

The Demon Catchers of Milan #2: The Halcyon Bird

OTHER EGMONT USA BOOKS
YOU MIGHT ENJOY

Contaminated by Em Garner

The False Princess by Eilis O'Neal

The Shadow Prince by Bree Despain

THE

Demon

Catchers

OF

Milan

KAT BEYER

EGMONT
USA

NEW YORK

EGMONT
We bring stories to life

First published by Egmont USA, 2012
This paperback edition published by Egmont USA, 2014
443 Park Avenue South, Suite 806
New York, NY 10016

1 3 5 7 9 8 6 4 2

www.egmontusa.com
www.katspaw.com

THE LIBRARY OF CONGRESS HAS CATALOGED
THE HARDCOVER EDITION AS FOLLOWS:

Library of Congress Cataloging-in-Publication Data

Beyer, Kat.
The demon catchers of Milan / by Kat Beyer.
p. cm.
Summary: After surviving being possessed by a demon, sixteen-year-old Mia leaves
her family in New York to stay with cousins in Milan, Italy, where she must study her
family's heritage of demon catching in order to stay alive.
ISBN 978-1-60684-314-7 (hardcover) -- ISBN 978-1-60684-315-4 (ebook) [1.
Demonology--Fiction. 2. Demoniac possession--Fiction. 3. Americans--Italy--Fiction.
4. Family life--Italy--Fiction. 5. Milan (Italy)--Fiction. 6. Italy--Fiction.] I. Title.
PZ7.B46893Dem 2012
[Fic]--dc23
2011034348

Paperback ISBN 978-1-60684-427-4

Printed in the United States of America

To Ann Carlisle Beyer
and Karl Fritz Beyer
who gave me books to read
and eyes to read them.

Table of Contents

	Della Torre Family Tree	viii-ix
1	*Before Milan*	1
2	*La Sua Carne Rimarrà*	6
3	*My Grandfather's Choice*	16
4	*The Journey East*	30
5	*The Candle Shop*	40
6	*La Famiglia*	50
7	*Arguing Historians, Sighing Candles, Unexpected Visitors*	63
8	*The Case of Signora Galeazzo*	80
9	*Gas Roses*	94
10	*How Little We Know*	108
11	*In Which I Meet More Gorgeous Italian Men*	117
12	*Alba*	125
13	*The Return of Lucifero*	139

14 Hot Chocolate   151

15 Enter Signora Negroponte   159

16 Signora Negroponte and I Start to Untie a Knot   172

17 The Festa di Sant'Ambrogio   189

18 The Novena   202

19 All Are Invited   208

20 Il Caso della Famiglia Umberti   213

21 On Guard   230

22 La Befana   235

23 A Soldier   250

24 The Case   255

25 The Bell   262

    Acknowledgments   273

    Author's Note   277

1200s Pagano DELLA TORRE

Martino DELLA TORRE, *capitano del popolo*

1300s Alcione DELLA TORRE
3 children, one who survived the Black Death

1700s G. DELLA TORRE
founded candle shop at age 21, 1733

Francesco DELLA TORRE

1900s

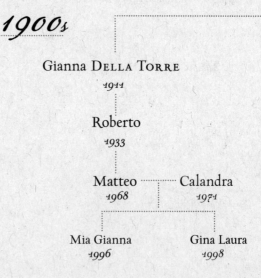

Gianna DELLA TORRE
1911

Roberto
1933

Matteo   Calandra
1968   *1971*

Mia Gianna   Gina Laura
1996   *1998*

Della Torre Family Tree

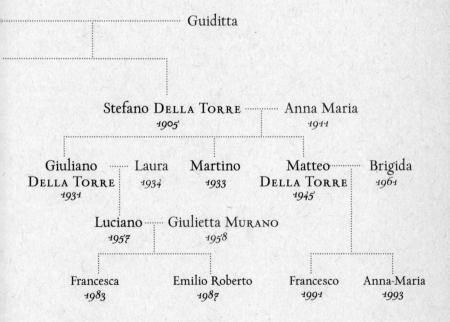

Guiditta

Stefano DELLA TORRE · · · Anna Maria
1905 · · · · *1911*

Giuliano · · · · Laura   Martino   Matteo · · · · Brigida
DELLA TORRE   *1934*   *1933*   DELLA TORRE   *1961*
1931   *1945*

Luciano · · · · Giulietta MURANO
1957   *1958*

Francesca   Emilio Roberto   Francesco   Anna-Maria
1983   *1987*   *1991*   *1993*

ONE

Before Milan

I used to be the kind of girl who would check under the bed and in the closet every night before going to sleep. Sometimes I would go so far as to slip out of my room, past my sister, past my parents snoring down the hall, and check every lock and catch in the house.

These days, when I walk into a house, I know at once who waits inside. I know who is quick and who is dead—and who among the dead does not want to leave. Even when I fear them, I know what to do. After Milan, I know.

I hated Milan when I first came here: principal city of the Italian north, huge, gray, industrial, possessed of polluted fogs and mad, narcissistic inhabitants. I could say I love it now, I suppose, but love is such a complicated idea. I'm pretty sure I'm not the first person to figure that out.

I've learned a lot in the last few months. I hope I get to live a few more and to keep learning. We'll see.

At the moment, I am leaning my elbows on the table in our family candle shop, in the Via Fiori Oscuri, in the Brera neighborhood of Milan. As I sit here, the streets are still full of light. Today's sun has a bit more than an hour left with us. In a few minutes, Nonno Giuliano will come back downstairs to check on me and ask if I have finished my studies, which I have, much to my surprise. He will reach into the battered wooden desk drawer, just like twelve generations of men before him, and pull out a large box of matches and begin to light some of the candles on our shelves. There are tall candles, short candles, candles the size of footstools with nine wicks, candles in the shape of Roman goddesses or antique columns. Some are already lit, the flames looking like fingertips beckoning to passersby.

Then he will go into the back room and return with a green bottle and three squat glasses. The bottle always seems to be half full. It never has a label, because we have friends as far away as the Veneto and Liguria who make their own wine and send us some. It's always a rich red, a good, red table wine, and he has to pour carefully because of the sediment at the bottom of the bottle. The wine has its own story to tell, about one hillside covered in grapevines, a yeast that one family has been looking after for twenty, thirty, one hundred, two hundred years.

After Giuliano pours the wine, exactly six minutes pass. Then a young man with curly, blond hair turns the corner from the Via Brera, quickening his step a bit as he comes within reading distance of the faded lettering on the window of our shop. He always loosens his tie just as he passes the big archway with the white moped parked outside, right across the street.

He always appears six minutes after the wine is poured, always. When he gets to the door, he pauses, resting his hand on the handle, as if he is asking permission. Giuliano looks up, not at the young man but at some place far away beyond the walls of the shop. He nods his head, pressing his lips together in the start of a smile—and the young man turns the handle and steps inside. The last words he says that can be heard on the street are, "*Buona sera, Nonno. Buona sera, Mia.*—Good evening, Grandfather. Good evening, Mia."

Then he comes in and sits down at the table with us, and takes a long sip of his wine. The sight of him makes my lungs seize up and my heart spit and cough like the engine of a *motorino*, always, the same way every time.

There's a sculpture in the Vatican Museum called the Apollo Belvedere. I want to go to Rome to see it, but I feel like I know it really well from the photographs. It's a Roman copy of the ancient Greek statue of Apollo, the sun god, and it looks like how he must have looked in his days of power, a prince with hair like the rays of the sun. This young man drinking wine looks like him, and I have seen women follow him as if he were a god. He's my cousin Emilio.

The first time I met him I was lying in a pool of my own urine.

I've never really gotten over that.

Here's how it all started. It was a warm, muggy evening, in a town very far away from here: my hometown of Center Plains, lost in the forests and factories of upstate New York. It's the kind of town that, if it got up tomorrow and decided not to exist, nobody would notice. School had just started, and the weather was unfairly reminding us of the best days of summer. I was doing my Algebra II homework. I hated algebra. I thought my life was hell. How wrong I was.

"I'm not good at anything," I said.

"You will be after this," said a voice.

"Who said that?" I asked. I looked around the room I shared with my sister, at the posters fading into the dusk, the stuffed animals leaning close together.

"Who's there?" I asked.

"A friend," said the voice at last, deep and gravelly, a man's voice, but there was no man in the room. How could there be? My father would have killed him before he made it up the stairs.

I felt each individual hair stand up, one by one, on the back of my neck.

Hundreds of times have I wished I had left the room at that moment. Perhaps nothing would have happened if I had gotten up, left my desk with the math homework that was making me feel hopeless and stupid, and gone downstairs to the living room, where my parents were watching TV.

But part of me was curious, and I stayed, even though my stomach was turning over and my hand holding the pencil had gone sweaty with fear.

Maybe if Gina had been there, not at some dumb rehearsal, none of this would have happened. If only Gina had been helping me with the math, making me feel even more stupid but at least getting it done. Gina could have kept out the dark.

"I don't think you could be a friend, actually," I said.

"Then I am someone who has something you need," said the voice.

"Yeah?" I asked, my heart beating so hard that my eyesight vibrated. My homework seemed to jump back and forth.

The homework pages rustled. The math formulas I had copied rearranged themselves, twining like narrow maggots into letters I could not read. I touched the paper and, beneath my fingers, it felt as if the whole sheet were crawling with worms. I yanked my hand back. The secrets I needed to know were right here on the page. If I could just read this, I would never again feel like I wasn't worth anything. I would never have that sinking feeling when the girls at school stopped talking as I walked by. If I could understand what was written here, I could get through being sixteen. . . .

I leaned closer and blinked. For a fleeting second, it looked like a piece of math homework again, and then—I leaned even closer.

That was how I didn't feel the blow coming.

TWO

La Sua Carne Rimarrà

First he pulls me into the air. Then he turns my bones liquid, so I'm easy to move. Then I hang, like a suicide. My feet kick together. I can see the carpet below them. My head hangs down. Once, I try to fight, but he's too much for me.

He buzzes like flies and flocks like bats—

My bones are liquid—

For one minute a glimpse: silent countryside, a man bleeding to death on the ground, quietly.

They are legion, and they knock to get in—

Fighting's a big mistake. What he does hurts all of me at once.

My bones are liquid, and they hurt, they hurt, like bones in an unquiet grave—

I *am* the grave.

They knock to get out, my bones. I don't blame them. I want to get out, too.

Too much to fight—

Yes, says the voice. And the worst thing about it, the worst thing of all about it, is that the voice isn't coming from outside of me anymore. The voice is inside me. It's as close as the lining of my brain.

> *But then I show you the power, don't I? Don't I? Answer. Answer!*
>
> *Yes, that's good.*
>
> *It's power to fly. It's power to see through the walls. It's power to see through the town. I go, I go. I hear the unspeakable things. I can see far. If only I had had this power before, when I was on Earth! Then justice would have been done, and so many things would not have happened. . . .*
>
> *I can fly far. Make the body go through the wall! Make it!*
>
> *It's stopped. Stopped at the wall. I can go outside this room like I always do, don't let it stop.*

I scrabble against the wall above the door. Then I know that the best way to open it is simply to open my mouth and scream. But a quiet scream. I don't need the voice for this. I stretch out my curled fingers. I open my mouth. The door blows open. I broke the spine of the hinges! That's power.

I come down the stairs. I see the stairs below my feet. I don't like the pictures on the walls. Down! Down! Every picture down. One by one behind me. Slam, slam, slam. That sound of shattering glass. Best sound, if you don't count breaking bone.

They're there. They're on their feet. Catch one, bash him against the wall. Yes.

She heaves him up and tries to run. I speak.

"The carcass slows you down, Mother," I say.

The look on her face is worth it all. She stares long enough for me to get in a blow.

But I miss. I never miss!

She goes out the door. She has him. The door is shut. When I open it—

It won't open. A man's familiar voice says, "Not there, you won't," and I stay inside and yell and scream.

I can see through walls. Not like they become transparent. More like they just don't matter.

I can see the things people are doing. I can see two guys fighting, a man hurting a girl. I can hear a husband and a wife lying to each other. I can slide close enough to hear them, inside their heads and out. That's how to tell someone's lying. Listen inside their head and out, and if the two don't match up, they're lying.

I can see high up over my town, to the edge of the baseball field, where four guys are beating up another guy in the dark, I can hear the sounds of their fists thudding again and again—while way up in a high building, I can smell the ink from a printer, where a woman prints list after list of names—and down another street inside walls prickling with rats I can hear someone say, "Make a fist. It makes the vein pop up." I can smell every stain, every sweat of fear and pain, I can smell it and taste it, hear it, feel it shuddering in the air. Now, that's power.

I go back to the room I'd begun in. I watch the wallpaper curl down from the ceiling in long strips like drying skin. I listen to the slow, ripping sound it makes. Sometimes I roar and the walls shake and posters fall, lamps fall and shatter. I throw the chairs across the room without touching them, because I can. They smash into the bookshelf. I make the books ripple back and forth like a domino set, slapping into the shelf sides like waves, and then I pluck them out, one by one, and send them floating, all without touching them, because I can.

When the sister tries to come in once, we throw her, too. She makes a wonderful noise hitting the wall. I hope we broke something. They get her out of the room, which is too bad.

One man comes, but I tell him things he has done, and he and his assistant run away. They call these priests? I remember priests, when they had the power of gods, the power of darkened rooms. This one barely gets past ringing the tinny little bell he has brought.

Another man comes, with more assistants behind him. They get us strapped down. They do tests with electric devices and their stupid holy water and their books, and I throw the books without touching them. The holy water stings like kindness. Why? Who believes it is holy anymore?

I hate the sting, and I know I have to be more cunning. It hasn't been hard to learn the tongue they speak. It is in the walls of the house, for one thing, though of course this is a new house, hardly half a century old, so the walls don't have a lot to say. I went inside the head of the first priest so easily. But this man, with his legion of assistants, is ready for us. He has set wards about himself and his legion. I can't tell him the terrible things he's done.

I have to be more cunning. I raise my eyes over the ocean and tell him what choices are being made about him. I tell him someone is dead. I show my power like great wings of blood over my head, like the depth of a pit dug for the nameless dead, like the husk of a genocide's heart. He goes. His assistants go. He warns me he will speak to someone of greater power, but I am not impressed.

I recognize the next one; yes, I do. He's gotten old. You all get old, you crumble into dust, and there's not a thing you can do about it. Not us. We don't get old.

He rings a small, silver bell. I come to see it.

I laugh and say, "Come to try like the last time?"

He says, "Yes."

I tell him the terrible things he has done.

He knows them all. So does the man beside him.

He says, "There's nothing you can show me of myself that

I have not seen. I don't fear you."

He rings the bell again, and it has a very sweet and tempting sound. I stay to listen.

"Listen to the bell, Mia. Listen to the bell."

I don't like him telling us that. I don't like him using that name. I roar. They leave. But they come back.

"Finished?" asks the old man, ringing the bell.

I opened my eyes and saw a stocky, gray-haired man standing over me. He spoke.

"Ascolti il campanello, Mia. Ascolti il campanello."

I had no idea how he had gotten into my room or why he was saying nonsense words. He looked familiar to me, but I knew I'd never seen him before. *"Ascolti il campanello. Guardi la candela."*

In front of my blurry eyes, a single tongue of flame fluttered. I thought, *Where it flickers, there is life,* and, as if in answer, it flickered away from me. Breath. I was breathing. There was life.

My ears were ringing, and my whole body ached. I felt desperately thirsty and wondered how long it had been since I'd had anything to drink. I wanted to ask the old man for water, but I couldn't seem to open my mouth.

The old man touched the bell again, and the sound of it was like sugar crystals on a pastry. I looked beyond him and thought I saw another face I recognized, gleaming, gold curls and watchful eyes. Behind him, I saw my family. Behind them were faces from photographs on our walls, the kind that people sometimes see on waking, until they notice with a shock that they can see the wall through the faces, and they wake up fully, saying, "A dream, a trick of the light," rather than believe that someone they love might have returned to gaze upon them in the night. At the very back stood an angry, dark-browed man: *Grandpa!* I thought. But when I caught his eye, he turned away from me and was gone before I could be sure.

The old man murmured, *"È ancora molto nell'altro posto,"* and above him the golden-curled head nodded in agreement.

The bell rang, bringing more sugar. I had to stay for the sugar.

But then the voice said, *I'm in your bones, you'll come with me,* and I knew I must.

"Mia Gianna Dellatorri, La comando di rimanere!" said the old man in a voice like the voice of gods. It echoed in hollows and spaces that the room did not have. I did not want to listen. I wanted to float, to rise farther. *I can still fly,* I told myself fiercely, but the bell began to ring insistently, constantly, and my eyes could not leave the flame. The old man spoke in his gods-voice, and now I could understand the words, as if some rough-voiced translator were growling them in my ears:

"Le Sue ossa rimarranno!"—Your bones shall remain!"

Though I could still feel the air beneath me, and I still cried out that I wanted to fly, I could feel every joint rattling inside me.

"La Sua carne rimarrà!"—Your flesh shall remain!"

I felt myself yanked down onto the bed. *You shall not control me! You shall not rule me! No one can own me!* I cried inside my head, knowing the ferocious truth of it in every fiber. I struggled to rise up.

"Il Suo spirito rimarrà!—Your spirit shall remain!"

I felt my lungs fill with sweet air and my nostrils with a bittersweet smoke—what were they burning in the room? Then I exhaled and something fled on my breath. I felt it running up my dry throat like a man fleeing an avalanche. There were roars and howls and darkness, and then only silence and the flame, which miraculously had remained alive in the midst of the rushing air and sound. In the silence, staring at the flame, I could smell that the smoke had faded, leaving behind another scent, like cinnamon.

The old man spoke, but I did not understand a word he said. Someone else moved into the light and translated in a warm, accented voice: "He says, welcome back, Mia Dellatorri. You are safe now. My name—his name, I mean—is Giuliano Della Torre."

Then I saw that I was lying in my bed. Over there was my sister's bed, and her teddy bear and her five Beanie Babies. I saw that I wasn't flying. The wallpaper was torn, and my books were in the wrong order on the shelves.

I realized that I was lying in a pool of my own urine. I hoped they wouldn't notice, but they had seen me shift and glance.

"It's normal," said the young man, resting a hand on my shoulder, and then looking beyond the old man for a moment. I followed his eye and saw my mother. She came forward quickly.

"Sweetie," she said, and wrapped her arms around me.

I couldn't seem to move on my own.

"Emilio," my mother said to the young man, "could you give me a hand?"

"Of course," he said, and helped her lift me off the bed. Mom and Gina got me out of my wet clothes, the same sweats I'd been doing algebra in, whenever that was. Dad changed the sheets and the mattress cover both, and I watched him from where I slumped in my sister's favorite chair in the corner. When he was done, he came over and carefully reached out to touch my face, just once. "I have to go to work. Be good," he said, like always, and somehow I thought this was funny.

My sister sat on the floor beside me and held my hand.

"Gina," I said. She looked up. "I'm so thirsty."

"I'll get you water," she said, standing up. Her voice was shaking, and there were tears in her eyes. She looked exhausted. I realized the morning sun was shining on her face. The last clear memory I had was of the evening shadows; how long had it—had I—?

The old man came in with a bowl. He passed it to my mother, and she knelt beside me and said, "This will help with the thirst. Plus you need to eat, sweetie. You haven't eaten properly for four days."

"Four days?"

Out of the corner of my eye, I saw my sister duck her head quickly. My mother smiled, the saddest smile I'd ever seen.

"Eat, and rest, and I promise we will explain. I promise."

I opened my mouth, and my mother fed me beef broth. Suddenly I remembered sitting on my high chair—or maybe I remembered seeing my sister sitting in the high chair?—opening my mouth for the baby food and turning my head away sharply when I didn't want any more. I remembered my mother used to make little airplane sounds and fly the spoon toward my mouth.

She didn't make little airplane sounds, thankfully. I was embarrassed enough. The broth was not too hot and had small bits of pasta in it. After one mouthful, I thought, like a baby, *I like it!* and I ate as much as I could.

"Piano, piano," cautioned the old man, Giuliano, and Emilio echoed him, "Slowly, slowly. You haven't eaten. You must not get sick."

After a few more mouthfuls, they carried me back to the bed, and I slept.

THREE

My Grandfather's Choice

"You want to do *what*?" My father was saying as I came down the stairs that evening, thinking that someone had replaced my legs with Jell-O. I wondered where all the photographs in the stairwell had gone. "Hi," I said unsteadily as they all looked at me.

"Gina!" my mother called sharply. Gina's head appeared around the kitchen door. She saw me and started guiltily. "You were supposed to be watching your sister," my mother said.

"She can watch me from here, Mom," I put in, and lurched my way to the couch. "You were all talking about me, I can tell."

Emilio was watching me, and I thought maybe he seemed pleased.

"Go back to your bed," said my father, and normally when he used that tone of voice I would have immediately done what he said. But something inside me was awake.

"Someone will have to carry me," I said. "Anyway, since you were talking about me, you should tell me what you were saying."

I saw him start to swell up, as if he were going to shout, and said quickly, "Come on, Dad, I've had a really hard couple of days. . . ."

Suddenly everybody started to laugh in a painful, edgy way. Gina came into the room and plopped down on the couch across from me.

"She's got a right," said Mom.

My dad gave in, deflating, but it was Gina who spoke.

"They want to take you back to Milan," she said.

"Uh?" I said.

"Over my dead body," said my father, speaking at last.

Emilio stared at him, but it was Mom who said, "Matt! Please don't say such a thing. Don't you think it will hear . . . ?"

Emilio nodded vigorously.

At this point, Giuliano snapped at Emilio.

"Ancora non siamo stati presentati," he said, leaving us staring. Emilio nodded.

"My grandfather wishes us to be formally introduced to you, Signorina Mia. I believe he feels that our first meeting was . . ." He shrugged, and I thought I knew what feelings he was trying to express. *Awkward as hell*, maybe? I turned to Giuliano.

Emilio said, "May I introduce to you my grandfather, Giuliano Pagano Della Torre, your first cousin twice removed. And I am Emilio Roberto Della Torre, your third cousin."

My what? I wasn't really surprised that they were related to me; that explained why they both looked oddly familiar.

"Piacere di fare la Sua conoscenza," said Giuliano gravely, holding out his hand. I shook it, conscious of his powerful, blunt-fingered grip. I looked at Emilio, not sure what to say. He smiled, and I almost forgot everything but his eyes.

"You can just say, *'piacere,'* " he offered.

I tried, but it didn't sound right at all.

Emilio held out his own hand, with the same blunt fingers but smooth, golden skin, his grip warm and nearly as strong as his grandfather's.

"Pleased to meet you. We're . . . cousins?" I tried to remember what he had said.

"Yes. It's complicated."

At this point, my dad decided he'd had enough.

"I'm telling you, she's not going," he said. "My father is turning in his grave right now. He never let us forget that he left Italy to get away from you. Now, I'm grateful for everything you've done for Mia, even though I still don't understand what went on in that room. But we will do what we need to do to take care of her, even move if we have to."

"Did your father ever explain to you why he left us?" Emilio asked.

"No. But I know something happened that made him really angry. I don't know what it was, and I don't think I want to, but you must be crazy if you think I'm going to let my daughter go back with you."

He looked around at all of us, then spoke directly to Giuliano.

"Before you came, our parish priest, Father Amadoro, tried an exorcism. It didn't work. He didn't say this, but I don't think parish priests are supposed to conduct exorcisms. I think it's against the rules."

"You told us that," Emilio said with grave politeness.

"I know. But that is not all that happened. I think I told you also that he sent for the diocesan exorcist. So this old guy came up from Albany with his team, and he did all these tests and said, yeah, this is a possession, not just some—your daughter isn't crazy. He also tried an exorcism. It didn't work. So he called some colleague of his in Rome, because he didn't think there was an exorcist in the United States who could handle this—this demon, or whatever it is. I didn't tell you that."

Emilio shook his head and murmured to his grandfather, who kept his eyes on my father and leaned forward to show he was listening very carefully. Judging from my mom's face, Dad hadn't told her that last part, either. Gina and I caught each other's eyes.

"You know what the guy in Rome said? He said that under no circumstances was an exorcism to be performed on a Della Torre."

I blinked.

Almost before Emilio translated, Giuliano nodded, his eyes narrowing. He seemed about to speak, but my father wasn't finished.

"So you tell me why the head guys in Rome are denying my daughter the rites of her Church."

I should mention that this is the most Catholic I had ever heard my father be. I don't think we had been to Mass since Easter. As far as I can tell, Father Amadoro, our parish priest, performed his illegal exorcism on me out of love for my grandfather, Roberto Dellatorri, one of his most faithful parishioners.

After my father finished speaking, we had to wait while Emilio translated for his grandfather, and all I could hear was his pure tenor, changing my father's words into rhythmic, poetical, meaningless sound. Giuliano nodded seriously and then began to speak. When Emilio translated, he echoed his grandfather's solemn tone.

"We should have been here sooner. We didn't get the warning in time. Rome doesn't like us, and it's better they don't know."

Giuliano seemed to realize this was not going to help his cause, and he thought for a moment. Then he spoke again, gesturing at me. "Matteo Delatorri, your father was a brave man, a good man, with a strong sense of justice. But you must understand: in our work terrible things happen. You have seen what happened to your daughter. Mia is very lucky to have survived such a powerful attack. We . . ." He paused, Emilio pausing also in his translation, and they looked at each other. Even without knowing Italian, I could read their eyes plainly—"How much do we tell?"

"I don't know how to say it." Giuliano went on at last. "Sometimes we have to take desperate measures. We are like doctors who have to decide—save the mother or save the child?

We had to do that with . . . with someone your father loved. We had to choose between the life of that person and the life of many people. Pray, Matteo Dellatorri, that you never have to make that choice. Pray." Giuliano's eyes had gone dark during this speech, and his voice sounded like the voice he had used during my exorcism.

"But you, and yours, you are still Della Torres, whether you like it or not. Roberto could cross the ocean but he couldn't change his . . ."

Here Emilio paused, frowning up at the ceiling, then went on, "What is the word—*genetica*? Is it the same?—He couldn't change his genetics.

"You could move house, you could fly over the sea, you could change your name—or misspell it in a new country—whatever you like, but you would still be Della Torres.

"The demon will still come for Mia. And the next time, we might not be able to find you in time to rescue her.

"We are having to revise much of what we thought we knew about this demon. We do know that it has come before, and that . . . that Mia is the first one to make it out alive."

We all sat silent for a moment. *You haven't answered the question about Rome,* I thought. *Why did they say no exorcism on a Della Torre?* Giuliano began to speak to his grandson again, answering as if he'd heard me out loud.

"As for Rome, of course they don't like us," Emilio translated. "You have seen how dangerous this work is. They think we are amateurs, that the work is too dangerous for us.

"We have one or two friends in Rome, and they help ensure

that the Vatican doesn't notice us. We have done our best, for centuries, to make certain that Rome doesn't notice: even now, they are perfectly capable of ending the lives of those they do not like. I wish we had gotten here sooner.

"You must understand. Mia is in danger here. We must take her back with us. Our home in Milan is very well protected. We must keep her safe there and prepare for the next assault."

"How did you find us, anyway?" Gina asked. "I thought Grandpa just left Italy and that was it. He never even wanted to talk about you guys."

Emilio surprised me by chuckling. He translated briefly for his grandfather, then turned to us and said, "I can answer this one. We used an extremely magical tool: an address book."

We just looked at him. None of us thought this was as funny as he did. I wondered how long I was going to have to live with these weird people, if my dad let me go. Emilio stopped smiling and continued, "Your grandfather wrote his family out of his life, but the family did not do the same. Many who left sent letters home to Milan, and those who stayed in Italy wrote back. I have seen the letters about your grandfather. I have seen the letter that announced your birth, Mia."

He held my eyes for a moment. I was the one who looked away.

"You've been spying on us this whole time?" my father snapped. "On top of everything else."

Emilio looked sharply at him but took a breath before answering in an even voice. "Not spying. We only knew what your names were, how to find you, and . . . who was still alive."

We were all pretty quiet after this.

"Wait. You knew how to find us, but how did you know that Mia was in trouble?" Gina pressed.

Emilio smiled at her. He said to Mom and Dad, "You have raised very clever children, I think. I can't tell you everything, but I will tell you that one way we found out was that a friend of ours told us that your bishop had called Rome in quite a hurry. So we hurried, too."

Gina nodded. "I wondered if the priest had told you. He was a good friend of Grandpa's."

Emilio shook his head. "No, not the priest. Most of them can't afford to associate with us."

He looked like he didn't want to tell us any more. After a moment, though, he chose to go on.

"This whole experience, as terrifying as it has been for all of you, frightens us for another reason: it's the first time this particular demon has attacked someone outside of Milan. We didn't even know it could. We have been struggling with it for so long," Emilio went on, and I could tell that he had meant to say something else, "that we thought we knew its ways. Now we find ourselves in the dreadful situation of knowing far less than we thought. That's another reason to bring your daughter, our cousin, back with us."

We just looked blankly at him. What was there to say? I could tell my father wanted to make some serious head-of-the-family pronouncement, but even he had to hold back and think.

Giuliano asked the next question in such a serious voice that I thought he was still talking about Milan or Rome. He wasn't.

"Perhaps we could take a break for dinner?" translated Emilio.

Emilio told me over dinner that Italians usually eat later in the evening than Americans, but that he and his grandfather had both been hungry, very hungry. We went out because my father could tell my mother was too tired to cook (that's my dad for you, right there—didn't offer to cook, even though he's perfectly good at it). I had expected them to want Italian food. But when my father asked, Emilio said, "We noticed an interesting-looking Chinese place on the way from the airport. Is it any good?"

So we went to The Unusual Luck, and I got to order my two favorite dishes even though I could tell my dad was still angry—at me, maybe—or afraid of me? Odd, anyway, about me. We were pretty quiet up through wontons and egg rolls, but then everybody started to look less shocked and tired right around General Tso's chicken. I was surprised to see that both Giuliano and Emilio could use chopsticks, and Gina asked, "So you have Chinese food in Italy?"

Emilio laughed.

"We have everything in Milan. My grandfather only started learning how to use chopsticks a few years ago, though. He's still very proud that he can, can't you tell?" he added, giving us the world's most beautiful one-sided grin.

We giggled and all three of us looked at Giuliano, who

frowned with his eyebrows, smiled with his eyes, and clacked his chopsticks at us affectionately.

Some Italian guy started singing to techno music in Emilio's pocket and he jumped up, pulling out his cell phone.

"Excuse me," he said, and headed outside, leaving his grandfather and the rest of us to stare at one another and wonder how we were supposed to talk without him to translate. Giuliano pointed after his grandson with his chopsticks, waggling his eyebrows and opening his mouth a couple of times.

"Curlfrond," he announced gravely at last. "Alba."

We waited politely.

"Oh!" said Gina. "Girlfriend! His girlfriend, Alba."

"*Sì*, curlfrond," agreed Giuliano, grinning at Gina. He launched into a complicated game of charades, mysterious English and Italian, and while we tried to follow it, I noticed a tiny, sad feeling in my chest. It couldn't be because Emilio had a girlfriend, right? I mean, of course he had a girlfriend; he was so gorgeous.

Emilio and Giuliano went back to the hotel they were staying at (Gina and I had been moved to the guest room because we were both too scared to go back into our own room). We went home, and Mom and Dad started the argument I could tell they were going to have. "Calandra," Dad began. He never uses Mom's name unless he knows she's going to disagree with him.

I knew I wasn't allowed to stay for the argument, and I didn't really want to. I walked back out onto the porch and looked at our yard.

We didn't take very good care of it. My dad has spent the last four years saying he's going to get rid of the rusty swing set we grew out of long ago. There was a dead lawn mower crowned with morning glories, and a plastic car, its red hood bleached pink by the sun, half buried in the weeds nearby. There were two plastic chairs for sitting in while you were minding the barbecue. There was a chain-link fence, one of the low kind, covered in more morning glories and dividing our yard from our neighbors, most of whom did not do much better than we did. In our neighborhood, yards are for putting the kids and the dogs out in, and they look like it and smell like it, too. We don't have a tree in our yard, but the D'Antonis next door do, a big, neglected crab apple that's good for climbing and shares its shade with us.

It was a Saturday in September, hot and muggy, still summer even though school had started. One day soon, we would wake up to find the temperature had dropped overnight, leaving the air clear and cold, and we would know it was autumn. I wondered whether I would be allowed to go to Italy, or whether the law said I had to stay in school here. What would I do there? How long would I have to stay?

Terrifyingly none of the adults seemed to know the answers. Part of me thought, *Thank heavens, no more essays on the beauty of poetry for Mrs. Beaumont.*

This is how I realized I had already made up my mind, not by considering the good and bad things about going or staying, but by noticing that I was already trying to work out what it would be like.

I remember everything about that moment, the sweat dripping down my neck and under the collar of my T-shirt, the way my cutoff jean shorts felt a little tight after another summer of growing, the radio blasting from the D'Antonis' driveway (their son, Tommaso, was working on his car again), the smell of cut grass and barbecue and a hint of dog poop.

I heard my sister come out on the creaky porch behind me. She had worn the same pair of flip-flops all summer, and I could hear them flapping on the wood. I turned around.

"Hey," I said.

"Hey," she said.

We sat down on the porch steps.

"Maybe you could come with me," I said.

"Maybe I could, later. We don't have money for more than one ticket."

We sat for a while, picking at the grass that grew in the cracks on the steps.

"I knew you had decided," she said. "I knew you would go."

I thought about not having her around to read my mind.

"Are you mad? Or maybe jealous?" I asked.

She thought about this, then shook her head.

"Yeah, I mean, I would love to go to Italy and everything," she answered. "But I saw what you were like."

She paused, pulling at a particularly tough piece of grass as if that were all that mattered. "It was terrifying. I don't know what it was like for you. I mean, I couldn't really tell whether you were there or not? Don't take this the wrong way."

"I'm not," I said. "I understand."

"Anyway, it scared the crap out of me, and I think what you'll have to do over there will be scary, too. It's going to be hard work, and I think it's going to take you to the edge, know what I mean?"

When Gina raised her face to me, the joking light gone out of it, that's when I really got frightened.

"Wow," I said finally.

"Yeah, wow. I guess we're all kind of still in shock. You too, I bet."

"Yeah."

I threw a clump of grass; it seemed to fall slowly in the evening heat.

"Gina . . ." I had remembered something. "I'm sorry about anything I did to you."

She closed a hand over mine, and her touch started my tears. They fell on my knees, one little splash, another little splash, another. When I finally looked up, she said, "It's okay. It's okay, because now I can see you really are back."

I cried even harder, letting her put her arms around me and hug me tight until I was finished.

"I still don't believe it, right?" I said. "But I have to. Things happened that I can't explain, Gina. But I'm starting to understand that I have to go with them. That is," I added, "when hell freezes over and Dad lets me."

Gina snorted.

"He has to let you go," she said. "We all do," she added, and I heard tears in her throat. Then she braced herself and went on,

"He knows it's the only way, and he doesn't like it. That's why he's shouting."

I stared at her.

"How come you always know this stuff, and I can never figure it out until long afterward? It always takes me, like, a year. I'm the older one, right? I'm supposed to be the one who figures everything out." I sighed and pulled up some more grass.

She shrugged and looked out over the yard. After a while she said, "I know you think I'm the smart one. But you know these things. And you know other things. You sell yourself short, Mia. You always have. Maybe it's *because* you're the older one, and they expect so much of you. I don't know."

It's always seemed strange to me that I'm the big sister. Gina is so smart, so pretty, so together—all the things I am not. Sometimes people think she's the older one, even though she's two years younger. It's like my parents got it right on the second try. Or maybe the first kid gets all the worry, and the younger one can relax more.

I turned my thoughts back to leaving and Italy.

"How soon do you think?" I began.

"As soon as possible." She grinned, poking my shoulder. "No, but really. I think you should go as soon as you can. We don't know when *it's* going to come back."

FOUR

The Journey East

The next morning, as I was waking up, I tried to see through the walls, but they were blunt and closed. I rolled out of bed, wondering if the world would ever make sense again. At least breakfast felt real and normal: orange juice, toast, bickering parents, my sister running late. I wondered if anyone would ask after me at school. Probably not.

I looked at myself in the mirror after breakfast. (My mom always teases me about that. *When you were a kid, you hardly knew mirrors existed. Now you're a teenager . . . making up for lost time, I guess.*) I was as pale as a Goth chick, with huge, dark circles under my eyes. At least I had lost a little weight; nobody in my family is chunky or anything, but I always feel kind of flabby next to my willowy sister. I saw the same old features:

huge, oversize mouth, eyes too close together, nose straight but too long, eyebrows that would be perfect if they weren't so thick, and mousy, thin hair that makes people assume I'm not actually related to my sister and my parents, all of whom have lustrous, thick, black hair. Sometimes I've suspected this myself. But my cheekbones, which would be interesting if I were thinner, clearly come from my dad. My sister has them, too, and I guess she must be thinner (she will never tell me how much she weighs), because they sure are interesting on her.

"I look like shit," I told the mirror. "I mean, more like shit than normal."

I knew my mom was out so I wouldn't have to put money in the swear box. I started to cry.

I suppose we must have done stuff to help get me ready to go. I remember Dad being glad my passport was still good, the one we had gotten for a trip to Jamaica ages ago. I don't know what they told the school, just that I didn't have to go. Gina and I shared the foldout couch in the living room, because I kept waking up screaming in the guest room. Gina wouldn't let me sleep alone; she watched me fall asleep every night and woke up before I did. I didn't think about it until later, but I guess she must have wondered what would wake up. If she was afraid, she never told me.

Finally my bags were packed with everything I thought I'd need, plus everything Dad and Gina thought I'd need, minus the things Mom took out after we realized there were too many suitcases.

On the way to the airport, we had one of those lovely family drives where everybody is silent for the first hour. Finally my sister cracked a joke, and things got a little easier. But my dad still glowered, and my mom touched her eyes from time to time. Emilio and Giuliano followed in their rental car, giving us a last few minutes alone.

The airport seemed unbearably loud to me. There were too many people whipping past. I almost thought I could hear each thought, almost see through the thick cement walls.

I tried to pick up my bags, but I was still too weak. Gina carried them, snatching them up in a way that dared anybody to try to take them from her.

"I love you, sweetie," said my mom.

"E-mail me when you get in," said my sister.

"Be good," said my dad.

They all meant the same thing. They embraced Giuliano and Emilio, and my father said, in a fierce man-to-man voice, "Take care of her," to which Giuliano replied in Italian. They seemed to understand each other. Gina hugged me one last time and whispered in my ear, "Find out anything you can about Grandpa, too." I squeezed her back to show I'd heard.

Then we went through security and boarded, waiting while everyone else got on and wrestled their bags and pointed out that someone was sitting in their seat. I had been on a plane a few times before: to Disney World in Florida, that one time to Jamaica, and stuff we had to do with my mother's family—funerals, weddings, reunions. But I had never been on a plane so big, designed to cross oceans, carrying so many hundreds of people.

Since we had bought my ticket separately, I was going to have to sit alone, but Emilio showed a streak of kindness and worked out that the elderly man sitting next to him would much rather sit in my seat, next to his daughter and grandchildren. He and Giuliano gave me the window seat, "Because you have never seen Italy before."

He didn't mention that first we would have to look at hours of ocean. It spread to the horizon in every direction, and I could clearly imagine being swallowed, thrown by the buffeting winds as the plane spun out of control. My palms sweated as I gripped the seat, and I shut my eyes and looked away. It occurred to me that I had felt exactly the same way when the demon had gripped me. I hadn't really known it until that moment over the sea, I think. I had been too numb to remember.

"Book?" said Emilio beside me. I turned around and stared, not comprehending him. It took me a second to realize he was holding out a novel.

I smiled, showing too many teeth, and said, "No, thanks. I'm fine," and then groaned inside. I had already decided that I always sounded like an idiot around him. He shrugged and tucked it in the seat pocket.

"It's called *The King's Last Song*. I just finished it," he said conversationally. "It's very good: very beautiful. It's set in Cambodia, but it's kind of a combination of Italo Calvino and Salman Rushdie—have you read anything by them?"

I really didn't want to talk. "I haven't even heard of them," I said. "We don't exactly study them in school."

He smiled. "Ah, yes, you study the American greats. But what do you like to read in your spare time? I expect you're a little old for Harry Potter?"

I was not going to admit that the last Harry Potter book was sitting in my backpack at my feet. My sister and I had exchanged copies before I left, so I had her copy with her name written in her careful, round handwriting: *Gina Laura Delatorri*.

"Oh, yeah," I lied. What I wanted more than anything at that moment was to take out that book and run my finger over her name on the flyleaf.

"Well, anyway, I'll leave it right here. This is a very long flight, Mia, and—Mia?"

Something else had said my name. I dragged my eyes to the window. At first I thought it was riding on the wing. Without knowing how, I recognized what I saw: a misshapen body, and a face too long for a human one, grinding its jaw and looking at me from under half-closed eyelids. It was naked, and too obviously male. I could see the airplane wing through it. Then it was gone.

I didn't know how strong Emilio was until I felt his fingers closing on my wrist, his grip so tight it hurt. I was standing in front of the exit door, reaching for the handle. Why was I there? Everybody was staring at me.

"Mia, look at me."

I couldn't. I looked at Giuliano, standing behind him, who

had closed his eyes and was murmuring a prayer that didn't sound like the words he had said before. It seemed to have a different rhythm, and the words had a different angle to them. He was doing something with his hands, too.

"Mia."

I raised my eyes to Emilio's.

"What did you see?"

I couldn't speak.

"Stay here, Mia."

Not again, not again, I thought. *Not here, on the plane, not in this closed space with the stale air, not here . . . Stay away, stay away!*

"Mia, so long as I keep hold of your hand he cannot come in. Stay here. Breathe, Mia. Breathe. No, ma'am, she's fine," he said to the flight attendant.

I remembered Giuliano speaking to me while I lay on my bed: *Ascolti il campanello, Mia.*

"She's no danger. Really. You don't have to restrain her. Please: I will be responsible. I understand," he repeated, and he must have persuaded them. I was learning that all Emilio really has to do to persuade most women is to exist.

I seemed only able to breathe in gasps. People were staring at me, and I realized the hacking sound I was hearing came from my own throat. All the way back to my seat, I looked straight down at the nasty airplane carpet, grateful for Emilio's firm grip on my arm as he walked behind me.

"Is she all right?" asked an American woman sitting across

the aisle. She hadn't seen me at the exit door, apparently, because she didn't give me the "you are obviously a terrorist" look the people by the door had.

Maybe embarrassment is a good tool in the fight against demons. I got control of my lungs and my brain and smiled my best fake smile.

"Yeah, I'm fine, thanks. I just get a little freaked out by flying, you know? But I'm fine."

She grinned and said, "I know exactly what you mean. I get freaked out by flying, too. At least you're with your boyfriend."

"Cousin, cousin," Emilio and I corrected her at the same time, and then the three of us laughed. This embarrassed me even more, but at least I was free of the terror for a moment. Whenever I am swimming in the seas of horror, even the island of shame looks pretty good.

After a moment, when the woman went back to playing cards with her kid, and everybody else stopped glancing over and whispering, Emilio reached down into his satchel. I'd never seen a man with a bag like that, with chocolate-smooth leather and brass fittings. All the men I knew carried toolboxes, except for my uncle, a salesman, who owned a hard-sided briefcase. I wasn't sure men were supposed to have something so soft looking. I thought he was going to pull out another fancy novel, but instead he brought out two boxes and handed them to me.

"Presents for you," he told me. "Grandfather thinks they're a good idea."

Apparently Grandfather did, because he leaned across and gave me a little wave.

I looked down and saw a cheap Walkman and a package entitled *Teach Yourself Italian,* which held a book and CDs.

I had forgotten the problem of language. Coming on top of everything else, it made me want to cry, but I wasn't going to cry in front of these men who had already seen me pee my bed. Besides, I still imagined traveling with these mysterious people to a magical city far from my smelly backyard, and this Walkman and language kit seemed so prosaic, so unmagical.

"Thanks," I said as politely as I could.

Emilio raised his eyebrows.

"You're welcome," he replied. I couldn't tell what he had been expecting, but I knew this wasn't it. "I had a look at them in the store," he said, "and they will get you a good start. They teach very proper Italian, which is important. Not like in America, where everything is slang. You will learn the slang from speaking, anyway.

"Why not get started now?" he added. "We're not going to run out of Atlantic anytime soon. I can help you with anything that seems difficult."

I stuck a CD in the player, slipped on the headphones, and made my first real attempts to understand the language Giuliano spoke.

I took a break for the in-flight movies, I admit. I had never been on a flight so long that there was time for more than one movie. Giuliano watched them both, too, with the Italian channel turned up on his headphones so that I could hear what sounded like a lot of tiny people chattering inside a tin can. I tried changing channels myself, to see if I could learn Italian that way, but gave up after about five minutes. Everyone talked too fast, rudely ignoring the fact that there was a foreigner listening. When I went back to the lessons, though, I forgot where I was and spoke out loud, asking the invisible person on the CD how their day was going. Emilio and Giuliano both turned to me.

"Good, good! Keep working on the pronunciation," Emilio said and, still grinning, turned back to his fancy novel, this one in Italian with some artsy photograph on the cover.

"A kilo of tomatoes, not too ripe, please," I intoned to myself. "Where is the bank?"

Learning one word made me want to learn another, and another, and stringing them together made me want to string more.

"Emilio," I said. He raised his eyes out of his book. "How do I ask what the word for something is, like, 'How do you say *book*?'"

"*Come si dice . . . ?* So, *come si dice* 'book'? Do you see?"

"I see." I smiled. "Wow. Wow."

He looked at me and then went back to his book with a shrug and a smile. Eventually I fell asleep with the lesson still playing on my headphones, so I made my entrance into Italy with my hair sticking up and my shirt and face both rumpled.

Once we made it through customs, and my passport and papers had been scowled at, turned upside down, argued over, and finally stamped, I was introduced to a small crowd of people, all of whom crammed (with me) into a tiny car and bobbed away down the highway. My first bleary-eyed glimpses of Italy were disappointing: the long, completely un-scenic highway, filled with crazed drivers who played the traffic lanes like a video game, and then, what seemed hours later, the city, with its steep-walled, dirty streets, filled with more crazed drivers.

Eventually we started bouncing over cobblestones, and I will always remember the first time I heard that sound, the sound of a foreign street. Then I was led up into a dark apartment walled with books. Somebody steered me into a small room, filled with more books, and pointed me to a soft, white bed.

I tried to remember what to say. At last it came. *"Grazie mille,"* I said to the blurry face, and fell down and went to sleep.

The Candle Shop

I couldn't tell what time it was when I woke up. The light that filtered from behind the long, heavy curtains looked gray. I stretched and slid out of bed, blinking down at myself. I was still wearing the clothes I had arrived in. When my feet touched the floor, I got a surprise: the floor was perfectly smooth and silken, cool, a wonderful place to put bare feet. It was tiled in some kind of stone, with little pebbles set in it that had been polished flat.

I rubbed my eyes and took a good look at the room. It was narrow and small, but with high ceilings. Tall, dark shelves full of books lined one wall, with a small gap for a desk with one drawer. A leather armchair stood by the one tall window, which turned out to be a door to a balcony, propped slightly open to let in the warm air of September. I stepped outside.

It was late morning, and the sun was shining, which I would not have guessed from the light that had managed to make it past the curtains. My first real view of Milan consisted of a small courtyard, built of yellowing stone and lined with balconies like my own, as well as a maze of back stairs and ground-floor archways. Almost every balcony was crowded with something—pots of geraniums and basil, big jugs of water, laundry frames with washing swinging slightly in the breeze, weather-beaten chairs and rusting tables with full ashtrays on top. The floor of the courtyard was paved with a pattern of flat cobblestones and edged with round ones, and had stone gutters that ran across it to a drain in the middle. It also had dog poop.

A herd of mopeds stood parked on one side, next to three cars, none of them larger than the car I had come in from the airport. A guy was underneath one of the cars, his legs sticking out. Two more guys stood nearby, smoking cigarettes and agreeing with everything the pair of legs said. They looked up when I emerged onto the balcony, and one said something to the others. I wanted to step back inside, but they soon looked away. I felt relieved and annoyed at the same time. What, a car was more interesting?

After a moment, I lost interest in them, too, because I needed a bathroom and had no idea where to find one. I went back inside to explore the apartment. My door opened onto a long hall, and the room I needed was two doors down on the right. I thought about how everything looked the same as in the United States and yet completely different. Every door, for example, had a lever instead of a doorknob, as if this were a library or a post office. Then there was the language I had heard all around me last night. Sometimes I had thought they were speaking English, because sounds had emerged that made sense, even if the sentences didn't, but when I listened more carefully, I couldn't understand a word.

Suddenly I wanted to cry. Sitting on the toilet, I bent my head and stuck my face in my hands. I wanted to go outside that door and find Mom and Dad and Gina at breakfast. I wanted to sit with them and eat my mother's horrible oatmeal and hear my dad growl at the radio news while he nursed a last mug of coffee before leaving for work.

I sat up again, remembering the reason I was here. Where was everyone? I didn't like being alone in this silent house. And how could I go about getting something to eat? After working out the hot and cold water faucets (I found out that *C* stood for *calda,* "hot"), I stepped back into the hall and looked around. I couldn't hear anyone moving about. I found the kitchen, full of more things that looked completely the same and totally different. It was much cleaner than our kitchen, with newly washed dishes neatly stacked on a drying rack and the counters wiped. I found the living room, lined with more books and some old-looking couches with wooden legs and clawed feet. I finally heard voices coming from below.

I found an open door that led to a narrow, wooden stairwell. A door stood partly open at the bottom, leading into a tiny room, full of files and leather-bound books and boxes, the small, remaining space taken up by a table covered in papers. It looked like the back room of a shop, and so it was, as I found when I stepped through the door.

I saw Giuliano first, and then a small woman whom I knew to be Laura, his wife, and then the shop.

I loved it from that first moment. I loved the paneled walls and wooden shelves full of candles; the scent of wood and wax and varnish; the faint, sharp hint of sulfur from matches; and above all the warm smell of flame. The whole shop felt completely foreign, yet precisely like home.

Giuliano and Laura looked at me. Then they both smiled.

"Buon giorno," they said.

"Uh," I said. "Uh. *Buon*, uh. *Buon giorno.*"

They both laughed. They started speaking quickly, and I tried to answer, which meant I got tied up in all kinds of mental knots while I tried to follow their hands and make sense of a blur of Italian at the same time. Eventually we all laughed, and Laura beckoned me upstairs. In the kitchen, I could tell she was trying to ask me what I wanted for breakfast, and I remembered words from the airplane. *"Pane . . . e caffè?*—Bread and coffee?"

Bread and coffee was what I knew how to say, but ten eggs and a pan full of bacon was what I really wanted. I wondered if they had eggs and bacon in Italy. I have since heard that lots of people learn how to speak a new language because they want to meet guys, or girls, or because they fall in love with someone from another country. I learned to speak a new language because I wanted breakfast.

Fortunately Laura was an experienced grandmother, so I got

more than bread and coffee. She set out freshly baked rolls and butter, and fruit, and little pots of yogurt in several flavors. I realize now that she must've thought this was a feast. When she heard, at last, what Americans eat for breakfast, she said it only confirmed her theory that all Americans are mad.

I felt guilty when she gave me coffee. What would my parents say? She served it to me in a big bowl, with sugar and hot milk, so much that I could only tell it was coffee by the smell. I know it sounds stupid, when they were so far away, but I felt bad breaking my parents' rule—right up until I took my first sip.

I spent the day trying to get over jet lag. Sometimes I would catch myself staring at a wall, or a shelf of books, or a photograph. I tried to study some Italian, because I could tell I was going to need it. So far only Emilio had spoken any English to me, and besides the family, there was an entire city full of Italians outside my balcony. At first my brain didn't want to face verbs and nouns, but then I pulled out *Teach Yourself Italian* and started naming things in the room I had slept in. I began to dance around the room to keep things interesting. I twirled around and pointed my finger at random objects—book, *libro*! Bed, *letto*! Desk, *scrivania*! Laura came and stood in the doorway, grinning, then took my arm and led me over the whole house. Kitchen, *cucina*. Sink, *lavandino*. No, no, not *lavanda* (pointing to the lavender on the windowsill), *lavandino*. Table, *tavola*. Living room, *soggiorno*. Sofa, *divano*. She fed me an amazing mushroom ravioli dish for lunch as a reward, and laughed her head off when I asked her to pass the Pope (*papa*) instead of the pepper (*pepe*). Then she remembered herself and reminded us both sternly that it wasn't all that funny (at least I think that's what she was saying).

Emilio stopped by my room in the evening to see how I was doing. He looked at me, taking in what I had already seen in the mirror—my skin even paler and sallower than usual, deep violet shadows under my eyes, and my cheeks and lips feverishly red. Laura had cheered me up so much that I had forgotten, for a while, why I was here, but my face in the mirror had reminded me, even before Emilio's close examination.

"Still a little fiend-ridden," he said as calmly as a doctor, and I shivered. "Plus some jet lag. You'll need a few days to get over that. The rest, just be patient. It takes a while. I've brought you some books," he added, and they spilled out of his satchel onto the desk. "Mostly history, in Italian and English, and a guide-book or two so you can get to know the city. Grandfather wants you to read all you can, and we will start you on other studies soon. But for now, get through these."

I stared at the pile. Some were brand-new, with shining covers in red and yellow and orange, and others were old and battered, bound in leather or cloth and lettered in gold.

"Okay," I said.

"The history is important," he said, watching me.

"Okay," I repeated.

He gave me an impatient look.

"In any case," he went on, "we will have to wait some time

45

before we can let you out of the house on your own. For now you can go around with us. We need to determine the best ways of keeping you safe, and you must rest and recover also. Plus you must get to know the city. So this will help you pass the time."

I wondered how long I would be stuck in the house. Maybe they had a TV. They had to have a TV, right?

"Sure," I said. "Cool. But, um, is there anything else to do around the house? I mean . . ."

This time he glared at me. He seemed to have a number of things he wanted to say, but he didn't say any of them. Instead he said, "Is that what you're wearing to dinner?"

I looked down at my jeans and T-shirt, totally at a loss.

"What's wrong with them?" I asked.

"Well, we're going out," he answered as if a whole bunch of things should have been obvious that weren't.

"We're going out?"

"Nobody told you? Of course we are. We're celebrating the return of our cousin."

The thought of more family to meet, after the hazy introductions last night, and of having to speak Italian with strangers, made me want to stick my head in a bucket.

"Which cousin?" I asked, trying not to sound exhausted.

Emilio blinked. Then he burst out laughing.

"You!" he said.

My turn to blink. I felt so dumb.

"So we will be going out at 7:30," he said, still chuckling, and patted me on the shoulder, "and in Milan, we dress up to go out, especially to a nice place. So, a skirt and blouse, or a dress, and some good shoes. If you need to bathe, the towels are—oh, I see, my sister left you one."

At home, my bedtime was ten. My stomach was already growling, partly because it was confused and partly because it was used to dinner at six. When Emilio left me, saying that I could get in some reading before dinner, I sat down on the bed again and stared at nothing.

Emilio knocked again, then stuck his head back in.

"Grandfather's on the computer right now, but tomorrow I'll get you a password and everything, so you can e-mail home. We should be able to get an Internet phone service set up, too, Skype probably. It might take a little longer."

I tried to picture Giuliano in front of a computer. He belonged in the old candle shop in the flickering light, quiet, sturdy and, above all, old school. I tried to picture him Googling demons. It didn't work.

I took a shower (*C* is for *calda!*), then tried to figure out which of my clothes would make me blend in the most. I laid out skirts and shirts, and my one dress, running back and forth into the hall to look in the full-length mirror. Someone was carrying on a conversation, and I found myself trying to catch their words as I scrubbed at a spot on my one good pair of dress shoes. I couldn't tell if they were in the apartment behind us, although sometimes they sounded like they were coming from the bookshelf, sometimes by the window.

A woman spoke most of the time. She sounded pretty

uptight and pompous. Someone else answered her in a gravelly male voice that made me feel cold. It sounded almost familiar. I listened hard over the sound of my heart pounding in my ears. I reminded myself that the Della Torres had said the house was well guarded from the demon. No, I decided at last, it wasn't the demon's voice, but it did sound an awful lot like him. Trying to make out their words, I leaned closer to the wall.

"She shouldn't wear that yellow shirt," said the woman. "It's so bright, yes, but with her skin it makes her look like a jaundice patient. I hope she tries the dark blue."

There was a yellow shirt lying among the choices on the bed, and a dark blue one, too. Could they see me? Where were they? I spent the next ten minutes investigating the wall to see if there were any peepholes, like in some horrible gas station bathroom on the highway. There weren't. As an experiment, I picked up the blue shirt.

"Yes, and that simple skirt, the one without the frills—very tidy. I really prefer more lace, and the whole business of raising the hem above the ankles is quite tawdry, but it will do."

"I like the white skirt," said the gravelly voice.

"Don't be ridiculous. You've never worn a stitch of clothing in your whole life, so you can have no opinion."

The one with the gravelly voice wandered around naked? Who were these people?

"I've been around you long enough to have opinions," answered Gravel Voice, which was just about what I was thinking. Pompous Voice ignored this.

I smoothed out the skirt she liked, which I had never worn with the dark blue blouse. I couldn't see how they would work together, but somehow her advice seemed worth listening to.

"Now, for shoes, are those all she has? Oh, dear. They might do in America, poor thing, but she is in Milan now. She must talk to them about shoes. For tonight, let's just pray to the Heavenly Queen that no one will look down. And jewelry: let's see. That plain gold chain, and the small cross. Nothing else for a girl so young."

With this strange help, I chose my outfit, but I carried all the clothes to the bathroom to change, just in case they could see me. When I stepped in front of the hall mirror again, I was surprised to see how nice I looked. So was Emilio, I'm afraid, when he came upstairs from the shop.

"Ready? Oh, you are. Very nice."

I saw him glance down at my shoes and start to shrug. I wondered if he could tell I had had help. As I followed him downstairs into the candle shop, a thought came forward. The voices hadn't been from an apartment behind me. They had been in the room. Of course.

six

La famiglia

The tiny shop was crowded, and everyone seemed to feel they had been introduced last night, when they came to the airport, so nobody gave me their name when they said hello. As we passed into the street, I tried to get them all straight: Giuliano and his wife, Laura, and Emilio; then a woman a little older than Emilio, with sleek, dark brown hair drawn up into an elegant chignon. She talked so familiarly to Emilio that I thought, with glum shock, that she must be his curlfrond/girlfriend, Alba—until the tall, dignified, African-looking man standing next to her kissed her on the cheek and took her arm in his as we started to walk away.

I caught up with Emilio and whispered, "I know I met all these people last night, but . . ."

He smiled.

"My sister," he said in a low voice, jerking his head toward the woman with the chignon. "Francesca."

"A model? She's so cool-looking."

"A model?" He seemed to think the question was hilarious. "No. A lawyer. The first woman in her firm. Do not tell her she looks like a model; she won't like that. The man walking with her is Égide."

I tried out the name in my mind, the way Emilio pronounced it: *Eh-gheed,* with a very soft *G* sound; it seemed kind of romantic. Later I learned that it was a French word for *shield*.

He paused.

"Our grandparents weren't very happy about him when he appeared," said Emilio. "We have some friends who still don't approve. But my sister doesn't care. And she always gets her way."

"My sister always gets her way, too," I told him.

"She looks like the type. It's impressive, but irritating, isn't it?"

"Yes!"

"But, Égide. A good man: Francesca doesn't choose any other kind. We had a good father." He paused and then added, "And a mother more than wise enough to pick him."

The way his voice softened and warmed made me want to ask him about his parents, but I didn't want to upset him. I could see there was a story there, and somehow, even before Emilio mentioned them, I had known I wouldn't be meeting them tonight.

Behind Francesca and Égide was a gawky guy with a huge nose and frizzy curls, whom I recognized as the driver from the night before. He was walking with a girl who was obviously his sister—a fascinating example of how the same features can be goofy or gorgeous, since on her the huge nose looked aristocratic, and the same gene that made him skinny made her slender and graceful. I really wanted to talk to her, since she looked almost my own age, but she obviously didn't want to be here, and ignored her brother and everyone else while texting rapidly on her phone, her perfect nails flashing.

"Anna Maria is the model," Emilio added, pointing a thumb at the girl on the phone. "She's only three years older than you, you know. That's her brother, Francesco, next to her."

Giuliano followed them, deep in conversation with a younger copy of himself—a man with dark hair starting to go gray, but just as sturdy and energetic. Beside this Giuliano-copy was a slender, big-nosed woman, who also whipped out her cell phone the moment we began walking.

"Those people walking with Grandfather are Uncle Matteo and Aunt Brigida. They are actually my great-uncle and great-aunt; Uncle Matteo is Grandfather's youngest brother."

"So was my grandfather the middle brother?" I asked.

"No, actually not. Your grandfather is—was—my grandfather's first cousin. Your grandfather's father died early in World War Two, and his mother, she died of grief afterward. He was raised by his uncle and aunt, Nonno's parents. We were all neighbors; the kids were already growing up like brothers."

This family seemed complicated. Back home, things were

simple: father, mother, sister, grandfather, and grandmother. Oh, and a few uncles and aunts. And their kids. And . . . oh.

Emilio started to tell me about my grandfather's family, who had lived a couple of streets away, actually in an apartment downstairs from the one he, Emilio, rented with Francesco. My great-grandfather had inherited the whole building, but the family had had to sell it in order to support his orphaned son.

Looking at these people, I thought how strange it was that I shared genes with all of them and had never met or even heard of them before. I noticed, too, that my grandfather seemed to flicker like a shadow from face to face. Uncle Matteo had his dark, thick eyebrows, and even drew them together in exactly the same way when he was thinking; Giuliano had the same eyebrows, too, though they were finer and grayer. When Anna Maria got a funny text on her phone, she laughed with a single, sharp bark, just like my grandfather had. Giuliano's face had the same expression when he was in repose: sad, a little angry, but with a measure of peace as well. I had always wondered how a face could spell out so many differing emotions at once, using the same alphabet of muscle and nerve.

I tried to pay attention to Emilio's story so that I could repeat it to Gina, but the sounds that had been scraping around the edge of my hearing grew too loud: a terrible clamor of voices snarling overhead, one of which I already knew too well. The horror snicked into my skin. A breath of freezing air spread between my shoulder blades, as if a path had been opened for frost to spill down into my body.

"Mia?" Emilio asked from somewhere over me. I looked up. I was squatting on the ground. I couldn't figure out how I had gotten there, but I knew I had to try to work my fingers in between the cobblestones. I had to keep hold of this world.

"Nonno!" he said, turning to his grandfather, but already Giuliano had seen, and when I could raise my eyes I could see various pairs of Della Torre legs rearranging themselves around me. I thought they wanted to hide my bizarre behavior from passersby. Probably this was true, but it took me a moment to notice that all of them also seemed to have a job to do. Some were looking up, some out. Some were speaking softly under their breath. Anna Maria had hurriedly put away her cell phone, but I caught a nod between her and Uncle Matteo, and saw her pull her phone out again and begin talking nonchalantly to no one. Laura and Francesca had drifted to the edges of the cluster, while Égide and Brigida stood quite close to me.

I heard myself saying to the ground, "He's coming back, he's coming back, he's coming back," like some choking mantra.

Above me, the shouting, snarling voices, threaded through with the deep, gravelly voice I feared the most, were joined by others, some high and light, some low and fierce, rising to a pitch so loud I thought everyone on the street would cover their ears; yet people just walked past, carrying their shopping. They didn't even seem to see me, on my hands and knees in the middle of a fashionable Milanese street. The circle of family tightened above me; I heard Giuliano chanting the way he had on the plane.

Then that was all the sound there was, just the noise of people's shoes, clattering by on the street. The terrible, invading voices were gone. In the silence, I realized I was glad that I had recognized only one of the voices; the people who had been talking in my room back at the apartment hadn't been among those snarling overhead.

I glanced up, still squatting where I was. Emilio was looking up into the evening sky between the buildings. He looked down at me.

"We drove them off, for now," he said in English.

He and Égide helped me to my feet. Égide asked if I was all right—I didn't need to know the words to understand them.

"Sì, sì, grazie," I said.

"You are all right?" Emilio asked. "We didn't expect that so soon, or we would have been even better prepared. But we did expect it."

Still fighting back the nauseating fear, I thought but managed not to say, *I wish someone had told* me *what to expect.* Instead I just walked on with Emilio, Francesca, and Égide close by to make sure I kept my feet.

I had so many questions I didn't know where to start. I felt so tired I didn't ask any of them.

What I did notice was that everyone seemed pretty shaken, and that they were trying to hide it from me, talking loudly to one another, even cracking jokes that sounded like they had to do with what had just happened. Then we arrived at the restaurant, and the mood seemed to get lighter. I felt safer than I had on the street. Maybe it was just an illusion, but it was very nice to have a roof over my head again.

The owner of the restaurant kissed Giuliano and Laura and shook hands with everyone else. Giuliano introduced me. Then he introduced me again, at the first table we passed, where half the people at the table seem to know half of the Della Torres. Then he introduced me again at the second and third tables, but not at the fourth, which held American tourists. (I had only been in Milan twenty-four hours, and already I could recognize them. What is it about us?) After the sixth and seventh tables, I got to sit down. I knew I would never remember anybody who had shaken my hand in the last ten minutes.

I recognized a few words on the menu, like *pomodori* (tomatoes) and *insalate* (salads), but then found a lot of phrases that translated suspiciously in my head as "cones with fungus" or "ovoid car parts."

"Would you like some help?" asked Emilio.

"Yes, please . . ."

He translated various dishes for me but in the end, between jet lag and street attacks, it was just too much, and when he said, "Shall I order for you?" I nodded.

"I will order typical Milanese food, for your first night here, so you can get to know the city."

"Okay, but nothing too weird," I said, trying to sound polite about it.

"This from a child of the land of peanut spread and jam on bread, and coffee that tastes like water." He laughed.

Uncle Matteo, across the table, called out to Emilio.

"He wants to know what I think is so funny," Emilio explained. Everyone laughed when he told them.

"Uncle Matteo says that you Americans are nothing compared to the English, when it comes to food."

"I don't know anything about English food, but I love peanut butter and jelly, and the only thing weird about it is that some people don't," I retorted, surprised at myself. It felt good to smile some more.

We argued about food. I missed most of the jokes that people made, since if they got translated at all they didn't arrive in time, and I would end up laughing long after everybody else was finished. By the end of the meal, though, I was catching more words.

Meanwhile, I ate real Italian food for the first time. Okay, Nonna's breakfast and lunch should count, I know. But.

The waiter set down a plate of small, toasted triangles of polenta with mushrooms on them. I had never tasted anything so wonderful. I bit through the delicious, bubbly crust, thinly coated in melted cheese, and found the soft, warm cornmeal center, with no hard bits like the kind that sometimes sneak up on a person while they are eating cornbread, and the mushrooms joined me there in a sauce that tasted sweetly of wine.

That was just the appetizer. I had no idea, even though I had watched everybody take a million years to order, that there was so much more food coming. I could remember one or two long meals with my grandfather in childhood. They came back to me after the third course, when I realized we weren't finished.

They had put the gawky, big-nosed cousin on the other side of me. I tried to catch his attention while he talked with Giuliano.

"Francesca?" I asked.

He ignored me, but Emilio's elegant sister looked up.

"Sì?"

"Oh, no—I meant—"

Why on earth did they have to have the same name, separated only by a vowel?! I looked down at my plate. She frowned and went back to talking with Anna Maria.

At that moment, a waiter swooped down with a risotto that wasn't anything like my mom's heavy, creamy mess. For one thing, it was yellow.

"Saffron," Emilio explained, between bites of his own. "It's a famous local dish."

By then, I was so much in love with the food that I paid attention when he told me things like this. Across the table, it seemed like everyone was talking about cooking. I asked Emilio.

"Yes, a national obsession." He smiled.

"What about *your* national obsessions?" asked Anna Maria.

Whether I just stopped hearing everybody else, or whether everyone else fell silent when she spoke this one English sentence across the table, I don't know. I was so excited to hear English that I didn't notice the glare in her eyes at first.

"Anna," said Emilio in a warning voice.

"Well, it has to be okay to ask!" she snapped at him.

"Um, I don't think we have any," I said. "None that I can think of, anyway."

"None?" She rolled her eyes. "What about the war on the terrorisms? What about this—this criminality, in Iraq and Afghanistan?"

My face felt hot.

"Anna, it's her first night here," said Emilio.

By then I'd figured out who she reminded me of: a friend in school who had gotten really involved in human rights and stuff. Anna Maria's eyes had the same look in them, like this was too important to wait for me to get over my jet lag. But what did she think, that I spoke for all Americans or something? And anyway, wasn't she a model? Did models care about politics?

"Uh," I began. "Look."

Now I noticed how quiet everyone was. I wondered how many actually understood what we were saying to each other. Not that I could think of anything else to say.

I hadn't expected to feel so angry and so sad at the same time. It kind of struck me from behind. It struck Anna Maria, too, I guess, because her eyes were softening.

I looked up at her.

"We were trying to do what was right," I said. "But now it's all messed up."

"We sent soldiers, too," Emilio cut in. "But I think that you, Anna Maria, ought to remember that Mia can't even vote yet, and she isn't responsible for everything her country does. Besides it will be a terrible waste if our osso buco gets cold. Please," he added as Anna Maria glared at him, "there will be time to talk about all these things."

"Okay," she said, and added something in Italian under her breath. It took me three tries to get Emilio to translate it, and even then he made me promise first that I wouldn't argue with her: "If the American voters are that ignorant, I don't think much of her country's chances."

By then, her mother had worked out what we were talking about and scolded Anna Maria into behaving better, so that between Aunt Brigida and Cousin Emilio, family peace was restored, if the arguing that continued around the table—about the best way to cook osso buco (veal in a crazy-good sauce)— could be called family peace. How little I knew!

After that, there was a salad made of tiny, sliced, raw artichokes and thin slices of Parmesan cheese. I would never have expected to like it, but I actually mopped up my plate with a slice of the wonderful restaurant bread, after I made sure with Emilio that nobody would laugh at me for doing it.

Then it was midnight, somehow, with all the courses of magical food behind us and my head confused, since this was the first time I'd ever had a second glass of wine. I was puzzling over dessert, which I had been looking forward to, but which turned out to be a bowl of fruit and a plate of cheese and nuts that excited the heck out of everyone else for no good reason I could see. Even when Emilio explained that the pears were at the height of their season and these were the first chestnuts and walnuts from the harvest, to which I wanted to reply that where I came from we could get them all year-round in the market, what was so special about that? But I didn't. Then Emilio said, "May I help you on with your coat?" which was another way of saying, "I have been standing here for five minutes with your coat in my hands." We passed slowly through the restaurant, saying good-bye at almost every table, of course, and stepped out into the sudden, chilly dark. It had gotten cold while we were inside; autumn was coming in, just like back home.

Only when the first shiver of cold struck me did I remember what waited in the street. The sleepy buzz of wine in my head stopped. I paused where I was, right on the edge of the sidewalk, and let the others flood out around me. Somewhere on my left, Giuliano spoke what sounded like quiet orders. The Della Torres shifted and shuffled, following Giuliano while they kept talking about dinner, or was it politics? Something, anyway, which seemed to involve important policy decisions, I thought.

When we started walking, we moved like a school of fish, with me as the littlest minnow in the middle. I wanted Emilio never to leave my side. He would protect me; he would translate what was happening for me, just as he had all through dinner. It was very hard to let him walk away with Francesco when we finally arrived at the door of the shop. Everyone kissed one another good night, and most of them kissed me, which made me nervous. Francesco hit my nose with his chin. Anna Maria smelled good, and startled me by smiling at me, as if she had never said any mean things about my country. Uncle Matteo smelled strongly of cigarettes and wine.

Emilio kissed me last. Afterward I knew the exact spot, right on the bottom ridge of my cheekbone, precisely an inch from my ear. He left behind a smell like pinesap, the kind I always managed to get on my feet and hands up at Lake George, that smelled so sharp and rich while I scrubbed to get it off. That stuff sticks.

We stepped into the shop, Giuliano, Laura, Francesca, Égide, and I, and I breathed a sigh of relief to be out of the street. The smell of warm wax was wonderful. Giuliano picked up a long, ornate candle snuffer and began putting out the few candles that were still burning. I watched the thin trails of smoke float up and swayed where I stood, until Laura led me up to bed.

Pompous Voice and Gravel Voice were talking when I came in the room. I was so tired (and probably slightly drunk as well) that I said, "Could you please keep it down? I need to sleep."

There was a shocked silence. I shut my eyes and smiled.

SEVEN

Arguing Historians, Sighing Candles, Unexpected Visitors

The next three weeks seem to involve an awful lot of verbs. *Essere, fare, uscire, venire, andare, capire:* to be, to do, to leave, to come, to go, to understand. I was amazed every time I managed to write a coherent English e-mail to anyone back home. But I studied, oh, yes I did; I studied as if my life depended on it, because I was pretty sure it did.

Hey, Gina-banana,

Psyched to hear you got the part. Does Ariel get to kiss anybody, and if so, is that anybody played by Luke? Life is pretty much the same here in glamorous Milan. At least I think it's probably glamorous, but I wouldn't know, since they still haven't let me out of the house alone yet. I have to travel with, like, five relatives to dinner or the Castello Sforzesco, a fairly interesting ruin in the middle of the city.

The rest of the time I sit on my balcony, if the weather is nice, and study millions of verbs and some other stuff. Apparently my balcony is safe. Why it is safe and the street isn't, I have no idea. They haven't really explained anything about what they do.

So, one thing they make me do is kind of odd. I have to meditate every day. Don't get the idea that I'm going to start wearing long, floaty skirts and smelling of patchouli. There isn't a statue of Buddha in sight when I meditate. There is a small sculpture of the Virgin Mary holding Jesus, which Laura brought me the other day. It's made out of painted wood, and it's beautiful. There are even tiny animals carved around the base of her pedestal: I think my favorite is the eensy bear with carved fur. The statue is supposed to be very old, owned by one of our ancestors.

That's the strange thing—everything in the house is "Uncle Martino's this" or "Cousin Maria's that." I get the feeling that except for Francesca's clothes, nobody in the family has bought so much as a coffee mug for a century. They used to have more, but they lost a lot of their stuff in the war. Milan got bombed pretty badly in 1943.

So I sit and look at this sculpture of Mary, and I'm supposed to empty my mind and picture her in total detail. Here's what it says in the ancient notes that Emilio helped me translate (he refuses to speak any English with me anymore, which is a total pain):

"The demon catcher would do well to meditate daily upon Our Lady, Queen of Heaven. The wise demon catcher will meditate for at least an hour a day, imagining her in her perfect form. He must picture her in great detail, from the stars upon her mantle and her robe blue as the sea, to her firm and shapely foot upon the sickle moon. He must picture her shining with a great yellow light."

Uh, okay. Whatever. Apparently this comes from a really old manuscript, written by yet another relative of ours. I don't know if it says "he" all the time because only men can be demon catchers, or because people used to (and sometimes still do) say "he" when they mean "everyone."

So besides Italian verbs and meditation and history, how else are they preparing me? I don't know. I don't even know if they know. I go along day by day, and then all at once I'm paralyzed with fear, so frightened I wear myself out. Gina, what am I going to do?

Sorry to freak out on you. I don't have anyone else who will get it, who I can really talk to, even if they could speak English.

Okay, freak-out over, for now.

Dinner is almost ready. I can smell it from the kitchen. That's one thing, Gina. I never thought food could be so important. It's a huge deal here. Every day Laura goes out to the shops and comes home with bags and bags of groceries and a Plan. Everyone else pitches in with the Plan when they get here, and the Plan is always delicious.

Okay, dinner's up. Give my love to Mom and Dad. Keep lots for yourself.

Xoxo,

Mia

Dear Mia-boBIA,

Sorry to answer your long one with a short one, but I have, like, ten essays due, and that's before I start memorizing.

Poor you. I don't even know what to say. This has thrown all of us for a loop. But I did get to see some of what they did with you, and I have to say, I think they have big plans, and they know better than anyone how to defend you. Maybe it's like school, you have to learn to count before you can add and subtract, and so on. And Emilio: he's way more than just good-looking, you know. He's the real deal, just like his grandfather.

On a completely different and more cheerful note, Ariel does not get to kiss anybody, least of all Luke, who is playing the Duke of Naples. Bummer. Ariel is Prospero's odd-job fairy, though, so I get the most excellent supernatural costuming and a twenty-minute makeup job.

The rest of your life sounds alternately boring and totally awesome, by which I mean staying inside all the time blows, even if inside includes the balcony, but the

food and the culture and the whole family history thing
are fundamental, it sounds like. If I wasn't insanely busy,
I would envy you.

Love,

Gina-banana

Finally one morning, about five weeks after I arrived, I felt
brave enough to start on the pile of Italian history books. I had
been avoiding them. I had tried one in the first week, but after
referring to my dictionary fifteen times in the first paragraph—
I am not joking—I decided they hurt my head too much and
exiled them to a corner of my desk, where they sat and glared at
me. Then one day I just reached for one of them, and I didn't
need a dictionary every five seconds, although, granted, it was
a children's history of Milan. I read. And read. And read. I
didn't take in a lot of what I was reading, because it felt a bit too
much like school, but at least I could read it—and that made
me ridiculously happy.

I noticed my progress in other ways, too, like at dinner at
night.

Francesca and Égide always came home at the same time,
walking in the door together, one or the other carrying a
battered grocery bag with orange flowers on it that always
contained something Nonna had asked for: fresh milk, fresh
bread, a half kilo of mushrooms, a bottle of wine. One night,
as often happened, Uncle Matteo and Aunt Brigida were with
them. Giuliano greeted them, asking, "No children with you

tonight?" To which they replied at the same time, "A date," and "A study crisis," meaning Anna Maria and Francesco respectively. It was easy to tell which was which, since Anna Maria had left school to become a model.

I was helping make ravioli. I am completely useless in the kitchen, but this did not stop Nonna, who ignored my pleas (I think she knew they were really protests in disguise). I never liked to help cook at home, but I was starting to enjoy filling the little pasta squares and running the cutter along the edges of the ravioli molds. Nonna hovered over a sauce on the stove, then darted away to shred endive for a salad.

Uncle Matteo opened a bottle he had brought with him, and poured out for all of us, tucking a glass in by my elbow with a smile.

"You're doing a good job," he said, patting my shoulder before thumping into a seat at the table beside his wife.

I could follow some of the conversation now; there were still lots of words that just flowed by as a river of sound, but even those were starting to puddle into the shapes of sentences. At least everybody here had the same accent. Sandro, a neighbor who sometimes stopped in at the shop, had moved up from Sicily, and I couldn't make sense of even the simplest things he said.

While they talked, Uncle Matteo pulled out a slim, battered, black case from his jacket pocket and opened it on the table, idly picking over its contents. I knew I had seen something like this before, but so much had happened, I couldn't remember where. I was pretty sure that Giuliano had one of these, and Emilio, too.

The case was bound in leather, with lines of gilded writing running down the lid. I couldn't read the words from where I was standing. The interior was made of light-colored wood, carefully varnished. Various objects were held in place between slats of wood or under leather straps, among them two candle stubs of different colors of wax, a book of matches, a tiny hand mirror, a small copper bell, a thin, leather-bound notebook, and a pen. I thought I saw nails lined up in a row, too, and some other things I didn't recognize.

"Brigida, help me remember that I have to get this strap repaired," he said, pulling on a bit of broken leather. I didn't need to understand all the words to see what he meant. Brigida nodded and turned to Giuliano.

"No Emilio tonight, either?"

Giuliano shook his head. "Alba."

"Ah," said Aunt Brigida, adding something else in a caustic tone that I wish I could have translated. I say I learned a language in order to ask for breakfast; I think I learned it in order to understand the gossip, too.

Well, really, I suppose I learned it for all kinds of reasons. I do remember that dinner, and Uncle Matteo's case, and I remember that the next day the history books started to make sense, although the history itself did not.

My teachers back in Center Plains were apologetic about teaching us history, but bravely tried to make it interesting by having us make dioramas, reenact important moments like the creation of the Magna Carta, or pretend to live in a feudal society in the Middle Ages. Sadly, the poor, brave history teachers, bravest among them Ms. Sadler, who once lectured dressed as Genghis Khan, never succeeded in making the subject relevant—just boring.

I could tell the people who had written the Italian history books would not be able to do any better. I gave up on the first one and tried another.

After an hour or so, I started getting really annoyed. The problem was that none of the books agreed with one another. I felt as if the historians were fighting in my head.

"The origins of Milan are lost in the mists of time," said one.

"No, they aren't," said another. "It originated with the Etruscans in the sixth century BC. But nobody knows what the name *Milan* means."

"Yes, we do," said another. "It's a shortened form of *Mediolanum*, which means 'middle of the plain,' as anybody can tell, and which makes sense because Milan *is* in the middle of a plain."

"No, it means 'land of the May' in Celtic, and in fact the Celts did conquer the Etruscans in May."

"You're all idiots! It's obviously a reference to *lana*, 'wool,' and to the sheep that were raised here."

Together, like some weird animal with too many legs and no brain, we lurched forward, the papery historians and I.

"None of that matters, anyway, because pretty soon the Romans decided that what northern Italy really needed was an aqueduct or two, and they were just the people to build it. The Romans were one of those peoples that just couldn't leave anybody alone. They were always invading you without asking. They would come in with their eagles and their big ideas and ruin everything."

Of course none of the historians was actually saying things this way. I wrote down "eagles and big ideas" and for a fleeting second thought about another country that had both. *Oh.* Wait a minute. These people I was reading about, with their total inability to sensibly name a city, had been *alive*—getting up in the morning and feeling disgusted about stupid politicians making stupid decisions, or eating their mother's horrible oatmeal and hating algebra, if they had algebra back then. They had hung out with their friends, had crushes on the cute Etruscan boy next door, had wondered whether the Romans would leave them alive. It looked like a lot of times the Romans didn't. The Romans weren't the only ones with issues about violence, either. When those early Milanese weren't rushing off to war, they spent their spare time poisoning one another or arranging for grisly executions or dying of disgusting plagues. There was so much blood, blood on every page.

Someone knocked on my door.

"Come in," I said.

"Ciao," said Emilio, and I remembered that another way the old name for Milan had been translated was "honeyed land." I felt like I was looking at it.

"Working hard, I see—that's good, good. What is it today?"

he asked, approaching my desk, then answering himself, "History. Yes, excellent. But don't neglect the language."

"How can I, when all of these books are in Italian?" I retorted, glad I could come up with the words fast enough. I wanted to tell him how sick I was of opening my dictionary for every other paragraph—and then finding every paragraph full of blood. I wanted to beg and plead to be allowed to do something else. I opened my mouth to start, then shut it again. More than anything, I didn't want to be embarrassed in front of him.

"It's coming fast," he said confidently. "May I sit?"

"What? Oh, sure."

He picked the one other chair in the room, the old leather armchair that sat by the window. When he sat, I saw the light on his hair and realized with a shock that it was reflected from the lamps in the courtyard outside. It was later than I'd thought. My stomach growled, loudly enough for both of us to hear, and he laughed and said, "Nonna won't be cooking for another hour, at least. Let's go down to the shop. I'll get an aperitif for us from the café. You can practice speaking with anyone who comes in. Let's go see if Nonna needs anything."

He stood up quickly, but I was the one who felt a rush of vertigo. I held on tight to the back of my chair. Suddenly and unreasonably I didn't want to leave my cocoon of language CDs and history books. But after I'd made my way downstairs to find myself standing in the shop, surrounded by the smell of old wood and warm wax, I knew I would be all right, at least for now.

"So what would you like? Prosecco?"

I must have looked blank, because he smiled. "I'll just bring back some different things, and some little bits to eat, and you can decide what you like."

At the door, he stopped, turned, and came back.

"Mia. Something very important."

I was still standing in the middle of the room, arms dangling at my sides.

"Yes?"

"You must not blow out any of these candles. In fact, don't breathe on any of them or try to touch the melted wax or the flame. Do you understand?" he asked urgently. "Tell me what I have said in English, so that I know you understand."

I repeated the warning back, haltingly but correctly.

"Good," he said. "But the books, you can touch."

After he was gone, I took a look at the books. They were mostly history, in very dense Italian. Oh, good. I walked around the room, looking at the candles from a cautious distance. They were very beautiful in all their varieties of shape, color of wax, number of wicks, and so on, but they looked like nothing more than candles. They smelled of honey, mostly, so I guessed they were made of beeswax, though I had never seen it in such a range of colors, from pale white to deep, dirty gold.

As I paced, I started to notice odd things about the candles. Like how one flame wavered as if it were in a high wind, while the one next to it burned straight and still, pointing perfectly upward. Or how two candles made of the same yellow wax burned with different colors—one with a blue flame, one orange with a green heart. When I stared at one, I thought I could hear music. Another one burned slowly down, the flame drowning in a sea of wax, and went out with a sigh. I heard it: a sigh.

Emilio came back with a tray loaded with glasses, little sandwiches, canapés, olives, and other pickled vegetables that I didn't recognize.

"Help yourself," he said. I tried the Prosecco but liked the other drink better: *aranciata amara*, bitter orange, a soft drink with a bite to it. I thought about drinking coffee, and how I drank wine at dinner now, way more than the two or three sips I was ever allowed at home. I felt guilty again.

A man came into the shop, moving so quietly that he startled me while I had an olive in my mouth. I sat up, the olive going one way and the pit going the other. The man looked at me as if he would rather not speak in front of a stranger. I asked Emilio, "Should I go?"

"What?" he said, startled. "No, no, you are fine where you are." He gave me a hard look. To the man, he said, "Don't worry. She's family."

The man gave me a searching glance, then sat down at the table. I was surprised Emilio didn't offer him anything from our very full tray, because up until that point, I had never seen anyone visit the Della Torres without being fed. His guest didn't seem bothered, though. He was a small man, with black, greased-back hair and fine, pale features. There was hardly any red in his cheeks.

"What is it?" Emilio prompted him gently.

"I have come from the street of Signora Galeazzo. You asked me to watch. I mean, your grandfather did."

"Yes, I know. What have you seen?"

"He told me the signs were already starting to show, your grandfather did."

The man was still looking at me while he spoke.

"I tell you: she's all right. Now, the signs are starting to show. And we have had signals here," Emilio added, gesturing to the room.

"Ah," said the man, lifting his eyes to the candles. Somehow I felt sure he didn't like them. "You asked me to watch," he continued. Then his voice changed, becoming sharper. "She's coming home. Soon. You need to know this. She's very angry."

"We thought she might be," Emilio nodded. "I would be."

"You know nothing about it," said the man.

Emilio shrugged, not put off by his strange manner. "Probably I don't."

"I could hear her, in the night. She's not far off, maybe only a few streets away. You don't have a lot of time."

"She has taken years to get here, so we may have weeks," Emilio said.

"I don't care about time," said the man, but he sounded sad.

"I know," Emilio said. "What can I give you?"

"Nothing you can spare," the man answered. "I bid you good evening."

"Thank you very much for your help. Good evening."

Emilio stood until the stranger left, then looked down at me.

"Did you catch all that?" he asked, sounding odd.

"I think so," I said. "There weren't really any hard words. Unless *Galeazzo* is a word? It sounded like a family name."

"It is," he said.

"That guy didn't really want me here, did he?"

"Not really. But that's all right." He smiled suddenly. "I think they are going to have to get used to you."

I smiled back.

"I think I would like that," I replied.

I was too caught up in the mystery of what had happened to actually ask about it, and Emilio didn't bring it up with his grandfather at dinner. I fell asleep wondering who this person was, this woman who would take weeks to travel a few streets, and whom the Della Torres had been warned about—by the candles?

In the middle of the night, I got up to go to the bathroom but had hardly opened the door when I heard my name from across the hall, in the kitchen. I stopped still. Giuliano and Emilio spoke just above a whisper. I strained to listen. They hadn't heard my door open, I guess.

"Mia saw him?" said Giuliano.

"I'm not kidding, Nonno," Emilio replied. He sounded fierce.

"You're sure?"

"She saw him. She heard him, too. She's got enough Italian now; I think she understood most of what he was saying. She asked me if *Galeazzo* was a family name or a word. That's pretty serious comprehension, by the way."

"You are proud of her."

"I am. But I haven't done much—she's been studying very hard. I think she understands that it may be a key to survival."

There was a silence. Then Giuliano said slowly, "Emilio, she's not going to survive. Not if . . ."

Another long silence, during which I felt my pulse pounding very clearly against the brass door handle. I didn't breathe. The funny thing was, I thought in Italian. *"Santa Maria, proteggimi, ti prego. . . .—*Santa Maria, protect me, please. . . .*"

"You know I still don't agree."

"It killed your father, and you don't agree."

They sounded like my mom and dad when they were trying not to fight. My demon had killed Emilio's father? What else hadn't they told me or my family?

Someone tapped his fingers against a wineglass, I couldn't tell who.

"We both know where we stand," said Giuliano. "You know I hate it—hate this. But there are so few choices. . . ."

"She should have choices, too, shouldn't she? *She saw him. She heard him.* She has it. She's one of us, through and through, even if she was raised in a mad country. Roberto's granddaughter, Nonno: this may be our one chance at his branch of the family, his powers. Can't we at least train her a little?"

"How can we be sure that these powers are not conferred by the demon?" asked Giuliano.

This seemed to stop Emilio, but only for a moment. "How can we be sure they are not her own? You tell me that when I was a baby I could see them and hear them. When I was a baby.

Before I'd ever even been present at an exorcism."

"Well then, if we do, who will decide which secrets to keep from her, my grandson?" said Giuliano. "Who will decide what the demon should not know when he comes for her again, as you know he will? Who will decide what he cannot hear?"

Giuliano sounded like he was taunting Emilio. He sounded cold, which was strange to me, because I thought of him as such a warm man. Emilio answered, "You will, of course, Grandfather." But there was an edge to his voice.

I heard them stand up and stepped back into my room as quietly as I could, hoping they didn't hear the door click. I tiptoed to my bed and sat down, resting my palms on my knees, and stared at the shelves of books in the dark. There was a lot to think about.

I wasn't going to survive. I saw the carpet on the floor of my room back home floating beneath my dangling feet, my heels hitting each other. I felt the power that had sent me floating into the air. I wanted to choke, to throw up. I wanted to rip every book from the shelves. I wanted to walk out into the hall and scream at them both until my throat was sore.

Instead I sat on my bed, palms on my knees.

They were thinking about training me, but they couldn't. Everything I might learn, the demon would learn. Something had happened today that had made them think. What did they mean, I had seen him? Of course I had seen him. He had come in and talked to Emilio just like anybody else walking into the shop.

Except he didn't, did he? said a voice in my head. That was when I remembered I had never heard the bells ring on the shop door, and then it all came together, somehow. He had come to the table, but I had never heard the scrape of a chair. Emilio hadn't offered him food, a breach of manners I couldn't imagine a Della Torre guilty of, even though I had only known them for about five weeks.

Our eyes see what we expect to see. I wondered what else I had thought I had seen. I had heard them talking. But had I seen them talk? Could I remember seeing Emilio's mouth move? I could very clearly remember how surprised he had been, when I had asked if it was okay for me to stay. He hadn't expected me to be able to see this person or hear their conversation, so of course it was all right if I stayed.

I kept staring at the wall.

Maybe the demon did give me these powers. I remembered the thrill of being able to hear inside people's heads. I remembered the horrible, sick thud of my sister against the wall. . . . What did Emilio mean, when he spoke of my grandfather, my branch of the family, our powers? I knew they were talking about me, but what about Gina? And what about my dad? I wanted to know, but the other thing Giuliano had said sent the rest of my thoughts into the shadows.

I wasn't going to survive. . . .

I sat on my bed, palms on my knees, and let the tears roll down my cheeks.

The Case of Signora Galeazzo

"Too many words," I wrote to Gina the next morning, in an e-mail. I was in a foul mood.

Dear Gina,

They wear me out. Learning a new language makes me hungry all the time. Trying to write you an e-mail in English is like this colossal task. I wish I could do what Emilio does, switching back and forth as if he's done it forever.

I wonder if I'll ever feel better. I'm starting to be able to imagine what it would be like to be normal again. Especially like I was before I met our bizarre Italian family, with their food obsession and their weird demon job and their house full of old stuff.

You asked me whether I have seen the demon again, since the plane, but I haven't. I don't want to see it ever again. Sometimes I think I can hear it, way out beyond where anyone should be able to hear.

Plus there are uncanny voices that float in the room, and miserable midnight conversations between a cousin I had a crush on and an old man I wanted to trust. But I didn't feel like telling Gina about those things, even though I wanted more than anything to talk to someone who would understand.

I miss you. Make Dad and Mom save enough money so you guys can come over soon.
Love and good luck with the twenty-minute makeup job and the Duke of Naples,
Mia

When I finished I put my head down on the keyboard and cried, so my sister told me later that she got an entire page of random letters, mostly *G*s, at the end of my e-mail, which I didn't notice because my eyes were too blurry when I clicked on the SEND button.

Eventually I lifted my head, went to the bathroom before anyone could see me, and washed my face. What else could I do?

I stayed in my room for most of the day. I didn't want to see Giuliano or Emilio, or anyone else for that matter. These people, who were so kind to me, thought I was going to die. My story was already written, and worse, they'd already flipped to the last page to see how it was going to end. Screw them. Screw everything.

I lay on my bed and thought about Grandfather Roberto. Maybe he'd been right to leave. Looking at the faces of my relatives, hearing their voices, noticing their mannerisms, stirred so many memories of him. I thought of how he had looked at Gina and me sometimes, with a frown on his face. I'd always assumed he was angry at us, even though he'd never said anything or treated us badly. Now I wondered if he had been thinking of the family he'd left behind. Had he seen echoes of them in us, the way I saw echoes of him in them?

I remembered one Sunday dinner. I must have been six or so. My father had told him about something odd that had happened on a job site. It was the first year after the factory closed, and Dad was proud of the fact that he'd found work right away as a carpenter. Dad thought I couldn't hear him over my mom and grandmother's conversation, but I could: how he'd gone into the dining room of the house his boss wanted to work on, and he'd felt someone—or something—there. He'd told his boss not to take the job. Marco hadn't listened, and sure enough, strange things had happened in that room. Tools had gone missing, and a saw blade had come loose and gouged Sal Manzetti's leg so badly he had walked with a limp ever since.

Grandpa had stood up from the table, thanked my mother for the food, and gone out to the porch to sit. Mom had asked Dad, "What's wrong?"

Dad had looked at Grandma as he answered. "I'm sorry. I didn't realize he still felt that way."

Grandma had just sighed. "That won't change," she had said.

After dinner, I had gone out on the porch to sit with Grandpa. He was staring at nothing, and I came up beside him and climbed into his lap. We didn't talk; he put his big arms around me, and I looked at his broad, strong-fingered hands and rested against him. For a moment, he had hugged me to him, so tightly I couldn't breathe; but whatever he felt, he always thought of us, so he had loosened his hold right away.

I'd forgotten all about that. I missed him so much right then, and Grandma too, even though she'd died six years ago, not too long after him. Why do we have to lose anyone?

After a while, I got up and went to the window.

The weather fit my mood. It was pouring, cold, miserable, late-October rain. What would Gina be doing? She'd decided to go as Ariel for Halloween and had charmed Mr. Berenstein into letting her borrow her costume from the play. The court-yard looked stained and drab. There was a pool of water in the seat of my metal chair on the balcony. Raindrops splashed into it; even the stupid pool of water never got a rest.

Instead of reading history or grammar, I pulled out my Harry Potter book from my shirt drawer and curled up on the bed, as far over in the corner as I could go. I read for a long time. Gradually, like the volume being turned up on a radio, I could hear Pompous and Gravel. They were arguing about the weather.

"It never used to rain like this," said Pompous.

"Yes, it did," said Gravel. "People always say that. According to humans, things are never like they used to be."

"You never paid attention to the weather."

"Yes, I did. I still do."

"No, because if you paid attention, you would know that the drops are much bigger now. I can hear them. It's like somebody throwing a bunch of coins on a tile roof. It's this global warming everyone's talking about."

"If by 'everyone,'" said Gravel, "you mean that man who stayed here last year, well, I read an article over his mind's shoulder."

"That's everyone, isn't it, including the people who wrote the article and the people who read it? That qualifies, enough, doesn't it, Mr. Pedantic?"

I shut Harry Potter.

"Do you guys have to argue all the time?" I asked.

There was silence, and the feeling of extra air in the room that I now knew meant they had gone back to wherever they went. I called after them, anyway, "How come you never talk to me? You only ever talk about me or just argue. We should talk sometime."

For the first time, I wondered how I'd always understood them. I had spoken to them just now in Italian, but I'd heard every word they'd said *the first night I'd been here*. I made a mental note to ask Giuliano or Emilio.

I got up and walked over to the balcony. The rain had finally stopped, and the pool in my chair reflected a small break in the clouds. I opened the door, sticking my head out to smell the washed city: the clear, wet, brisk air; the last leaves on the basil plant one balcony over, where the quiet man often sat reading the paper and stubbing out cigarette after cigarette in a lime-green glass ashtray. I could smell the sodden butts and ash, and the last gasp of fumes from someone's *motorino*—moped—that had just driven out through the echoing gate underneath the street apartments, and the gorgeous rush of cooking garlic from the apartment where the young guys who liked to work on cars lived with their mother and sister.

My stomach rumbled. My bad mood was gone, and I didn't feel scared to see Giuliano or Emilio anymore. I didn't even feel particularly angry. I went downstairs to the shop, where my best chance of a pre-eight-o'clock-dinner snack lay, since Laura always frowned when I came into the kitchen to raid the fridge after she'd already started cooking. It was around wine-pouring time.

"Ah, Mia," said Giuliano, too cheerfully, as I entered the shop. So much for my new, good mood. I had something I wanted to ask him, but I couldn't remember what it was, something to do with my room. Emilio was standing, facing one of the candle shelves, with his hands clasped behind his back. He turned around when I came in and walked slowly to the table, where the bottle and glasses sat.

"We're just waiting on Égide; he's going to take over here so we can run some errands," he said, and his smile seemed much more real to me than his grandfather's.

"I can watch the shop for you," I volunteered, even though I wanted to go with them.

"No, you should come with us. It's not good for you to be cooped up here so much," he said, and I couldn't hide my delight. Cooped up? More and more often, I felt I could hardly breathe.

After Égide arrived and we were out on the street, I could tell Giuliano was watching for something. Emilio had fallen back, on the phone with the curlfrond again, the unseen Alba. I think I would have spent a lot more energy trying not to be jealous if Giuliano hadn't been scanning the street this way and that.

"Uh . . . Nonno? Do you expect another attack?" I finally asked, nervous as heck.

"What? No, no," he replied. I didn't get much more out of him while we visited the baker, the greengrocer, the tobacconist's—where he bought not cigarettes but bus and subway passes—and the odd shop that sold everything from salad spinners to cheap kitchen magnets. While I was staring at a plastic Nativity set in the window, Emilio's phone rang again.

"*Pronto. Ciao*, Signore Galeazzo. Now—slow down. Right. Are you at home? No, we're not at the shop. Where are you? Ha! We're just around the corner from you. Wait right where you are."

Just then, Giuliano came out of the shop, handing another bag to his grandson.

"Paolo Galeazzo's around the corner," said Emilio. "We need to go to his grandmother *now*."

They both looked at me, no doubt wondering what to do with me.

"No time to take her home," said Giuliano shortly.

We were already out the door of the shop.

"Call Francesco, Anna Maria. Tell them our route. We need them to walk with us. You have your—?"

Emilio nodded and touched his chest pocket.

"I think we can manage," Giuliano said thoughtfully. "Yes, Francesco and Anna Maria, both."

Of course: to protect me. Emilio nodded. Stunned, I watched him struggle with bags and cell phone for a moment. Then I took the bags from him so he could call.

A few minutes later, we found Paolo Galeazzo standing outside a bookstore. Giuliano made hasty introductions as we began to walk.

"I was coming to get you," said Paolo. He was a skinny guy, almost thinner than Francesco, his narrow face white with fear. He and Giuliano began to speak together in low voices as we hurried forward. My stomach knotted with fear and excitement. I didn't like seeing Giuliano so focused on Paolo, and with Emilio still talking on the phone, I felt unguarded. I hunched my shoulders.

After Emilio had spoken to Francesco and Anna Maria, he put his phone away, looked at me, and shook his head.

"We have to find another way," he said. "This is ridiculous."

"Tell me about it," I rolled my eyes. My shoulders loosened.

"Ah, well, even if there wasn't this problem . . . When we do let you go out alone, Mia, you should still be very careful. It's a big city."

"I know," I said, and I couldn't keep the longing out of my voice. He laughed.

"Of course you want to explore. Well, we are working on it."

I wanted to ask how, but as we turned the corner onto the Via Monte di Pietà, a more important question plagued me. I couldn't stop thinking about the conversation of the night before.

I asked Emilio, "Should I really be tagging along?"

He smiled his one-corner-up smile. "Do you have a choice?"

"Well—"

We hurried forward in silence. Finally I gave up and said, "I'm just afraid I'll be in the way. I don't know anything about what you do."

The word I used—"afraid," *timoroso,* was too small to do the job it had to, and I felt the same way.

"But you want to know," he stated simply. "You must know. At least I think so."

"Yes." My voice shook even though I didn't want it to. "Emilio . . ."

"Yes?"

I lowered my voice, pretty sure we shouldn't be talking about this stuff in the street.

"In the shop, last night . . . I've figured out that I wasn't supposed to see that guy."

I didn't tell him how.

I believe Emilio was never a fool, not from the moment he was born; yet the look he gave me then made me think that perhaps he had never really seen me before. He lowered his voice, too.

"You did, did you?"

He smiled at me. I waited a moment, then asked, "He said that your grandfather told him to watch that street."

"Yes."

"And you said that the candles had warned you."

"Yes."

"So the candles tell us things?"

I had never said "us" like this before. I wondered if he noticed, or if it would bother him that I spoke of myself alongside him and the other demon catchers.

"That's one thing they do," he said, nodding just like Giuliano. Again I was struck by the similarity between them, a family likeness of gesture and habits of speech far more than feature. Left to myself, I never would have guessed that the short, gray, elderly man heading down the street in front of us bore any blood relation to the young man beside me, with his eyes like storms and his fallen-star hair.

"What else do the candles do? And the—that guy?" I asked.

"Think about it some, and tell me what you think, and I will tell you whether you are right," he said.

"Why can't you just tell me?"

My words stopped Emilio dead in the street.

"When your government tells you your city is safe, do you

believe them? When your mother tells you a boy is bad, do you believe her?"

"No, yes, sometimes, but—"

"But should you?"

"I don't think so, but—"

"Your government can't see everything, and your mother judges boys by the standards of her youth. This doesn't mean your government is wrong or that your mother is not wise, though, does it?"

"No."

"Yet it does mean that you don't just take their word for everything. So why should we just tell you things? Would you be wise to take our word for it? Why should you trust us more than your own senses?"

Why indeed? I wondered if he knew I had heard them in the night, whispering in the kitchen about how I had seen that spirit guy in the shop, had understood what he'd said. I went on, "But you know you know more than I do. Your grandfather, too. Your senses know more than my senses."

"Maybe they do. But I wasn't born that way. We all had to train our senses. So do you.

"Our family mostly tells the truth, Mia, but you should not just believe what you are told. You're not a child. You must become accustomed to seeing the world with your own eyes, catching the details that everyone wants you to miss."

"What details?"

"Keep watching. But, Mia, you already don't believe what

you're told. Why should you believe me or my grandfather? Keep watching. Keep your eyes open."

"Okay." I sighed. Great. I couldn't have a tiny amount of security in this crazy situation. I waited a minute before pursuing another subject.

"So. Signora Galeazzo. That's who that guy was talking about, right? Her house. Somebody was coming back. Somebody was going to take a long time to get there. So, if I'm using my own senses here," I added sarcastically, "I'm guessing not some living person."

"Definitely not living," said Emilio.

"And?"

"We don't know much else. We know a bit about the history of the neighborhood. We've known she was coming for some time, but we've only known where her thoughts were bent a little more recently. There's a way. You can tell. . . ."

For a moment, I pitied him as he paused—I guessed he was trying to decide what he could and couldn't tell me—and then I got mean. My sister hates it when I do that, but I figured I was justified.

"How?" I asked, sweet and completely innocent. Right.

He looked over at me.

"It's hard to explain, especially right now," he said loftily.

Sure, Emilio. Sure. I frowned and kept walking until my curiosity took over again.

"So, are we talking about another—another demon?" I asked, lowering my voice even further. *Demon* was one of the first Italian words I had ever learned, even though I hadn't really wanted to. I had run across it in the dictionary one night looking for something else, and since it was very similar to the English word, just an extra *E* on the end, *demone*, my eyes had been drawn to it like some miserable lodestone.

"We don't think so," Emilio replied. "We're not entirely sure, but we think instead it's a *fantasma*."

"A fantasy?"

"A ghost. An unquiet spirit, a restless spirit," he said, speaking in English for the first time since he had warned me about the candles. *"Un fantasma. Uno spirito irrequieto."*

"An unquiet spirit"—what a phrase. I felt as if somebody had touched the back of my neck with fingers that had been frozen under the earth for a long, long time.

"Ciao, Anna Maria. *Ciao,* Francesco," said Emilio, for our cousins had just caught up with us. Anna Maria goggled at me like I was a dish she was going to have to send back to the kitchen. I tried to ignore her, but it was hard; she was so cool, so amazingly dressed, such a model. She looked like she'd just come from a photo shoot. It was odd to think she was only three years older than me.

"Ciao, Mia," said Francesco, patting my arm. "Remember, I'm the boy, so I get the *O*."

He laughed. I tried to.

"A thousand thanks, Cousin," I said, and getting to say that little word, *cugino,* cheered me up a little.

Anna Maria fixed that.

"Why are you bringing her, anyway?" she asked Emilio, just loudly enough for me to hear.

"Because it's time she learned what we do," he answered calmly. He glanced over at me and added, "From the outside."

"What does Nonno think?"

"He thinks," said Emilio slowly and deliberately, "that if she can see messengers, guess correctly about the candles, and come out alive from the possession of one of the most powerful demons we confront, she has as much right to be here as you do."

"*Maria*, Emilio! Take it easy," Anna Maria said as if she hadn't meant to totally question everything, but of course she had. Still, his words warmed me, even if there wasn't much truth in them, since I was only there because they hadn't had time to take me home.

"Ah! Signora Galeazzo's house," said Francesco, sounding relieved.

NINE

Gas Roses

We stopped at an old stone building, its facings scarred and pitted where many mopeds had parked and scraped along the wall. Iron rings were set in some of the stones; I knew from my reading that people used to tie horses to them. There were marks higher up on the stones, too, round pits and other scratches and scars. A sturdy rosebush grew out of a tiny bit of fenced earth, cigarette butts clustered around its roots, a few last blossoms glowing against the dirty wall.

Giuliano faced the house, examining it. I wondered why we didn't rush inside, and Paolo Galeazzo, shifting anxiously from foot to foot, clearly did, too. Emilio put a hand on his arm and said, "In a moment. It's all right," in a voice that could have calmed an earthquake. Paolo stood still.

Giuliano stepped forward and smelled the roses, then nodded, frowning. "Emilio," he commanded, gesturing at the roses.

Emilio smelled them. "Ah," he said, sounding slightly surprised.

Next was Francesco, whose giant nose ought to be useful here, I thought, although I also wondered why the boys got to go first. Maybe because they were older?

"Oh," said Francesco, looking thoughtful.

Then Anna Maria stepped up, looking as if she thought what I thought—that this must look like a very weird family to anyone passing in the street, with all of us taking turns smelling roses. Just the same, she bent down and inhaled deeply.

"Huh," she said, and glared at the roses.

As everyone else turned to go inside, I thought, *Hey, what about my turn?* So I darted forward to smell them myself.

The roses smelled, well, like roses. They smelled wonderful, in fact, despite the autumn cold, which should have sapped all their scent away by this time. Except—

"Almonds?" I asked aloud. Then I laughed at myself, adding, "Almonds, but bitter. Odd. And there's something else, something cold."

My relations, already at the door, frowned at me as if I'd done something wrong, and too late I realized I should have just grunted, if I was going to smell the roses at all. Paolo Galeazzo was staring at all of us. But didn't this concern him, too?

Giuliano jerked his head at the door, giving me a look that was hard to read. I obeyed and followed everyone in.

Once inside, we paused in the entrance hall to the apartment. All the Della Torres reached into their coat pockets and pulled out small, battered, black leather cases like the one I had seen Uncle Matteo open at the dinner table, each one with gilded lettering running in columns down the front, and brass or iron fittings. I noticed small differences: Emilio's had a deep scar on its underside; Francesco's had a very short column of lettering; Anna Maria's just looked tremendously old; Giuliano's had scorch marks.

"Emilio book, Anna Maria bell, myself candle," ordered Giuliano. "Francesco, I need you to look after Mia."

Francesco grunted. I could hear his disappointment.

"Mia," said Giuliano. "I need you to watch and keep hold of yourself. Keep out of the way," he said kindly enough that it didn't hurt to hear it. "Use your meditation." I wondered what good that would do, but Giuliano held my eyes for a moment until I nodded. Oh, *Santa Maria*, how hard was this going to be? What was going to happen? He just scared me more. Then Paolo opened the door to the next room.

The ceilings were high, the room dark. I couldn't figure out why we didn't just turn on the light. Old, heavy, wooden furniture stood like a sinister audience in the shadows. After a moment, my eyes adjusting to the dimness, I raised my head.

A woman floated high in the air.

I'm not a screamy girl. I don't squeal at spiders or rats. I screamed now. I was surprised how little sound came out.

Someone clapped a hand over my mouth. Francesco—I saw his eyes glint toward me in the dark. He pulled his hand away as soon as I got hold of myself. Only Anna Maria flicked her head impatiently. Everyone else was too busy looking upward.

She was seated in a chair, her head nodded to one side. Her old, tired hands hung over the armrests. I remembered a lame documentary from history class about the oracle at Delphi, seated on her tripod, breathing vapors from a vent in the earth, ruled by a force far greater than herself. They did a horrible, cheesy voice-over to make the oracle sound awe-inspiring.

But Signora Galeazzo, slumped in her chair, ruled by a force far greater than herself—that was just plain terrifying.

"Nonna," breathed Paolo.

Her head jerked up. She spoke with a voice that could not possibly have come from her throat, a voice stopped with earth, a voice that came from all the lost places. She didn't speak to us; she spoke only to herself, coldly, like a madwoman talking in the street. Gradually the angry muttering started to rise in pitch, accompanied by whistling gasps.

She began to sing something in a minor key. Paolo stepped back beside Francesco and me and whispered, "What language is that?"

"Hebrew," Francesco replied quietly.

"She doesn't know Hebrew," whispered Paolo. "She's never spoken anything but Italian, like a good Catholic."

"This is not uncommon, for a possessed person to begin speaking or singing in languages they don't know. It's part of how we know that someone else is inside them," explained Francesco.

Giuliano had moved forward, placing his open case on a table near the center of the room. Emilio and Anna Maria followed. They conferred too softly for me to understand them. I whispered to Francesco, "What are they doing?"

"Deciding which ritual to use. I know Emilio and Giuliano have been talking about it since they found out she was coming, but I guess they hadn't figured it out yet. Sometimes you have to change, anyway."

He shrugged, glancing nervously over at Paolo. But Paolo wasn't paying attention. He was looking up at his grandmother, working his palms against each other, squeezing and knotting his fingers. Now I knew what people meant when they used the phrase "wringing his hands." Francesco reached over and laid one hand over Paolo's.

"You're tangling up the web," he whispered to Paolo. "Take some deep breaths. She is in good hands—my great-uncle is the best."

"I hope so," Paolo whispered back.

Giuliano had set out a small, yellow candle in a silver holder. Emilio had taken a black leather book from his case. He showed his grandfather a page, and Giuliano nodded. Anna Maria held a round, silver bowl, hardly bigger than the hollow of her hand, seated on an equally small, red cushion. In her other hand, she held what looked like a little, silver stick, wrapped with red cloth. They looked up at the floating woman and held very still.

I wondered what they were waiting for. Obviously not to figure out whether she was possessed.

Giuliano nodded at Anna Maria. She set the tiny bowl on the table and tapped it with the silver stick, bringing forth a surprisingly big sound for such a small object. She struck the bowl three times, letting each peal fade before she struck again.

The old woman on the chair above us stopped singing on the second stroke.

Moving as if she wasn't quite sure how to use her head, she rolled it down to look at us, and I was surprised to see, as well as I could see in the dark, that she looked content. She certainly looked more peaceful than any of us. I started to feel bad. We were upset over nothing. She was fine. Why were we here?

"Well," she said, still in the harsh voice from the lost places, "I'm back, anyway. I expect Ludovico has made a mess of everything, hasn't he? Hopefully I can make a start on the depositions. I need to get back to work, it will help. Straight back to work."

Of course she should. Emilio raised his book; I saw his hair glitter in the dark as he lifted his head, before his grandfather laid a hand on his arm and stopped him.

"Work is good, always good—provided you don't work too hard," Giuliano said to the floating form above him. He sounded as if he were chatting with an acquaintance in the street.

"Provided you don't have useless, lazy assistants and an equally useless husband," she said, adding bitterly, "People who have good help can afford not to work hard."

"That's the truth, isn't it?" said Giuliano, smiling at the terrible creature who hung above him. I couldn't believe he could smile at her.

"True as the soil," she agreed. "Inevitable as winter."

"So," he continued in the same easy voice, "where have you been?"

There was a rushing, roaring sound, as if all the little light left in the room were being sucked out of it. We were left in a darkness so complete that I could feel my skin itching. When the voice spoke again, it was a dreadful, enraged hiss.

"If you dare send me back, I will kill her. She won't survive me. You can't make me go back."

In the dark, with nothing to go by but the breathing of Francesco beside me, I felt as if I were back in my old room, with the voice coming out of me, the candle flickering in front of me, the longing in my heart to fly—

Something brushed against me. At that moment, Signora Galeazzo began laughing in triumph.

My whole body cramped, and I went down on my knees. The smell of bitter almonds filled my nostrils again, this time overpowering, suffocating; I knew if I could not breathe fresh air I would die. I gasped for breath, clawing the rug.

"See how you like that," snarled the voice, rattling the old woman in her chair.

Paolo and Francesco were holding me. Giuliano stood with his back to me, facing her. Didn't he care that I couldn't breathe? Or Emilio, holding his book before him, or Anna Maria, ringing that damned bell?

"Steady, steady," said Francesco, but still I couldn't breathe. I felt my lungs cramping.

"Yes! Yes!" shrieked the voice. It seemed to boom even deeper, as if it came from far inside the earth. "*That's* how it feels. She knows how it feels. If I kill her, if she dies with it in her lungs, she will understand before she dies! And you, you will know what it is to lose what is precious to you! To lose the ones you love. I didn't come all this way so that you could send me away! I didn't come all this way not to be listened to, after all this time!"

She was shrieking now, thundering. Her words pounded in my ears and then faded, as if someone were turning the volume up and down. I felt like I was about to vomit, but I felt sure that if I threw up, I would choke on it. I understood the smell of almonds outside too well now.

Then: peace. Snow was falling on my face. *Thank goodness I'm awake, at last,* I thought. I stood up but it was hard, as if I had forgotten how. I looked down and saw myself lying down, another snowflake settling in my hair.

My face was not my own, and yet I knew this was me. I bent down to look, and I saw that my skin had sunken into my cheeks, that my eyes remained open and bloodshot, but that instead of being red, the blood was turning brown, and my lips were blue, with no breath parting them. In the moment I understood that I was dead, I noticed another still hand resting beside my own, already dusted with snow. Raising my eyes slowly, I looked out across a patch of ground covered in bodies, all still, all quietly kissed by the snowflakes, one at a time. The only sound was of wind in pine branches—I was not on a plain after all, but in a broad forest clearing.

Then I could hear the rumble of boxcars in the distance and, incongruously, the sound of music—a little orchestra of violins, violas, and flutes. These sounds, though I did not know why, filled me with terror.

Oh, God, I thought. *Oh, Santa Maria*, as the horror soaked into me and seized my heart.

"Majdanek," I whispered, and the wind rose in the pines; "Majdanek," I repeated as my eyes opened. It sounded like the name of a demon.

My cheek was pressed against Signora Galeazzo's rug. In the dark, I could feel all the spiky bits of hard Persian wool pushing into my cheek, could smell dust and dirt. My whole body was covered in cold sweat.

"There, you see, *she* understands," said the terrible voice above us, rasping in its borrowed throat. "*She* knows. I knew she would.

"We thought they would never come and take us, you know. We were Italian. Besides, Mussolini was busy with other things. My people have been Milanese citizens these five centuries. But we heard from friends, from relatives; we heard whispers about what was happening in Germany, and of course we were allies.

"So when the Germans asked the officials, the officials would say, 'Jews? Oh, I don't think we have Jews here, do you? Have you seen any Jews lately? Not me. We don't have the proper forms, anyway. Can't get them, it's wartime, you know.' Nobody can drag their feet like an Italian bureaucrat!" she said, sounding proud. "But then came the bombs, and after them, German soldiers, with their terrible black eagles, their terrible ideas. Then, when you heard the boxcars in the night, it was the most frightening sound.

"I think that nosy bitch down the street told on us. She never liked us. But it might have been the boy next door, who kept finding ways not to starve.

"When they came for us, I was almost relieved; now the worst has happened, I thought. They took us to that cavernous underground railway at the Stazione Centrale. There were dogs. . . . I still couldn't believe that they weren't just imprisoning us. Even after all the pogroms and the burnings my family has lived through, I couldn't believe, you know? The dreadful trains rumbled north, to a place we had not heard of."

Her attention had drifted into her story, and I could feel my lungs loosening.

"Auschwitz, Auschwitz!" she growled, turning to me again, and the thunder came back into her voice.

"You cannot imagine it! You cannot, you cannot, you who remain! They made some among us, the musicians on the trains, pick up instruments from the dead and play them, an orchestra to soothe us as we came off the boxcars. Can you see it? They took trouble over their cruelty, they wrote it down, they made lists and plans and came up with schemes like the horrible, sad orchestras.

"I wasn't going to take it, was I? We planned work slowdowns. We fought. But they found out which ones were the troublemakers, and they sent us East, to another camp, a camp they said no one ever left alive. . . . Majdanek."

"Majdanek," I repeated, understanding.

"But even there, we never gave up. A few of us, we planned an escape, and some of us made it. Me, I've taken longer to come back. . . . Longer . . ."

She began to laugh, heaving, gasping, Signora Galeazzo's throat wheezing with the effort.

"Majdanek," said Giuliano, and turned to look upward again.

He walked back to stand by Emilio and Anna Maria.

"I will not go back," she whispered in that lost voice, filling the whole room with sound.

"We will not make you go back," he said gently.

He said it again, and again, and again in the same soft voice. Sometimes she raged at him, and sometimes she whispered. Giuliano repeated himself so many times that Emilio had to send Francesco for a glass of water for his grandfather's parched throat, leaving me to lean against the wall.

At last she fell silent. The chair jolted lower with a nauseating jerk. The head rolled up again.

"You won't?" she asked.

I fought the urge to laugh hysterically.

We sat in the dark, so I never knew if the others were crying like I was. Sometime around three in the morning, she and Giuliano finished talking. He had helped her to understand that whatever long and painful journey she had taken, she had yet another one before her, one that we all hoped would lead to peace.

"We could banish you out of this body you are in," Giuliano told her very gently. "We could put you in a place where you would remain until transformed. But this thing I would not want to do. It would be better for you to set out on your own."

"But where am I going? What comes after?"

"I do not know," Giuliano replied. For a moment, I saw the abyss of death in my mind, of not being, and it was as lonely as her voice.

I leaned against the wall and slipped in and out of a haze of exhaustion. Giuliano, Emilio, and Anna Maria seemed tireless, patiently turning the spirit's thoughts toward leaving Signora Galeazzo's body. I had to struggle to stay awake and focus on what was happening, so much so that I didn't realize that Signora Galeazzo's chair had nearly floated to the floor.

When the voice finally departed, it didn't flee out of Signora Galeazzo's throat like an avalanche, as my demon had left mine. It expelled itself softly, on a sigh. The chair landed on the floor with a scrape and a thump, Signora Galeazzo's rigid body falling limp, her head and chest slumping. Giuliano and Emilio ran forward at the same time to keep her from sliding out of her seat.

"Bed is best, now," Giuliano said to Paolo, who nodded and showed them the way.

I noticed that there had been a lamp on in the room the entire time we had been there, yet somehow the gloom of possession had prevented it from illuminating anything at all. Now it gave out a small pool of yellow light, warming the walls and the stately old furniture. I used it to find my way to a chair (not the one Signora Galeazzo had been sitting in), feeling tears starting again in my eyes. Francesco sat down beside me. Anna Maria stood at the table, packing her tools away in their case. She clasped it shut and began on Emilio's, turning to us to say, "I have a shoot in four hours, and all I want to do is lie down and sleep."

Francesco ran his fingers through his wild hair and replied, "Can't you take a bunch of drugs like the other ones do?"

She snorted (again I was reminded of my grandfather). "Been there, done that. It just makes you ignorant. Anyway, I can't afford a habit. . . ." She gestured to the air where Signora Galeazzo had been. "I need to keep my wits about me," she added fiercely.

"*Basta, basta*, I didn't mean it," he said, waving his hands to placate her.

I wondered why anybody with a glamorous job like hers would want to bother doing her family's work as well. I knew I wanted to do it, though I wasn't sure why exactly, but I couldn't see why Anna Maria felt so passionately about it. It didn't seem quite the profession for somebody who had to keep their nails perfect, not to mention their hair and skin and all that. But then my thoughts drifted back to the spirit, the woman who had come so far. Had she made the painful journey back here for nothing? What would happen to her now? Were there thousands like her, their rage and grief unnassuaged? Did each body I had seen lying on that stretch

of earth house an angry spirit? What about all the other holo-
causts?

I thought about these things all the way home, too tired to
try to ask them out loud. We took a long time stumbling home.
Sometimes I could hear whispers above me in the alleyways and
streets, but I was too tired to care how vulnerable I might be.

I think Giuliano steered me to the door of my room; I
remember opening it and falling into bed. Only as I slid into
sleep did I realize that we had never learned the spirit's name.

TEN

How Little We Know

I didn't want to get out of bed the next morning. Granted, half my time in Milan, I didn't want to get out of bed; sometimes I still woke up with my feet kicking together. This morning, I felt like I had a legitimate excuse.

"I've only had three hours of sleep," I complained to Nonna Laura as she opened the shutters in my room with fierce, bearish bustle.

"You can nap later," she replied. "You need to get up, eat something, feel the sun on you. It's very important after a night like that. Everyone else is already up and out."

I groaned, pushed my way out of the covers, and squinted at the window. "There is no sun," I complained.

Laura put her hands on her hips and glared at me.

"Call on the brave blood of your ancestors, stop whining, and get out of bed, Mia," she said shortly, and walked out of the room. I heard her rattling pots in the kitchen like an angry poltergeist.

I waited for Pompous and Gravel to agree with her, but they weren't around. As I dressed, I grumbled to myself. Laura didn't get it. She hadn't looked out over the plain of frozen bodies. She hadn't been there, listening to that woman. I sat down on the bed for a minute, thinking about how someone could really make someone else walk into a gas chamber and die there.

Neither of us said anything about it when I came into the kitchen a few minutes later, more or less washed and dressed. When I looked at Laura, I thought about how she must have lived through that war as a child, she must have heard about the boxcars, known about the Jews, maybe even had friends who were taken away. Maybe she did have some idea.

I watched the frown lines on her seamed face. My head still hurt, like the time I snuck two whole beers at a Fourth of July picnic when I was twelve. She set coffee, pastries, soft cheese, olives, honey, jam, and a sliced pear in front of me. I'd forgotten that I'd missed dinner, along with everyone else who had gone to Signora Galeazzo's house.

"Thank you so much," I said, right at the same time that my stomach spoke for itself, and we both laughed. "Thank you so much" in Italian is *grazie mille*, "a thousand thanks," a courtly expression among many courtly expressions in my new language. I was getting used to sounding (at least to myself) like a Shakespearean actor whenever we went to the grocery store. I was starting to like it. She nodded shortly. By now I knew her well enough to know she felt the matter was settled.

She sat down across from me with the last of her own coffee and hot milk in her bowl.

"Where is everyone?" I asked. "Did Emilio make it to work?"

"He always makes a point of going in after an exorcism, if it's a weekday, obviously. I think that's too much, myself, and so does Giuliano, but Emilio is very like his father."

"Can I ask—" I began. "I don't want to—"

"You can ask about Emilio's father, Mia."

"Thank you, Nonna. What was he like?"

She pushed her bowl around in a small circle, watching the coffee swirl, like a sibyl who could see the past in a bowl of water.

"Luciano was—he was one of those children a mother longs for and yet is afraid to give birth to, one of the kissed children—kissed by the Virgin. He was a sweet, easy baby, and he grew up into a man who did everything well."

I watched her face soften and thought I knew what she meant. I had a sister like that, one of the kissed children. Yes, that's exactly what Gina was.

"But he took our duties, our family duties, very seriously. He pushed too hard."

She looked at me for a while then, and I had the usual, frustrating sensation that like every other Della Torre, she was waiting for me to hear what she *hadn't* said. I took a wild guess.

"I will try not to push too hard, Nonna," I said.

She nodded, approving, and everything was all right, if just for a moment. It seemed to me that I'd lifted part of a burden off her shoulders, though I couldn't quite see how; I only knew it had to do with the sadness in her eyes when she spoke of her son. Maybe that's why I remember the rest of the day as full of sunlight, even though it was dank and overcast outside. Just one day of sunlight.

Giuliano had taken to marking a spot in my books he thought I should reach, but in so casual a way that I didn't resent it, and that day I got even farther, easily. When I shut the last book, I slipped down to the shop, where I found Giuliano sweeping the floor. I took the broom from him and picked up where he had left off.

"It's good to see you up after last night," he said. "How are you doing? How did you find it?"

I paused, leaning on the broom.

"Amazing," I said, meeting his eyes. "Scary, but . . . amazing."

I thought maybe he looked pleased; it was hard to tell.

"Ah," he said. "Well."

"I have a lot of questions," I ventured.

He took a seat at the desk. "Ask them," he said, "and I will see which ones I can answer."

"Well," I began, "are demons really just angry ghosts? Is the demon that attacked me a spirit who is just really angry about something?"

Giuliano gave me the same measuring look Emilio had

when I had asked him questions on the way to the Galeazzo house. It looked to me like both of them had to think how much information they wanted to give me, just as they had considered every answer to my parents and sister and me back in Center Plains.

Finally he replied, "When we use the word *demon* in this family, we are generally referring to any spirit or emanation that takes over bodies. There are so many kinds, Mia. Some are just sad or angry ghosts of human beings—and sometimes these are not just one spirit, but more than one, twined together by the pain of the events that connected them.

"Other demons arise out of human emotions. Some areas of Italy and Crete, for example, have trouble with demons that arise out of vendettas: nurse that kind of anger for a couple of centuries, and you get trouble. Some demons, we don't know where they come from at all. Living in our modern cities, we forget there's a whole world out there, full of beings we don't understand, both corporeal and incorporeal. How many people really understand a bear or a wolf? You know that wolves have come back to our forests here in Italy? Or perhaps never left? So, we guess there also are other creatures, beings we can hardly imagine or understand.

"The Della Torres deal mostly with the kind of demons that arise from human beings in Milan. We are of this city. Sometimes we get called into cases elsewhere, but not very often." He frowned for a moment. "But in answer to your question, there are many kinds, and we don't know even close to everything about them."

"It seems bizarre to me that we can't know everything. Haven't Della Torres been studying these things for centuries?"

"Over a millennium, actually." He added dryly, "Some subjects take more time than others—to know them completely."

Was he mocking me, I wondered. His voice changed, and he went on, "In my experience, every possession is a voyage into the unknown. We have our notes, we have our rituals, but what we find when we arrive face-to-face with a demon, whether purely evil or simply angry, may not be in any notebook or aided by any chant. It may be something we have never faced before."

Francesco had said something like that, though less poetically. My thoughts returned again to the woman who had spoken through Signora Galeazzo's throat.

"But a lot of them, they're not just evil—instead, they need our help?" I asked.

Giuliano looked at me with a light in his eyes I hadn't seen before. He smiled at me.

"You might be very good at this," he said.

I looked down. "Thank you," I said, even though what I really wanted to say was *I think I've been waiting to hear that my whole life*. I finished sweeping the corners, putting extra work into them, then put the broom away and sat down.

"That woman, that spirit, last night," I asked Giuliano, "is she gone, not just gone from Signora Galeazzo? Or is she like my demon? Will she come back?"

"She's gone."

"I thought so," I said. "It felt like it. But I couldn't be sure."

"Well, we're never sure, not completely," he replied calmly.

"Our ancestors were wrong too many times for us to be completely sure, ever. But yes, I am as sure as I can be that she is gone."

"Where did she go?"

He knit his eyebrows together like my grandfather used to. "Full of questions this afternoon."

I smiled at him.

"That one," he went on, "I don't know the answer to. I don't know if anyone truly does. We know they go on a journey, the same one you and I will take, one day. Where do you think it goes?"

He looked thoughtfully into my eyes.

"I don't know," I faltered. "Heaven, maybe. But I don't feel sure about that."

He smiled.

"Enough. We had a long night, we deserve a moment of rest from these thoughts. Would you like a coffee?"

He went up and got us coffees from Nonna Laura, and we sat over our cups for the rest of the afternoon, greeting Sandro the Sicilian, and Beppo from up the street, and Signora Strachetti from the butcher's, as well as an actual legitimate customer who just wanted candles, one of two or three I'd seen since my arrival. Giuliano gestured graciously at the shelves, explaining that these were only display models, and he would be happy to send his assistant (me) for fresh ones. He did have to come back and show me the correct boxes to take ordinary candles from; I stored up more questions to ask him later.

All the neighbors drank coffee with us, until it got close to wine-pouring time, at which point we all switched over. Emilio showed up six minutes after, of course, looking as fresh as if he'd had a full night's sleep, and stayed for dinner.

After we ate, I came back down to the shop. For a second, I thought it was empty, but then I saw Emilio sitting at the table, a glass of wine and a book in front of him.

Something made me stay where I was in the dark office. He didn't seem to have heard me.

He turned a page, reading on, self-contained in the small pool of light from the lamp and a couple of candles.

He took a sip of wine and stared off into the distance, obviously thinking about what he'd just read, completely lost in his thoughts. No, people say that, they say "lost in his thoughts," but really, he looked *found* in his thoughts.

He didn't glow like Apollo. He looked a lot more like his grandfather, the family features exposed now: I could see the generous Della Torre mouth, the high cheekbones, the far-seeing eyes with their amused expression. He looked both older, because he did not look like a god, and younger, because he sat still, relaxed, open.

What would it be like to lose my dad, as he had? And not just lose him, but lose him to the very forces my family struggled with? He had been through so much, yet it didn't really seem to have touched him, as far as I could tell.

I noticed something else. I didn't feel all melty looking at him this way. He looked like a regular cousin, somebody I could be friends with; he looked almost ordinary, an unusual thing for a Della Torre, I thought.

I looked at him so long that I thought he must surely feel my gaze, first because he was a demon catcher and second because he was human. But he did not, and it frightened me to see him so vulnerable.

I wanted to protect him. I wanted to leave him this moment of peace. Besides, I admitted to myself, I did not want to watch him close up, to lose this image of him as a different man entirely, at peace with himself and the world.

I slipped away upstairs.

ELEVEN

In Which I Meet More Gorgeous Italian Men

If I'd still been in the States, I would've noticed the way the last two weeks of October slipped away after Signora Galeazzo's exorcism, because Gina and I would have gone to get pumpkins with Mom, and we would both be planning our costumes and hoping to get invited to parties. Then Halloween would have come and gone, and dorky-looking cartoon turkeys and Pilgrims would have started to appear in shop windows.

In Milan, the air got colder, and the fall fashion shows finished up. People brought out elegant, sleek winter coats and exceedingly tasteful scarves.

Hi, Gina,

I never said thank-you for that e-mail. Tell Mom thanks for the package, and thank Dad for remembering that Almond Roca is my favorite. I let everybody try a piece last night, and for once nobody said, "Oh, but blah blah blah from the Abruzzi is so much better," so I think it was a hit.

It was really hard to Skype with you guys the other day. Just the sound of everybody in the background made me so homesick. I am psyched that Luke the Duke came over, though! "Not that into me." Whatever! I'm glad he's coming over for Thanksgiving. I can't believe it's almost that time of year. Have I really been here that long? It seems longer, and shorter, at the same time.

Anyway, I heard Luke say once in English class that Thanksgiving at his house mostly involves a case of Miller, so I bet he is pretty pleased not to have to be there. Uh, my English is all confused now, because I only use it with you guys. Sorry!

Do you think Aunt Maggie will bring the creepy sweet-potato-and-marshmallow casserole?

I told everybody here about the holiday. Anna Maria was over having coffee and said something like, "Yeah, they fed you and you gave them smallpox and took their land." I was so stunned I didn't even cry—or jump up, grab a lamp, and smack her over the head with it. Whenever she says something like this, her brother, Francesco, just says, "All models are rude." I guess she got a Della Torre Talking-To, because she stopped by around dinnertime with some kind of a squash tart (pumpkin pie) and told me that she had looked all over the city for it. It tasted really good, though not a thing like pumpkin pie.

I know you would say she was right. But still, do you know what I mean?

I love you. Tell Dad I'm being good.

Love,

Mia

A couple of weeks before the Thanksgiving I was going to miss, I got to go shopping for dinner with Francesco and his father, Uncle Matteo, the one who looked like Giuliano. Because of me, we had to walk fast and we didn't go far, but I still was embarrassingly excited to be outside, even if it meant listening overhead every minute. We had to walk around ladders on the sidewalk where people were stringing up Christmas lights; we blew puffs of frost in front of us. I found myself laughing just to be able to do that.

As I handed Laura the bags of bread, artichokes, pasta, milk, and cheese, it dawned on me that Uncle Matteo and Francesco had let me do most of the talking, and that I had gone from baker to vegetable shop to grocery without a single hitch, a single missed word, a single butterfly in my stomach as I pushed open the door to each shop. I hadn't even thought about it. I gave her a huge grin of triumph, and she smiled back, saying, "Who crowned you queen of the May?"

"Oh, I don't know. Just my Italian is getting better, I think."

"It certainly is. Giuliano called and said he'd be home around five, and that you should take a look at that history of the Visconti if you've finished your other work."

I nodded. History made a lot more sense after Signora Galeazzo. A demon catcher had to know everything about the place they lived, otherwise when a case like Signora Galeazzo's came up, they wouldn't be able to make sense of the situation. Giuliano had told me a few days before that after the Galeazzo exorcism, he had finally found his grandfather's notes for some other cases on that street.

"All long before the war—but at least we could know what wasn't going on," he had said.

"And when we—uh, you and everyone—smelled the flowers outside the house," I had asked, "is that something that tells you what's going on? Because I smelled gas. Like they had in the . . ." I was thinking, *In the concentration camps*, but that sentence was too hard to finish. "Anyway, I smelled gas."

"What do you think?"

Argh! Worse than his grandson! Even though he'd just poured out almost more information than I wanted, a few minutes before.

"Well, I guess it would make sense," I hazarded, buying time like I did in algebra class. "But maybe it's only for ghosts, not for demons? And maybe it's only if they lived in that house? And if the flowers aren't in season, do you check something else? The leaves?"

Giuliano had started to laugh, then checked himself.

"Enthusiastic," he said at last, looking sad. "These things do interest you, don't they? But you shouldn't have to see anything so . . . terrible again. We'll have to be more careful. There's too much at risk."

As if I needed reminding.

"I just wish there was something I could *do*," I told him.

He looked surprised.

"But you are doing so much," he replied. "Studying, learning the language so fast, and sparing us a great deal of fear and worry while we try to solve this problem. Mia, you are doing a lot."

This was not a satisfactory answer, to say the least, but I didn't know how to reply. I hated feeling so helpless, hated it, hated it.

I thought about that conversation, about the need for history, on the day of the shopping expedition. After I'd finished helping Laura unpack the groceries, I went down to watch over the shop so Giuliano could step out. I walked around checking candles, always very careful not to breathe on them, and swept the floor, cleaned the glass in the door, and dusted the shelves.

I don't think anyone ever asked me to take care of the shop, or showed me where the brooms and rags were; I just started one day. My parents would have been shocked, but then, cleaning my room had never calmed me down like this did. After I finished, I sat down to my books. I didn't like being disturbed by the jingle of the bells over the door, even when a couple of gorgeous guys walked in. Especially when a couple of gorgeous guys walked in. Gina's the one who can handle guys; I've only ever been kissed twice, and both times were kind of failures. My usual method with somebody good-looking (Emilio got around this by being a cousin) was to let someone else talk to them, and steal glances when I was sure they weren't looking. I shrank back behind the pages.

"Good afternoon, Signorina," said one of them, smiling at my discomfort.

"Good afternoon," I answered, taking refuge in my shop voice. "Let me know if I can help you with anything."

Even that sounded a little too suggestive to me. I looked down at what I was reading. *The Era of the Visconti.*

"What are you studying?" asked the smiling one, standing right over me. I almost jumped out of my chair.

"J-just the history of Milan," I answered, hating my stutter. He was so beautiful, broad-shouldered, with high cheekbones and black, curly hair that had that windswept-on-purpose look. He looked like he was about Anna Maria's age.

"Ah, very important. The history of thousands of fools and a few wise leaders," he said. My eyes flicked to his hand, resting on the side of the table. His index finger was moving in a tiny pattern—what was he doing? As soon as he saw me looking, he stopped.

I didn't know what to say, so I shrugged as if I didn't care one way or the other.

His companion was picking up candles and putting them down. He took hold of a lit candle and tipped it back and forth, watching the liquid wax turn around and around in its pool.

I nervously launched into Giuliano's usual speech about the candles: "Please be aware that these are only display samples. We'll be happy to get you a fresh candle, if that's the model you'd like."

We? I thought to myself. *I'm the only one here.* I think they must have thought the same thing.

He looked down at the candle in his hand, looked at me again, and set it down reluctantly, glancing over at the dark-haired man in front of me. *You envy your friend,* I found myself thinking. *A lot. Why?*

They both gave off the same feeling, even though they looked very different, two separate varieties of handsome, in fact: the one with his dark, mysterious curls and the other with a Roman beauty, an elegant, high-bridged nose and flat, triangular cheeks. They both looked familiar, which meant they were probably models whose photographs I had seen in some magazine or shop window.

"We came to talk to Signore Della Torre about a candle order," said the dark-haired man at last. "Is he in?"

"No, he won't be back until around five," I said, and then wondered if I should have given him even that small piece of information. The room seemed cold. I couldn't stop feeling jumpy; I was pretty sure it was more than just the fact that I was standing close to two cute guys.

"That's all right," he said.

"Would you like me to take a message?" I asked, hating every minute that passed.

"No, no, thank you." The dark-haired one smiled. "Good afternoon," he added, his friend echoing him in a sullen voice.

"Good afternoon," I forced myself to say.

Something seemed to strike the dark-haired guy as funny,

and he turned to our guest book by the door. After they left, I went to look at his signature. He had signed himself *"Lucifero."* The sight of his scrawl sent chills up my spine. But not all the chills were scary.

"Satanists," Giuliano said briefly that evening, when I told him about their visit. He shook his head.

"They're always interested in us, of course. I know this 'Lucifero.' That's not his real name. Very pretentious, to name himself after his chief god and to use the name openly. He and his friends are Satanists, devil worshippers—amateurs, I'm guessing, rather than members of an established cult. Bernardo Tedesco's brother-in-law's cousin overheard them in a café, once, talking about 'harvesting demons' from us. What more dangerous occupation is there? You have seen a bit of what we deal with. Can you imagine the price someone would have to pay to control that kind of power, the power of a demon? If you *can* control it. We only manage for a short time, and with another end in mind. Besides, as you know, it's a certain kind of creature that answers the call of black magic, one that has its own, selfish, bloodthirsty plans.

"If they only knew . . . but they're like a lot of people interested in the occult. They like the dark and the excitement. Everybody wants to be part of a secret society, a special group. More than that, they want quick power. They don't have patience."

He frowned. "Patience," he repeated, and for a split second he looked strange, almost hungry. I didn't think about that until a long time later.

TWELVE

Alba

Later on, Laura sent me to get Giuliano for dinner.

"He's taking forever to close tonight. Beppo's probably stopped by. Tell him I've put the pasta water on," she said, the universal Italian code for "get your butt up here." It's a major sin to let the pasta overcook or to eat it less than piping hot.

I came banging down the stairs and burst into the shop, not expecting anyone besides Giuliano and one of the old guys from the neighborhood, any of whom could see me with my hair in a total mess and my patchy jeans.

There was no Beppo with Giuliano; instead, there was Emilio, who was supposed to be out. There was also a girl. She seemed as startled as I was for a second, and then she gave me a slow, assessing look, taking in my clothes, my overgrown hair, my breathless state. My stomach coiled up.

"May I introduce my little cousin, Mia," said Emilio, touching her lightly on the waist and turning to me. She continued to look at me, managing a smile and putting out her hand.

"So pleased," she said distantly. "My name is Alba."

She didn't want me there, and I didn't want her there, either. The worst part about it was how beautiful she was: some animal side of me wanted to love her just for that, for her enormous eyes and long, graceful neck and perfect mouth.

I thought about going back upstairs, sticking my head under my pillow, and crying until I died of dehydration.

"Well, we should be going," said Emilio.

"What restaurant?" asked his grandfather.

"Nobu," said Alba, smiling so warmly at him that I would have been jealous if I were Emilio and his grandfather wasn't such an old guy. It was kind of gross.

"Ah! All that raw fish and not a drop of olive oil in sight! You should take her to La Lanterna, the next time you go to Cinqueterre," he said to his grandson. "That's real sushi. That's Italian sushi. Go, go, have a good time," he said, patting them both on their backs and steering them toward the door.

"It was nice meeting you, Alba."

I tried to make it sound true.

"Nice meeting you, too. The little American cousin."

The next minute they were out in the street, Alba's perfectly cut white coat outlined briefly against the stone of the Brera.

"The pasta water's on," I said to Giuliano.

"Ah? Good," he said, shooting me a sharp glance as we walked back through the office, he with a sheaf of papers and me with a mood. He didn't ask any questions, though.

After dinner, I helped Laura with the washing up, while Francesca spread her work all over the kitchen table and opened up her laptop. Laura folded the dish towels on their rack and wished us good night.

"What are you working on?" I asked Francesca while I finished wiping the counters.

She rapped the brief with the back of her fingers.

"A big case."

"Really?" I asked, fascinated. "Are you finishing up Signora Galeazzo?"

She looked blank for a minute, then gave a little half-corner smile, very like Emilio's, which I had already learned was the closest she got to a laugh.

"No, no. A court case."

"Oh! Oh. Sorry, I—"

"It's fine," she said.

I didn't think it was, though. Nonna had left us; there was no one to help me read her expression as she looked out the darkened window. Before I could stop myself, I asked, "What kind of case? A murder?"

She frowned at me.

"No, no, nothing so . . ."

"Good," I put in, jabbering to cover my latest mistake. "My

mom had to sit on a jury in a case like that, and it was awful. Her cooking was terrible for a week."

She looked up at me in silence for a moment, then smiled the half-corner smile again; yet she looked so sad and so far away that I felt like a complete jerk. I realized now that we were both outside the family business. Then again, the reasons were so different.

Francesca rescued me. She smoothed out the papers and said, "Actually, it's a civil case." She sighed. "Property, property, property. People can never agree on it."

She looked up, her eyes tired. "So you met Alba," she said, changing the subject. I leaned against the stove.

"Yes," I said, grateful.

"Wine?"

"Thank you, I would love some," I said, and pulled up a chair.

She got up, took a couple of glasses off the shelf, and poured until I said, *"Basta, grazie."*

We drank in silence. Francesca pushed her briefs away, leaning back in her chair and straightening her chignon. The pool of kitchen light around us felt like a spell I didn't want to break. She'd let me say *basta* instead of deciding how much wine a young girl should get; I liked the feeling that gave me, of being an adult, an equal, casual and cool. I wondered if adults felt this way all the time, or even most of it.

"What did you think of her?" she asked at last.

"She's gorgeous." I hadn't meant to say it, but it snuck out before I could stop myself. All that casual cool evaporated.

Francesca snorted, a very unladylike sound that I didn't expect from her.

"Gorgeous is not significant with Emilio. Gorgeous is every-day. Since he can have anyone he wants."

I looked down at the table.

"Yes, that's true," I said, trying to keep my voice light. "It's funny walking down the street with him, all the women look-ing. They never stop, do they?"

"They never did."

We each took another sip of wine. Then she said, "Alba hates me."

My head shot up.

"Really?"

"Yes. Does she hate you, too?"

"We only met for five minutes, but I didn't get the feeling she was that into me."

"It would surprise me if she was. Don't take it personally. She hates Nonna, too."

"She hates Nonna? But why? Who could possibly hate Nonna?"

This time Francesca gave me a truly warm smile.

"I know, it's hard to imagine, isn't it?"

"I don't get it. I don't understand anything here. Speaking the language does not help."

Francesca reached across the table and touched my hand lightly.

"So young," she said.

I scowled. That was so not what I needed to hear.

"I didn't mean to offend you," she said. "I forget; it's just the most awful thing to hear at your age, isn't it?"

"Pretty much," I agreed. We both smiled.

"Think about it, *cara*. If Alba doesn't like me, doesn't like Nonna, probably doesn't like you, doesn't that tell you something?"

I bet in the Stone Age, while facing some rampaging mastodon, our Della Torre ancestors said to their kids, "Work it out for yourself." Argh!

"Um, no," I said. "I just can't figure it out."

Francesca rested her chin on her hand, the kitchen light picking out red gleams in her smooth, dark hair.

"Hmm. I think there must be some things Italian girls just know—and some things American girls just know. But Alba. The way she hates us all, it tells you not to take it personally. It's the women in Emilio's life. She's jealous, Mia. See?"

I could relate to that, remembering how I'd felt the moment I'd seen Alba.

Francesca went on, "She's really horribly nice to my grandfather, to Francesco, to Égide—God, it's so annoying!—Égide is normally so perceptive, *so* perceptive about these things. He acts like a fool around her."

"Yeah," I joined in. "She smiled at Nonno in this icky way. It made me really uncomfortable."

"Yes! So don't you dare feel bad about it, if she comes to dinner and gets to you, somehow. She's just awful, that's all."

I looked down at my wineglass. Alba stirred up such scary feelings in me. I raised my eyes to Francesca.

"You know," I said. "Granted, demons are unbelievably terrifying. But sometimes I feel like actual living human beings are so much more frightening."

She laughed, nodding.

"I know what you mean," she said.

"Could I ask you a really personal question?" I said shyly. "You don't have to answer it."

Again she gave me the smile so like her brother's, her eyes friendly but a little guarded.

"Give it a try," she said.

"Can you tell me about your mom? I know your dad is— gone, but what about her?"

The smile went out like a candle. She gazed far beyond the kitchen walls.

"My mother," she said, and her smile relit. "She is still alive, Mia. Don't worry about being tactful about that at least, although it's probably best not to talk about her too much, especially with my brother or my grandfather." She paused. "Let me tell you about her," she said, but she didn't start by doing that.

"I was nine when my father died, my brother was five. You've seen a photograph of him, on the wall of the living room; you asked who he was, and nobody said anything right away."

"I was so embarrassed," I said.

"You couldn't know," she replied simply. "That's not the best picture of him. There are some where you can see the light coming out of him. Luciano, like *luce*, light. He was so loved, Mia. My grandmother tells me that half the girls in Milan ran after him, and that he was too good-natured to turn them away." She gave me a naughty grin. "No, though. I heard from my great-uncle that he never played with anybody's heart—he wasn't a Don Juan, just a very handsome man with a good heart that shone out of him, irresistible. Uncle Matteo says he walked out with this beautiful girl, then that beautiful girl, and the neighborhood said, maybe he'll marry this one, that one, every time. But then one day he started walking out with Giulietta Murano, a medical student at the university, and everyone was so surprised when he asked her parents' permission to marry her.

"For one thing, she was a foreigner—from Rome, you see. For another, you can see from that photo of her with us that she's not—she's not like him. She doesn't blind you. But if you ever get to meet her, Mia, you'll see why each one of us looks sad, then joyful when we talk about her. I miss her so much. I see her about once a year; Égide and I go to Rome. Emilio always says he's going to join us, but he's only come once. I think it was too hard for both of them. He looks very much like my father.

"Everybody always thought that whoever married Luciano would be so lucky. But when our family got to know my mother, they realized *he* was the lucky one. He had finally found a woman whose light matched his own. You can't see it in photos—her smile, her light.

"Her heart broke when my father died. She tried to stay, to keep going, to raise us. But for years, there were days when she could do nothing but weep. And she was angry, too. At my grandfather, at the family trade, at everything. The most peace-ful and loving woman I had ever known, weeping with rage. I often wonder, Mia, how many wives of demon catchers have their hearts broken.

"And then, when Emilio was thirteen, he told her that he wanted to become a demon catcher."

"To avenge his father?" I asked.

"Yes. But it was more than that. I think we always knew he was going to be a demon catcher, long before our father died. It was like it was written on his forehead when he was born. Back in the old days, you know, most families had a trade, and you just grew up in it and went on in it. Our family has just stayed like that, so that even in my generation it hasn't really been discussed. If you're a man, you go into the trade. If you're a woman . . ."

She pressed her lips together.

"Did you want to?" I asked carefully.

She shook her head quickly.

"I watched my father die after the possession," she said. "Besides, I wanted other things."

She didn't say what those were. But watching her work in the evenings, I thought that maybe her quest for justice, her fasci-nation with the law, was just another kind of demon-catching, whether she admitted it or not.

"Anna Maria—" I began to ask, and Francesca interrupted with, "Pushed and nagged and followed along and even snuck into an exorcism when she was eight. They finally just gave up and let her. It's all terribly sexist, I know. And it's curious to me that most possession victims are women—not all, by any means, but most. I don't think that's just nature."

I thought about this. "What if it's the demons? I mean, the one attacking me sounds and looks male. Are they mostly male?"

She shook her head.

"No, there have been some quite famous female demons. They say that Lilith was one, you know, Adam's first wife. Of course, one of my professors used to say she was a goddess who got a bad rap, so I don't know. But our family has dealt with several female demons, they tell me."

She didn't look like this conversation was annoying her, so I kept on, partly because I was enjoying talking with her about deep subjects for the first time, and partly because I just felt more comfortable asking her some of these things, rather than Giuliano or Emilio.

"So maybe there are just more male demons, and they are more likely to pick on women?"

"I don't think so," she answered thoughtfully.

She poured us each more wine and went back to her story.

"So, at thirteen, Emilio announced his intentions. Giuliano gave him the case he still carries, the one from G. Della Torre, our ancestor who opened the shop. Our mother just fell apart. She had such mixed feelings, you see. She was a doctor. She knew how we helped people. She had always known where Emilio was headed. But then when it happened, it was still unbearable. She went back to her parents in Rome, got a job in a clinic there, and left us to finish growing up in our grandparents' house.

"I knew that it was best for both of us, in a way. I was finishing my examinations, and I already wanted to go study the law. We wouldn't have to sit under a cloud of anger and grief at the dinner table. But how we all missed her, Nonno included—especially Nonno, even though he had to bear her anger for so long.

"He loved her for her own sake—who wouldn't?—but he also loved her because the light that shone out of her reminded him of the light that had shone out of his son. The light that was put out."

She fell silent. I nodded. "Put out by my demon," I murmured.

She looked up sharply. "Who told you that?"

Too late I remembered that nobody had—I had overheard it in the dark. I had to think fast, and I had to lie.

"Nobody," I said. "I just guessed it. It's not too hard to figure out, the way everybody acts, you know," I added.

She looked at me carefully. "You seem to think you're slow, but you're not."

"I am about most things," I countered. "Like other girls, other women," I added, thinking of Alba again.

She shook her head. "That's different. There's always more to learn about other people. My grandfather says that about demon-catching, too. Incidentally, there's the answer to that question you asked: we know at least one male demon has attacked one man."

"Yes," I said. That silenced us for a moment.

I went to bed not too long after that, though I took quite some time to fall asleep.

I woke up to the sound of voices—which, frankly, happened much too often. Unlike some of the others, these sounded urgent, and embodied.

"*Carino*, do you need anything to eat before you go?" Nonna Laura stage-whispered.

"No, thank you, I'm just back from dinner," Emilio replied.

"Have you seen my turtleneck sweater?" Giuliano asked.

"No. I'm fixing you both sandwiches," Laura said from the kitchen.

Emilio laughed. I crept from the bed.

"Anna Maria picked a hell of a time to turn off her phone," Giuliano grumbled as he came into the hall.

"It's the new collections," Emilio reminded him.

"More likely a new man," Giuliano replied. I heard the rustle of his coat. "Ah! I'm just waking up. Have you pulled the notes yet?"

"Yes."

"I'll read them in the car. I think, though, that we're looking at a combination, like the Albertinelli case, with some aspects of the old Roman problem. Did the candles tell you anything?"

"Only what you've already worked out," Emilio answered with a smile in his voice.

"Ah? Let's see. One, two, three, four—I must have left my matches at Signore Sforza's, can you grab me a book? Thank you. And a second stub, this one's nearly burnt down. We should bring a big one, too; this may involve imprisonment."

"Nonno, we should go."

"All right, yes, yes. We'll still get there in time, *carino*."

I decided to go ahead and show myself, hoping it wouldn't bug them, so I opened the door and stuck my head out in the hall. Giuliano saw me first.

"Mia? Did we wake you?"

"It's okay," I said, since he sounded apologetic. I noticed that neither Francesca nor Égide had emerged. "Are you going out on a case?"

"Yes."

"Cool," I said, then realized that must sound unbelievably inappropriate, and quickly added, "Good luck. Hope it all goes well."

Emilio's mouth twitched, but Giuliano bowed and said, "Thank you, Mia."

I didn't know what to say to that, so I stood stupidly while they said good-bye, then hurried back to my balcony to watch them go. Emilio stood in the courtyard, muffled in his long coat, breathing frost, his golden head gleaming in the darkness, waiting as Giuliano made slower progress across the cobblestones. Francesco hurried toward them from the big archway. He asked softly if he should call his father, and Giuliano nodded and climbed into the passenger side of Emilio's Audi. Even though it was cold, I stayed outside, wrapped in my bathrobe and a sweater.

I hated them all for a minute. *They* could go out in the middle of the night and save people. They could go out *anytime* they wanted. They could stand down there, by the car, without waiting to hear the whisper of angry voices overhead; they could leave the stuffy apartment, could go and just get a coffee at the Café Fiori Oscuri—*a coffee, damn it!*

My hands gripped the ice-cold railing so hard they hurt. I waited until the Audi had growled through the archway before I went back inside and started throwing the history books at the wall.

After six books, I realized that the noise might wake Francesca and Égide so I stopped, sitting down on the bed, thinking about tearing the sheets. I heard the light, careful tread of Nonna Laura in the hall, and I held as still as I could. I heard the rustle of her bathrobe, and after a moment, she went back to her own room.

"Good," I said out loud. I wanted to feel both free and safe again. I looked across the room to the statue of the Virgin on my desk. I went over and picked her up, turning her slowly in my hands, running my fingers over the folds of her cloak and the wild beasts on her pedestal. I touched her calm face. For a minute, I thought of throwing her at the wall, but I didn't; the thought suddenly horrified me. I set her back down on the desk and began to breathe more slowly, starting to meditate before I realized I was doing it. Finally I went back to bed, feeling a bit better and thinking there might be something to the meditation exercises after all.

The Return of Lucifero

Sometimes I think it was Laura's coffee that saved me during that time. No matter what was happening, what I'd seen or heard or felt the day before, the smell of coffee would reel me out of my room and into a seat at the kitchen table every morning like a fish on a line.

It occurs to me now that Nonna might have planned it that way.

She gave me the same cup each day, a bright yellow one about the size of a cereal bowl. My Italian having progressed to the point where we could have real conversations, she would catch me up on the news: the case had gone well; Francesca might be getting a cold; Alba and Emilio had had an argument, but everything was all right now. I couldn't tell for sure, but I think

Nonna wasn't all that happy about their reconciliation, either.

Cured by coffee, more or less, I could sit downstairs in the shop, studying and doing my meditations on the Virgin (now making more sense), slowly learning my few and pitiful methods for confronting the unknown.

Giuliano might not want to take me to cases, but at least he would talk to me about what they fought against.

"There are at least as many kinds of demons as there are human faults," said Giuliano. "And like human faults, some of them can be corrected or changed, while others prove very hard to defeat. I think that the unquiet spirit who took over the unfortunate Signora Galeazzo was at least as upset as the signora herself to find herself where she was. I think her first thought was, 'Wait! This is not my body! What has happened?' She was lost for a long time, you see. Terrible things had happened to her in life, and she was still angry about them. Some spirits, it seems, find it very difficult to let go, while others move on or vanish without a trace."

"But why?" I asked.

He shrugged. "Well, you and I, for example, we have different spirits, yes? We behave differently in the world, don't we? My character, for example, might be a more clinging kind when the end comes for me. I might choose not to leave this world gently. Especially if I have suffered a great injustice, like the woman of Majdanek."

"Do we have to call her that?" I asked suddenly, remembering for a moment what it had been like to look out across that plain of bodies. "I'm pretty sure that's not the place she wants to be associated with. Can we call her by another name?" I continued shyly. "I mean, I know it doesn't matter to her anymore. . . ."

"It matters to you, however," he said. "I think it is a very good idea. What name shall we call her by?"

I thought. "What about the 'woman of Signora Galeazzo's house'? That's where she used to live, wasn't it?"

He seemed pleased by the idea, so we left it at that. Sitting in the shop with him each day, I met people, too, such as Marie Franco, American wife of an Italian lawyer in Francesca's firm, who told of the strange mishaps that followed her daughter wherever she went: chunks of stone peeling off buildings to fall just behind her; a street vendor spattered with his own hot oil. I sat as an old woman, a neighbor whom I will not name, whispered descriptions of terrible torments. When she walked out the door, Giuliano turned to me and raised his eyebrows, asking, "So? What did you think?"

"I don't know, Nonno. . . . None of the candles moved. Plus the room didn't change, I mean, you know, go dark, like it did when the other people were here, or like it was at Signora Galeazzo's."

"Exactly." He nodded. "What do you think?"

"Well . . . if I didn't know better, if I didn't know why people came to us, I would say she wasn't telling the truth . . . ?"

"Still so reluctant to believe the evidence of your own eyes, of all your senses."

"Well, why shouldn't I be?"

He looked irritated, which meant I had raised a good point, considering that an unquiet spirit had recently convinced me that I was being gassed. "Yes, yes, but you must learn to differentiate. Today, you were listening to someone who made up lies for us. Even the story itself was inconsistent—not in the way that someone suffering from possession can be inconsistent, forgetting things, mixing things up—but inconsistent because she didn't keep her story straight."

"What a waste of our time! Why would anybody do that? Can't they see that they could be taking away from someone who's facing life and death? I can't believe she would do that," I finished angrily.

"That is because you are young and have no idea what it would be like to live alone in a dark apartment, growing old with sore bones, not able always to get out and do what you like, and with only one dutiful son visiting whenever he can get away from his work in Torino," said Giuliano. "You had better learn some compassion. This will not be the last time you have to listen to someone like her. From each person you listen to, you will learn something. Patience, for example."

This was too much. I snapped.

"What do you mean, I don't understand? I know exactly what it's like to be stuck in a dark apartment, to not be able to get out and do what I like! I know *exactly*."

I could hear my voice rising. It felt good, so good, like being able to put out my hand and break the hinges on a door. His eyes widened, then narrowed, and I wanted my words to slap him. "Patience?! Oh, I'm learning patience."

I'd gone too far.

"PATIENCE?" he roared suddenly. "You think *this* is difficult? You have no idea, no idea at all. *Patience?* You haven't even *begun* to learn it."

He stalked away into the back room. I stood where I was, fists balled together, shaking.

When he didn't come back, I went to the door and looked out into the street, the forbidden street, my head full of comebacks and arguments clamoring to get out.

The candles around me flickered. The early winter dark was setting in. I watched a student flutter past, portfolio under her arm. I stroked the door frame, feeling the old nicks and cuts in the wood, smoothed over by layers of varnish and by the touch of other hands. I breathed in the scent of melting beeswax and warm flame.

I felt like my feet were stuck to the floor, but I turned them anyway and made them go to the office, where Giuliano sat at the cluttered table, gazing at pages of thick, yellowing paper covered in brown handwriting. He looked up, and we stared at each other. His face wasn't hard anymore.

The words didn't taste right in my mouth, but I said them anyway: "Nonno. I'm sorry."

"*Cara*, I'm sorry, too. I should not have shouted," he replied, standing up to come and take my hands. Unlike me, he didn't have to fight himself to say the words. "I know how much we are asking of you. But believe me, it would be much harder . . . There are risks we cannot take, not yet."

"But couldn't you teach me? Just some small stuff? Just get me started, so at least I could go out in the street?"

He smiled very sadly at me.

"I promise you, we are working on that. I will try to think of something we can do in the meantime. But—it's very difficult."

I knew what he meant: they couldn't give any knowledge to the demon. I didn't say that, though, because I wasn't ready to admit I had overheard him and Emilio.

Molto difficile: very difficult. Yes, it was. He looked at me carefully, so I pretended everything was okay now, because I knew talking more about it wouldn't help. I am not sure he believed me, but at least he played along, coming back to the table, letting me change the subject, and answering my questions about the history of Milan. After a while, he asked me to watch the shop by myself for a bit because he had to help Laura with the Plan for dinner.

"Call me on my cell if anyone needs a serious consultation, yes?" He patted me on the shoulder. "And keep on with the book about the Visconti. They gave our family a bit of trouble back then, they did." He smiled as if he could remember the thirteenth century himself and headed upstairs for final instructions.

To keep myself from thinking about what had just happened, I considered what he had said about the Visconti. None of my relations had bothered to mention that we had actually run Milan, way back when. They had let me find out for myself. According to the books I was reading, we weren't dukes, because that came later, but we ruled the city.

I checked the candles and turned on the lamp, wondering whether anyone in Milan outside our family actually remembered.

The bell jingled, and a customer came in. It was Lucifero, he of the dark, windswept hair. *Great.*

He looked around the shop with the same hungry expression he'd had the last time, then his face softened when he saw me. I don't know what I had expected, but it certainly wasn't for him to come forward and say gently, "Bad time?"

Did it still show on my face?

"Sort of," I answered, before I could stop myself.

"I'll go," he said softly, and half turned away.

"No," I found myself saying, "you don't have to go, it's not that bad. Please. How can I help you?"

He smiled as if this were a very complicated question. "Well, I really came to talk to Signore Della Torre, but . . ."

"I'm afraid he's out—upstairs, I mean. He'll be back in a while, I think, before he goes shopping."

I didn't want to go get Nonno. I looked up into Lucifero's handsome face, still not quite able to believe the kindness I read there.

"Would it be all right if I waited?" he asked.

"Of course."

He stood, shifting his weight, uncertain, until at last I worked out what he wasn't saying and offered him a seat. It was strange, sitting across from him, no longer looking up at his cold face but eye to eye across the table. Suddenly I noticed every detail about him: the pulse in his neck as he pulled his scarf away from his shirt collar, the way his dark hair curled against his cheek, the faint, rough shadow where he had shaved, the soft light in his eyes, dark blue like Emilio's.

"Settling in, are you?" he said. "You seemed frightened of me the last time I was here."

I looked down at my homework.

"You were reading about the Visconti then, too. I remember."

I looked up at him and, prompted no doubt by the hidden spirit of Gina, I said with a smile, "You said it was the history of a few great men and many fools."

"You remember!" His eyes flashed.

"Yes, because I didn't agree," I said.

"I say foolish things sometimes." He shrugged. "I don't know what possessed me. In this country, you may have noticed, men say foolish things around women quite a lot."

I looked down at my homework again, my face hot. He seemed to think he had gone too far, because, after a pause, he said, "Your—grandfather?—may not be down for some time. Perhaps you would permit me to run up to the café up the street and get us a coffee?"

Permit him? No good-looking guy had ever offered to run up the street for a Kleenex for me before, let alone coffee. Emilio didn't count.

"They do have good coffee there, don't they?" he persisted when I said nothing.

"Oh, yes, yes—it's very good. Yes, please."

He stood up, winding his scarf around his neck again, and slipped out into the street. I sat there, waiting for him, feeling startled and happy. I hoped Giuliano wouldn't come back down. For a moment, I thought about his warning. He said

Lucifero wanted to harvest demons. Well. Maybe he did, but wasn't it worth finding out? And maybe he was not as he had appeared before. Before I decided what he was, he was back, setting a tray laden with coffee, milk, sugar, and pastries on the table and once again unwinding his scarf. I couldn't stop looking at him. Somehow he had grown handsomer in the moments he had been gone.

I looked at the tray. "I still haven't gotten over that people will just let you carry dishes out of that café. It's so funny. I've never seen it before."

He glanced up, stirring his coffee. "Really? They don't do that in New York?"

He said New York like "Nuyyorke." I wanted to hear him speak English, just for the accent. I noticed that I was tingling all over and hoped it didn't show.

"No, they don't."

"I've never been there. I've always wanted to go. No, that's not true; that's what people say to be polite, isn't it?"

He smiled at me. "Actually I've always wanted to go to the East, the Orient," he continued. "The world may be growing small but we are still strangers to one another, and I would like to know more about the yellow people."

This wasn't the first time I had encountered the casual racism that would have shocked most Americans, with our own open wounds from history. Even Nonna the all-forgiving had warned me against Albanian pickpockets the first time we had gone out.

Lucifero was still speaking. ". . . their ancient traditions, their philosophies, their magic."

At the word *magic*, he looked at me, his eyes holding mine.

"Does any of that intrigue you?" he asked. "With your family's work—studying the Eastern traditions might be useful."

I hesitated. Nobody had specifically said anything, yet I had noticed that we avoided talking about the work outside the family. We might have a low conversation in the street or talk about technique in front of a client, but otherwise, we took great care to hide what we did.

On the other hand, he already seemed to know about my family. And more than anything, I wanted to find out what he was thinking.

"Yes," I agreed, thinking about it for the first time. "There's so much missing, it seems. Like we're just feeling our way forward." I rolled my eyes. "So much to study."

"Yes, but you study with the best." (I didn't correct him; it stung too much to think about what I wasn't studying.) "Giuliano Della Torre is known far outside Milan. Your whole family has an ancient reputation among those who know, those who care about such things, who realize that there is more to this world than what we see."

"Really? He's known outside Milan? I know the Church doesn't like the Della Torres."

"Ah, the Church doesn't like anybody. They want to have it all to themselves, the power. They fear people like your grandfather for good reason. I believe he has a greater understanding of the netherworlds and their inhabitants than the men of the Church. He may have a greater understanding than anyone alive."

I sipped my coffee. Under his gaze, my mouth and my hands needed something to do.

"How much do you really know about your family, Signorina Della Torre?" he asked gently.

Signorina Della Torre—that sounded good. *I'm in the family business,* I thought, though it wasn't true at all.

"Not much," I admitted. I was still considering what Lucifero had said about the Church, and what he had said about Giuliano and my family's reputation. I could tell from our neighbors that we were known and loved here, in this little corner of Milan, but I hadn't really thought outside of that, except for that one bit of information my father had given Emilio, about Rome forbidding an exorcism on me.

"Your grandfather is a great man, indeed," said Lucifero. (I still did not correct him; it felt oddly good to hear him refer to Giuliano that way.) "I hope he will talk to me sometime soon. But even he has made mistakes. You might ask him about a young brother of his, named Martino, who died about thirteen years after the war." (I knew by now he meant World War II.) "Has he told you about him? Has he mentioned a cousin of his named Roberto?" He went on, watching me. "Have your cousins said anything?"

Did I know of a cousin named Roberto? I couldn't decide how much to let on. Could he know that Roberto was my grandfather?

"No," I said. "I never heard of anybody named Martino. I think I know of Roberto."

He saw the shadow crossing my face and said quickly, "I

don't wish to turn you against them. I'm sure they will tell you in their own time."

He looked down at his empty coffee cup.

"Well, I think your grandfather won't be back soon, and I should go. But," he said, rising, his voice muffled for a moment as he dressed for the cold outside, "but—"

He stopped, uncertain again.

"Perhaps you would meet me for coffee sometime? There's a place in the Galleria that does very good hot chocolate."

When I didn't answer, he added, "Pardon me."

"No, no!" I said. "I mean yes. I would like to."

His face lit up. "Are you free on Thursday? Maybe five o'clock?"

"Yes, I think I could be."

"Zucca, in the Galleria, then. You know it?"

"I think I can find it."

"Good, I look forward to it."

He was out the door before I thought, *I don't even know your last name. Or your first, for that matter.*

FOURTEEN

Hot Chocolate

I could hardly eat dinner that night. I couldn't stop thinking about Lucifero. In my mind, I turned over different solutions to the problem of getting out of the house alone, of traveling safely outside, of being safe at a café. As Monday, Tuesday, and Wednesday passed, I found Zucca online and more or less figured out where it was in the Galleria. I had the nightmare again, about my feet swinging and kicking together, about drifting up and out of the bed.

Each day during my meditation practice, I stared at the Madonna. Her blue cloak, draped over her head and falling to her feet, had golden stars painted on the inside of its wooden folds. Her expression was complicated: mournful and joyous, serene and startled, at the same time. Her son didn't have the same mixed, arresting expression on his face; instead he looked happy waving one hand around like babies do, pleased to be in her arms, under her protection.

Must've been hard to be her, knowing his whole story to come.

"Did you ever have crushes?" I asked her.

No matter how paranoid my dad was, or how sure my mom was that I was the most beautiful kid in the world (after Gina, obviously), boys were not a problem I got to have. A kid named Jimmy had kissed me twice in the third grade before moving to New Jersey, and then basically nobody had come near me, unless I counted Tommaso D'Antoni. One Friday afternoon, after I had watched him work on his car for two hours, we had shared a soda and a kiss. I think he did it as an experiment, and I'm guessing it didn't work, because after that he went back to not acknowledging my existence.

Like with everything else, drugs, alcohol, all of it, I was just too scared. Maybe the boys could tell. I wondered when I'd last had a crush on a guy. Sure, I had one on Emilio, but that didn't really count, did it? He was an untouchable god, and also a cousin, even if a distant one.

Lucifero had looked at me like I was real.

"Um," I said to the Madonna, trying to address her politely, "um, *Santa Maria*? How would you go about getting to Zucca if there was a demon chasing you?"

When I spoke, I remembered that I was supposed to be meditating. It was hard to meditate on anything but Lucifero.

"I've got to get out," I explained to her. "Plus," I added,

weirded out by the fact that I felt shy talking to a wooden statue, especially one that might not approve of my motives, "I've got to see this guy. I think I was wrong about him, I don't know. Either way, I need to know if he's up to something. Also he's really cute. How can I do this?"

She didn't seem to have any answers. I didn't ask her what to wear, since she obviously had no fashion sense. I thought of asking Pompous, but on reflection I decided that would be a really bad idea. I was pretty sure she was—had been?—part of the family, and she would want to know what was up. Any explanation would lead to a lecture, the way it did with living adults, too.

Instead I waited until everyone was away or asleep and tried on every single item of clothing I owned, about five times. At least it distracted me for a while from the problem of how to get to Zucca—and whether I'd be safe there.

In the end, I lied. I guessed that I would be safe once I was under a roof, because any time we went out to dinner, everybody relaxed once we were inside. Then, by pleading that I was desperate for a change of scene (okay, not a lie at all), I got Francesca and Francesco to walk me to the Galleria on their way to a lecture, and promise to pick me up afterward. I figured I'd work out how to get rid of Lucifero before they saw him; I'd think of something once I got there. Once outside, I still waited for the whispers, the cold, and a part of me couldn't believe that they never came. Was it really this easy?

Despite the fact that I was walking with two relations, I felt glad to get off the streets and under the high Galleria roof. It didn't seem like quite enough, but I told myself I would be in the café soon.

The Galleria Vittorio Emanuele II is what every American shopping mall wants to be when it grows up. It was built in the 1800s, I think, so it's also a very old shopping mall. It feels so real, so right, that it seems that all the other malls I've ever been in are just trying to imitate it, from the elegant ground-floor shops to the intricate glass roof arching high above.

Francesca and Francesco left me at the door of Zucca, and as grateful as I'd felt for the roof of the Galleria, I appreciated the low ceiling of Zucca even more. I appreciated most the sight of Lucifero, rising from a table near the back, one hand stretched out toward me.

"The hot chocolate is very good," he reminded me while I looked at the menu. "I didn't think your family would let you come," he added.

"They don't—" I was about to say, *They don't know I'm meeting you*, but I caught myself before I let it all the way out. "They don't really care one way or the other. I guess they trust me."

"Well, they should," he said to me, and to the waiter, "Two hot chocolates."

"Verdi used to come here," he told me when the waiter was gone. "Along with everybody in his scene."

"How cool," I said. We hadn't been to an opera yet, but Nonna and Emilio had both promised they would take me when the season opened, and by now I knew who Verdi was.

I could picture him and his artsy posse, the hipsters of their day, spending hours over their coffee, messing around and flirting like we did down at the mall back home (less coffee and hipness, more McDonald's fries and braces). Or maybe more like the Milanese and the tourists all around us, shopping bags clustered at their feet, tinkling their spoons in their coffee cups. Sometimes when we went to restaurants now, I found that I no longer had to focus entirely on translating every word the Della Torres spoke, so I could listen around at the other tables, hearing snatches of gossip about people I didn't know, coming into conversations that didn't quite make sense: Had that baby really joined the circus? Did her friends really wear newspaper? The words gradually resolved into more familiar shapes as I got my translations right.

I didn't listen to anyone in Zucca. I looked at Lucifero, and he looked at me.

"So, do you miss your American boyfriend?"

"Me? Right. No, I don't have one." *Great*, I thought. *Why don't I just write "loser" all over my entire body?*

"That's crazy," he said, laughing. I stared at him. He said, "Are the American boys just blind?"

I blushed, wishing I was the kind of person who could come back with something really snappy and cute. I couldn't really believe him, me with my eyes too close together and my mousy hair, but I wanted to.

"I can't figure you out," he said, leaning his hand on his chin.

"That's okay," I replied. "I can't figure me out, either."

He laughed again, and I started to feel a little more confident. The hot chocolate came, not at all like American hot chocolate but thick, kind of like our pudding but not as sweet. It always came with a glass of water and a spoon, Lucifero explained, and if you left it too long it thickened up so that the only way you could drink it was to eat it, which I suppose is what the spoon was there for.

Once again it was great to have something to do with my hands. I felt so awkward, and neither of us was talking. I was too nervous to try to carry out my plan of finding out what he was up to. As I snuck a look at him across the table, stirring his hot chocolate, his long, strong-fingered hand dwarfing the tiny spoon, I began to wonder whether he was up to anything at all.

He looked up at me, catching me staring at him, and pointed his spoon at my cup, saying, "Good, isn't it?"

I nodded.

"First they take the best cocoa beans you can buy. They roast them carefully and grind them up into a very fine powder. Then they mix this with an equal amount of sugar, and mix that with an equal amount of milk, or maybe some more. They boil it once without scalding it, and then strain it; then they boil and strain it again; then they boil and strain it a third time. That's how you get what we are drinking."

"A lot of trouble for a cup of hot chocolate," I pointed out.

He shrugged. "It's worth it, isn't it? The most valuable things are worth the trouble."

He looked at me, and I felt as if I might be worth the trouble.

I said quickly, "How do you know how they make the chocolate? Everybody here seems to know so much about making food."

He smiled.

"Worked at my uncle's café when I was a kid. Le Due Farfalle, near the Pinacoteca Ambrosiana. My uncle is one of these hardworking types. A little too Protestant for me, you know? All the guilt and none of the fun. Protestants don't get it. They confess first and sin later, if they dare to sin at all," he went on, and I wondered why this seemed to matter to him, since he was a Satanist. Wasn't he? "Sin first, confess *later*, that's the point. I don't understand Protestant countries."

I thought of Signora Galeazzo, and the woman who had spoken through her, that abyss of sorrow. I was about to say something, but Lucifero was on a roll.

"Even your America," he went on, launching himself into a full-blown lecture about the puritanical values of my country. I surprised myself by arguing straight back, starting with the point that I was actually raised Catholic and, from what I could tell, I was about as devoutly Catholic as any random Italian on the street.

We went back and forth, first about Puritan America, then about the separation of church and state. Gina, the good student, would've been proud of me, but frankly I had learned a lot sitting at Nonna and Nonno's dinner table every night. I even pointed my finger upward when I really wanted to make a big deal out of something. He did the same thing, leaning forward, poking the air with one long, strong finger to make his case.

"*Tu sei vivace*—You're feisty," he told me, looking immensely satisfied; he had some color in his face now, probably from the argument. I smiled at him, and we both got very quiet. I looked down at my cup, hugely shy again, and when I looked up at last, he was watching me so intensely it scared me.

I looked away across the restaurant, my heart thumping. The clock on the wall caught my eye: it read 6:32. I jumped. My cousins would be back soon.

"Is that really the time?"

"Yes, it's really the time." He laughed.

On the spur of the moment, I came up with a plan. It wasn't much of one, but it could work. I would get us to walk around the Galleria, and if he didn't leave me before my cousins got back, I could just say I'd run into Lucifero while I was hanging out.

I wasn't sure that was the best idea, but I wanted to keep him by me a bit longer. On the other hand, though, I hadn't figured out if he was up to anything. It didn't seem like it. He seemed pretty into me, that was all.

I found it surprisingly easy to convince him to wander around the shops with me. He paid our bill and helped me into my coat, making my stomach feel jumpy and shiny somehow, when he stood so close to me.

We stepped out under the great arching glass roof.

My enemy dropped from above.

Enter Signora Negroponte

I knew my demon as surely as if he were in my bones again. I felt him plummet toward us. I said, "It's too late."

"I know," said Lucifero. He showed his white teeth in a smile. He took my arm as he, too, looked upward.

Then somehow I was several feet away from him, staring while he opened his hands as if to catch what was flying down. For a moment, I saw everything around us with vivid clarity: the bright heights of the Galleria, the dark evening sky between the arches, the dimpled marble floor spreading away from us, interrupted here and there with circular mosaics. A cluster of shoppers turned to look at us, one holding a bag with Gucci limned in gold on it. I saw a trio of girls in identical jackets, and an older, square woman in an olive-green sweater with a gold brooch standing perfectly still, facing us both.

Lucifero kept looking up, smiling as if he were greeting an old friend. The next moment, the force that I could feel but could not see this time had dropped into him. His smile folded up as if someone had crumpled it from the inside.

I was on my knees, puking, a puddle of chocolate inside a larger puddle of spit on the marble floor.

"Get up, get up," said a rasping voice. "You can't help him this way."

A strong hand yanked me to my feet. I stood facing the woman in the olive sweater.

"Do you know what's happening?" she asked, glaring fiercely at me.

I knew that she knew even before I started to lie. She shook my shoulder.

"Don't waste time pretending," she snapped. "You do know, don't you? Did you want this? Do you want to save him?"

I had no idea.

"I can hold him for a very short time. Very short. You are a Della Torre?"

I nodded.

"Good. Call them. *Now.* Tell them."

I gaped. How did she know who I was?

She slapped my face.

"Call!" she said.

I stared at her. "I don't have a cell phone!" I cried. She snorted and pulled out her own, thrusting it in my face, Emilio's name blinking up at me from the screen. Her hand had many rings on it. I pressed the CALL button.

"Pronto. Chi parla?" said Emilio's calm voice on the other end of the airwaves.

"It's Mia. Emilio. The Galleria," I panted. "Lucifero. She said to come get you."

"What? Who?"

"Lucifero," I cried.

"Mia, calm down," he told me sternly. "Now, is someone in trouble?"

"Yes. He, he's got him. He's got. I mean, he's got Lucifero."

"Your 'he'? I'm in public."

"Yes!"

"Got it. Now, you are where? In the Galleria?"

"Yes. There's a woman, she says she can hold him for a short time."

"She *what*? What does she look like?"

"Uh, older." I tried to think. "Olive-green sweater. Square face . . ."

"I think I know. Wait with her. We're coming."

He hung up and an eternity began. Every heartbeat seemed to take an hour to arrive. The woman in the olive-green sweater stood near Lucifero, staring straight at him as he held terribly still, her purse on the ground beside her. I couldn't see her hands, but she was obviously moving them, holding them low and close to her body. Lucifero's face was changing shape as if fingers were pushing and pulling it from the inside. I knew the dreadful light that looked out of his eyes. He had wrapped his arms around himself, his teeth chattering, his eyes roving.

People were gathering around us. I started to hear a buzz of questions—"Is he all right?"—"What do you think?"—"It has to be epilepsy. He's going to fall down."

He opened his arms and began screaming. Everyone backed up except for the woman in the olive sweater. And me.

Then I felt a wave of power burst away from Lucifero, and the woman rocked on her heels. Everyone around us began to back up in a hurry. She snatched up her purse, turned, grabbed me, and pulled me with her into the crowd. By now the noise had attracted three police officers. They looked like superheroes in formal dress, with their capes and white gloves. Near them, in a strange, still space of his own, a Catholic priest stood in his narrow, black robe and white collar.

"It's not normal," said a woman near us.

Her friend snorted. "Well, no, he's crazy. Not normal."

"No, I mean . . ."

I could see that many people were looking toward the priest, even while holding their Gucci shopping bags. Part of me wanted to yell, *This is the twenty-first century! We don't have demons!*

Which, of course, I, more than most people, knew wasn't true.

The police didn't even try to interfere when the priest came forward, removing the cross from around his neck. He walked straight up to Lucifero and pressed the cross to his forehead. I realized he was speaking Latin. Lucifero went on screaming, but his voice took a different, even more urgent tone.

That was where Emilio, Giuliano, Francesco, and Francesca found us. Nonno took me by the shoulder.

"There are many questions I will need to ask you, but not now. What happened?"

"We—we stood in the Galleria, and he came down from the roof, and Lucifero looked like he wanted him to come down. He held out his arms, he was smiling. . . ."

I heard a snort each from Emilio and Francesco. Giuliano just blinked. He shook his head.

"Idiota," he said. "And now, *him,*" he added, looking at the priest. "Difficult," he said after another moment. He turned to all of us, and I understood his look as well as any of the others: do nothing foolish. It came to me clearly how much they stood to lose by practicing the family arts in public, in front of what looked to be a hundred people, and in front of a priest. But at the same time, I saw Lucifero, twisting in agony, screaming and spitting.

I wanted so badly to hate him. I could remember the smile on his face as he looked up. That wasn't the face I saw now.

We kept stepping back, using the fading crowd as shelter, until there were too few people around us and Giuliano said, "Francesco, I need you to stay and see what happens. Try that café there, maybe—sit, watch."

Francesco nodded and turned away as the rest of us headed for the great open arch.

"Some people were suggesting that they take him into the Duomo," said Francesca.

"Madness," said Emilio.

"I hope they won't be that stupid," Giuliano said. "With Father Agostino there, I don't think they will."

I could hear voices around us, various shoppers, already talking as if nothing had happened.

I asked in a small voice, "Will this be on the news tomorrow?"

The others looked at me and blinked.

Finally Giuliano said, "I doubt it. People don't remember what they don't understand, it seems. There might be something about a madman in the Galleria. In any case—Emilio, you'll call Marco and make sure? There you are," he added to someone standing in front of us—the woman in the olive sweater.

She looked at me.

"You didn't move fast enough," she said to me. "The old crow and the police were there too quick."

I felt angry color rising in my cheeks.

"I called as fast as I could!"

She shrugged. "It still wasn't fast enough," she pointed out. "He would have been better off in your family's hands."

"What will happen to him now?" I asked.

"If he's lucky, they'll entrust him to the priest and not put him in jail. If we are all very unlucky, he will be put in jail. You were lucky," she said, looking at me again. "You chose someone weak. That's an uncommon thing for a Della Torre to do, you know. I am right, am I not—you are the young American cousin who must not step out into the street?"

"Uh, yes."

We had reached the car. All my cousins were looking at me. I was in big trouble.

"Yes, we must talk about that," said Giuliano in a grave voice. He turned to the woman. "But not now."

Great, so I could writhe in terror awhile longer.

"In the meantime," he added, "may I introduce to you Signora Marcella Negroponte. *La mia cugina di quarto grado,* Mia Dellatorri."

I couldn't quite follow the Italian for how we were related, but nobody else seemed confused.

"So pleased. We were supposed to meet this evening, anyway, you know," said Signora Negroponte, and we shook hands as if she had never slapped me across the face. I wondered if Giuliano had said Mia Dellatorri or Mia Della Torre. I wanted to know: it mattered to me, now, whether he used the Old World name, or the one that had been misspelled in America. I wanted the old name.

I couldn't believe it wasn't time for supper when we got back. My blissful evening in the sheltered café had seemed so short, my terrifying evening in the open Galleria so long. Signora Negroponte crowded into Emilio's Audi with Giuliano, Emilio, Francesca, and me. I felt the tears start in my eyes, and my hands shook as we slid smoothly back over the streets. I couldn't stop shaking, but neither Nonno nor Francesca reached out to comfort me.

At the shop, two glasses stood on the table, one full, one empty to the dregs. The bottle of wine had aired for quite a long time now. Emilio brought down three more glasses as Giuliano said, "Let's try it, anyway," and poured for all of us.

I helped drag in the office chairs. We sat down around the desk.

"Now." Giuliano looked at me. "Explain."

He saw me glance at Signora Negroponte and added, "Anything you have to say, she ought to hear also."

I just sat there with my mouth open. I had no idea what to say. There were so many reasons for why I had done what I'd done, and all of them seemed idiotic right then.

Giuliano slammed his hand down on the table and roared, "Explain!" We all shook. "Explain what you were doing out, alone, with a man who means us only harm! Explain! *Were you betraying the family?*"

That brought my voice back to me.

"No!" I cried. "No! I would never betray you! Never!"

I could feel the tears in my eyes again. I was not going to cry.

"I've been stuck in this house! I never get to do anything on my own! He was different, you didn't see him. . . . He was . . ." I looked for a good word to describe what he'd been like. "He was nice," I finished lamely.

They were all staring at me.

"You got mad at me, that one day when I didn't like the crazy lady, and he came in, and he gave me coffee. . . ."

My voice dwindled away. I sounded like the fool I was.

"He said even people outside of Milan know you, know your work. That you are very great."

I looked into Giuliano's eyes. They stayed hard.

"He asked did I know about a brother named Martino, who

died thirteen years after the war? Did I know about a cousin named Roberto?"

Giuliano's nostrils flared. I had no idea why I was telling him this stuff. It didn't make much sense, and it certainly didn't make my case for me.

"He said you were not perfect. But the thing was," I added quickly as he opened his mouth to speak, "the thing was, he was different. I wanted to know what was going on. I wanted to know who he was, what his plans were. So he asked me out to coffee and I said yes. I don't know why!"

My face was in my hands, and my hands were soaking wet. I sat up and looked at them, unable to figure out why they were wet.

"I don't know why. I'm sorry, I don't know why."

In Francesca's eyes, there was a kind of painful understanding; in Signora Negroponte's, a hard look I couldn't read; in Emilio's, great sadness; in Giuliano's, judgment.

But I did know why I did it. I didn't really want to explain to them about the way he looked, the way I felt sitting across the table from him. So I clung to the other reason.

"I wanted to do something for the family. I sit inside, and I learn how to speak your language, and I study history, and I try to talk to the people who are already in my room—" Here Giuliano gave a start, and I wondered how I'd been finally able to tell him about them at last. Was it because everything else was coming out? "And nobody tells me anything, and I don't get to do anything. It isn't even safe for me to step outside, you can't imagine what it feels like—you can't imagine. You say you can, but you can't."

"I think I might be able to," said Giuliano in an even voice, if not a kind one, and I got a glimpse, as if I were looking over his shoulder and down the years, of soldiers marching past in the street.

"I'm sorry," I said, and this time I knew that the drops falling on my hands were tears. "I'm sorry."

"I'm not," said Francesca suddenly. "I'm furious. Not at you, Mia. Tell me," she asked gently, "is this the first time anyone's asked you out?"

All the others looked at her. It was plain that nobody else had thought to ask this.

"No. Kind of. Well, yes."

"Whose fault is all this, really?" she said, looking first at her grandfather and then at her brother. "Not hers, perhaps."

"Hmm, yes," said Signora Negroponte at last. "Am I to understand that you have not taught her?"

"We can't," Emilio put in quickly. "You saw why, today. What came upon Lucifero has come upon her before. We can't lose to that. We can't let it know what we know. It has already learned too much, from others—" He stopped.

"I am not saying," said Signora Negroponte, clearly trying to avoid a breach in the family by saying what she felt Francesca must wish to say, "that what Mia did today was not foolish in the extreme. It was." She awarded me a severe look, but softened it as she added, "But her ignorance, that is more dangerous, isn't it? At every step of the rather confused narrative we have just had, ignorance has been the cause. Yes?"

Giuliano got up and paced to the window, one hand tapping against his trouser leg. I saw his face reflected in the glass above the flickering candles, frowning.

Francesca stood up and went to her grandfather, pausing before she touched his shoulder, her face no longer closed with anger but open, beseeching: "Nonno. Surely there are some things her demon already knows—from—" She stopped as Emilio had, her face convulsed with sorrow, and then she went on, "Could she at least learn those?"

I saw his face change in the window. He turned and took her hand, and I knew there would be peace.

Signora Negroponte laughed shortly. "Out of the mouths of babes and lawyers," she said.

When Giuliano came and sat down again, he leaned across and cuffed me under the chin. He didn't look any less angry, and the cuff kind of hurt, so his next words surprised me.

"I accept your apology, and I, I am sorry, too. But now, you must not keep things back from us. Not anymore. You see now how unsafe it is. So. Tell us from the beginning."

He poured me more wine, and Francesca slipped up the street to bring back a tray of various panini, olives, and caper berries. I told them all I could; I couldn't help leaving out some details, like the way he looked at me. They guessed, anyway, not the least Emilio, who smiled faintly.

"They sent for me, you see," said Signora Negroponte. "So

that we could find a way to make it safe for you to walk in the street."

By then I felt brave enough to ask, "What is it you do? Are you a demon catcher, too?"

She laughed her hard laugh again. "No, no. Though my work brings me to the same places often enough. I untie knots. I also tie them."

I didn't know what to make of that.

"Which do you think this will need?" asked Giuliano thoughtfully. "A knot, or the untying of one?"

"I'm not sure," she said, and looked at me in a way I was used to by this time, as if I were as easy to see through as the window of our shop, faded lettering and all. She leaned back in her chair. "It's been a long afternoon."

"So it has," Giuliano said. "There will be plenty of time to talk after dinner."

Emilio and Signora Negroponte stayed for dinner.

"I don't want to discuss this while we eat," commanded Giuliano. "It'll ruin our digestion."

I think mine was already ruined. Nonna served us a wild mushroom risotto, one of my favorite dishes, but I couldn't really taste it.

"These must be close to the last of the season," said Signora Negroponte. "This is delicious."

"They are the last," said Nonna. I seemed to be the only one who noticed the coolness in her voice or the way Giuliano looked relieved to step out of the room when Francesco called.

He came back quickly and said only, "The Ospedale San Giuseppe," to which everyone nodded. I didn't dare ask what he meant.

They let me go to sleep after dinner. I went to my room and bawled for an hour, for Lucifero, and for myself; but then I slept.

SIXTEEN

Signora Negroponte and I Start to Untie a Knot

When I came into the kitchen for breakfast, Francesco was there, cleaning up a bowl of coffee he had knocked over and apologizing to Nonna. After I had had a few sips of my own coffee, he said, "I just stopped by to tell you what's happened to your friend."

"He's not my friend," I said quickly.

"Yes, I wouldn't think so. You said he smiled when the enemy came down toward him?"

"Yes, smiled like a welcome."

Nonna slammed dishes into the drainer behind him, before turning and catching my eye and giving a derisive snort to tell me what she thought of Satanists.

"Wow," said Francesco. "I wonder how he knew it was there."

"I don't know. He knew at the same time I did. But, you know, later, everybody seemed to know. In the crowd."

"Well," said Francesco, "we're certainly learning a bit about his nature."

"Yeah, thanks. I think I've already figured out the guy is a jerk."

"No, I mean the demon. Each one is so different. Sometimes, especially with the powerful ones who keep coming back, you really need to pay attention to everything they do, to learn them. So that someday you can stop them. As you can imagine, it doesn't always happen right away."

"It can take generations," put in Nonna, sitting down.

"Centuries," said Francesco, nodding respectfully.

"Oh, great," I said.

"Well, not everything can happen in a minute, like your empty vee," said Nonna. "Demons can be like wine, Giuliano says."

(*Empty vee?* I was puzzled by the almost English sound for a second, until I realized she meant MTV.)

"Yes." Francesco laughed. "It's a good metaphor. Lots of demons come about because somebody crushes something, over and over, and then leaves it to rot in a tight place. . . ."

Even though it all made me feel sick, and I was kind of irritated by Nonna's comment about MTV (I mean, who watches that?), I was fascinated.

"Really? Like wine?"

"In some ways," said Francesco.

At Francesco's "leaving it to rot," for one second, I could feel the tail end of a memory—but all I could keep hold of was the smell of dust on a hot hillside and then the scent of cinnamon.

I asked, "How do you get it out of the tight place?"

"That's the trick, isn't it?" agreed Francesco as Nonna nodded vigorously. "It's not like just drawing a cork from a bottle, or pulling out the bung in a barrel, is it? You have to get it out, in the air, have a look at it—but at the same time, as you already know, it's terribly dangerous, and you could lose everything, not just your life, but who you are. It could overrun you, a flood, a river of bad wine. . . ." He added, "You saw. At Signora Galeazzo's. We look for the way to let it out safely. Without being destroyed or letting it destroy the person it has taken over. They are kind of the bottle, the barrel—not quite." He ran his fingers through his mad, curly hair. "Ah! Metaphors only go so far."

Nonna asked him, "What time is your lecture?"

"Nine—oh, no, is that the time? Mia, the news about Lucifero: they put him in a locked ward at the Ospedale San Giuseppe, and Father Agostino, the priest we saw at the Galleria, worked on him all night. The demon went from him at sunrise. He's in a coma. My contact says that the demon was angry with his choice."

We both felt a warning stillness from Nonna. Francesco seemed to ask permission with his eyes to go on. After a moment she relented. "She should know," she said, shrugging.

"He says the demon wanted you, which of course we know. But that Lucifero invited him in. And the demon found

Lucifero too weak. So," he said, looking at my face, "it's quite a compliment, Mia. This demon wants someone strong, and it wants you."

"I could really do without the compliment," I said, laughing weakly.

"I know," he said, standing up. He squeezed my shoulder reassuringly before kissing Nonna and me both good-bye on our cheeks and darting down the stairs, knocking a book off a shelf on his way.

Nonna and I sat back down at the table, swirling our coffee in our bowls, as had become our habit. I felt the air fill with unspoken words, and it seemed as if a few might actually spill over and get spoken after all, when we heard a step on the shop stairs, and Signora Negroponte came into the kitchen. Nonna stood up immediately. They looked at each other coolly, and I remembered how last night at dinner they had hardly said a word to each other.

"Good morning, Signora Negroponte."

"Good morning, Signora Della Torre."

"Can I get you a coffee?"

"No, thank you. I was looking for your cousin here. May I borrow her?"

"If you wish."

"Have a good morning, Nonna," I said as warmly as I could. "Thank you so much for breakfast."

She smiled at me with real friendliness and waved me away.

Signora Negroponte took me into the office behind the shop

and sat me down at the table, covered in papers. She cleared a space in the sea of receipts and notes, and I saw the color of the tabletop for the first time, a dark, close-grained oak, like the desk in the shop.

"So," she said, "you will have heard the news about that which troubles you. Your moment of freedom from it has gone by."

The dark wood grain fascinated me.

"I don't think I'll ever be free of it," I said.

She laughed. "The blind pessimism of youth," she said, but somehow I didn't feel offended. "On the bright side, this means we can start trying to find out how to protect you out in the open.

"Let's have a look at you," she added, sitting across from me and tipping up my chin.

"So young," was her next comment.

This morning she was dressed in a well-cut, moss-green tweed jacket and skirt, with the white cuffs of a silk shirt peeping out, and a silk scarf in a complicated knot at her throat, pinned to her jacket with a brooch that looked like it had been woven out of brass. She smelled like someone's rich grandmother, though I wondered if she would be a little young to be a grandmother. I found myself staring at the knot in her scarf.

"Yes, the knot," she said, following my eyes and smiling her hard smile. "I untie them and tie them."

She let the silence in the room broaden and deepen. Outside, through the shop door, I heard the bells of Santa Maria del Carmine ring the hour.

"Can I ask you a question?" I said.

"Of course," she replied, but there was no promise in her voice that she would answer it.

"How come I'm safe in the house and on my balcony, but not safe in the street—and yet again, safe in restaurants, cafés, even Emilio's car? How does that work?"

She laughed her grating laugh at so many questions; then her eyes narrowed as she thought about what to say.

"You do *think*, don't you? Something the demon probably already knows. . . ." she said, musing. "Tell me, Mia. How long have you been here?"

"About three months."

She blinked. "Your Italian is very good, for three months."

"Thank you." I laughed. "They won't let me speak anything else. I'm pretty sure they don't even approve of me writing e-mails or talking on the phone with my family."

The hard smile again. "I don't know that they disapprove or approve. Half of them have never studied another tongue. Only those serious in your family's profession have done so—and they are not so interested in English. Except perhaps Emilio."

"He has beautiful English," I said.

"He has beautiful everything," she said. We both laughed.

"But you have not been in Italy long. It takes time to know a place. A lifetime is best. Most of us don't even have that in one place, these days. I don't know what it's like in America, but in Italy everyone's moving around, Sicilians coming to Turin to work in the factories, farmers moving from the plain to Milan.

And yet, here place still matters—maybe because it has mattered for so long. For millennia, we have worshipped the gods of the places in which we live. You study art history, don't you?"

"A little."

"Yes, Signora Laura would see to that," she said cryptically, looking out beyond the walls at some place or time I could not see. "So you will have noticed that the statues have place-names. The Nike of Samothrace. The Venus of Mílos. Even the great gods were local, and the local gods became great. There are saints, saints of the cities. You know your saint here, in Milan, Sant'Ambrogio. His festival is coming up the week after next."

I had read about him, but I couldn't really see what she was getting at yet.

"Even in the times when we forgot the saints and the gods, we still called ourselves by the places we came from. If you talk to people here, I think you'll find that they won't say, 'I'm Italian.' They'll tell you they come from Florence, or the Abruzzi, or Lucca, like me. Our gods belong to a place also. We are all bound to one another, the land, the gods, the people."

I thought of the shoppers, holding their bags, looking at the priest. This world was such a strange place, if it had both gods and cell phones in it.

"Your family belongs, not just to Milan, but to this house. The first time I ever walked into this shop, I knew it. I could feel the centuries. Giuliano owns this, perhaps; but it owns him as well."

She seemed to like saying Giuliano's name. I thought of

his embarrassment the night before and wondered what had happened to make Nonna Laura and Signora Negroponte so cold to each other: I could begin to guess, but it seemed so unlikely—after all, all three of them were so *old*.

"His ancestors," she went on, "they each guarded this place in their time. There are other places, too. This city has burned to the ground more than once, little one, and each time a Della Torre was among those who shoveled the ash and relaid the stone.

"Where your family lives, they guard. They have set the wards upon this house and renewed them year upon year, century upon century. As long as your feet touch the cement on your balcony, you are even safe in the air above the courtyard. Some of your ancestors have stayed, as well, committing some part of their spirit to these walls."

I remembered Pompous and Gravel. Again, I wondered how it was I could think about them now, outside my room. I meant to ask. Signora Negroponte continued talking.

"Therefore, you are safe two ways. You are safe because of how well guarded this house is. You are also safe because of your blood, because your family chooses to guard you. But of course you must be careful. For it doesn't matter how well warded a house is, little one—if someone of the house invites a being, woman, man, demon—into it, there is nothing in the world that can stop that being from crossing the threshold. This is another ancient truth. Your demon knows it, and you should know it." She laughed shortly. "Francesca said a wise thing yesterday. Giuliano should listen to her more often, and so should her brother."

That was something to think about.

"So what about the restaurants and cafés?" I asked.

"The same thing, more or less. There is a law that prevails over households, do you see? A very similar law prevails over places where people are offered food and shelter, even if food and shelter are given in exchange for silver."

"But there's no law in the streets," I put in, slowly comprehending.

"Oh, no, there's a law," she replied gravely. "One of the oldest laws. Roads were magic, they always have been, because journeys are magic."

I can see what she means, I thought; my own journey to Milan had seemed pretty magical.

"It's a different law, the law of the road, different from the law of shelter and household, do you see? The gods of the house, they are *lares,* hearth gods. The god of the road is Mercury, the prince of thieves, the lord of messengers. A road may take you where you want to go—but it will take everyone else, too. No one needs an invitation, no one can be refused: that's the strength of roads and, at the same time, their weakness. Placing household protections on a road, it would be like trying to place wards on a river. You might succeed, for a time, but sooner or later all things are washed away in a river, and sooner or later all things on a road move on. It is a weakness, as I said, but it is also a strength. Yes?"

"I think I see," I said, hoping that was true.

I waited for more until I realized she was finished. She changed the subject.

"Now, I spoke with Giuliano. Your family has been watching this demon for a very long time, as I think you know. Its nature is still unclear, for all that. It cannot be only a demon of place, no?"

She spoke as if I would know what she was talking about, and I really wanted to act as if I did. Once again, I felt horribly left out of all my family's doings and all their knowledge. But I couldn't fake it with her.

"Why not?" I asked.

"Well, because he came to you over the ocean, for one thing. He came to a place where your people have lived for little more than half a century, right?"

"No, America is a lot older than that. . . ."

"But your family's roots there, they are hardly three generations deep."

I wasn't sure, but it was probably true, or close.

"We know he is a demon of family—your family."

"I didn't know that. Not really."

"Well, you do now," she said, irritatingly calm. "What I'm trying to work out is what the best protection might be. The usual forms have worked, but they are impractical. I mean, you have remained safe while you are inside your family's house, guarded by its powerful wards, but you can't stay there forever. You need something different. We may have to try a few things.

I wonder if the protections of place would work after all," she finished.

With that, she opened her handbag and began taking out a series of small, everyday objects: acorns, rings, twigs, and bits of fabric, along with a couple of small pieces of jewelry that didn't look even slightly interesting. While I sat still, watching her, her questions about the nature of my demon started me asking my own. Before, I had just wanted to know how to make it all stop; now I wanted to know where he came from, what laws governed him, what secrets he had that could help us defeat him.

"*Mia? Stai ascoltando?*—Are you listening?" said Signora Negroponte, and I realized she'd been speaking to me. She held out something to me, letting it fall into my hand: an acorn.

"From Lake Nemi," she said, then added, "A lake near Rome. Sacred to Diana. Her oaks still grow near there."

"Uh-huh."

"Now," said Signora Negroponte, "I want you to step outside the door to the shop, holding that in your hand, and wait. Do you remember what it felt like when he came for you before?"

"The first time?"

"Any time. When he came for that man, Lucifero, even."

"Yes. I know exactly what it feels like," I shivered. "Different each time, but not that different. The first time, that was a surprise."

"But now, if he came for you, you would know in time to get back in the shop?"

"I think so," I said, remembering how ambushed I'd felt

when he'd come near me on the plane. I had nearly opened the exit door and gone out to him; maybe what Lucifero had done made sense, in some crazy way. I thought about the time in the street, too, when all the voices had rushed at me and I had felt the cold pouring down my neck.

"Yes, I thought as much myself," said Signora Negroponte. "So we will do it this way. Try the acorn, first, and then we'll have a look at some other objects; we have many choices. The one that keeps him from coming for you is the one we want."

I felt disappointed. This seemed more like a science experiment than a mysterious, powerful ritual. I got up and went into the shop. Signora Negroponte gathered up her various talismans and followed me, settling her purse and notebook before her on the desk. She looked up at me where I waited by the door.

"Right. Go," she said.

My hand on the door handle felt clammy with sweat. I turned it, listening to the shop bells jingling, and stepped out into the quiet street.

For a full minute, nothing happened. Most of our neighbors had already gone to work; the first classes of the morning had already started at the Brera, and the delivery trucks had come and gone. I breathed frost on the air, making a mental note to go upstairs and get my coat if I was going to be doing this all morning, then realized the cold pouring down my back wasn't the December air.

I felt pinned. Signora Negroponte must have seen the change in my expression because she jumped up and leaned out of the door, pulling me back inside.

I took a deep breath of beeswax and flame-smell. Sometimes it's good to be stuck inside.

"Not that one, then," she said, holding out her hand for the acorn.

"No." I smiled, feeling slightly hysterical. The acorn jittered out of my palm and rattled across the floor, and I realized my hand was shaking.

She caught me with that hard gaze of hers.

"Can you try the next one?"

I looked straight back.

"Do I have a choice?"

She smiled.

"Anyway, I think I can get the hang of this," I said, even though my voice faltered.

Thus began the strangest time yet in my new life. Signora Negroponte came over from Lucca once a week, for a couple of days at a time. We suspended my studies on those days, because I was just too tired to concentrate. Every morning, Signora Negroponte appeared shortly before the bells rang nine and politely refused coffee from Nonna. We began right away: I could put talismans in my pocket, hold them in my hand, wear them around my neck. Once there was a paste I had to smear over my heart. I would wait outside for the feeling of ice pouring down my back, or listen until the whispers began, and then I would dash inside, where she would make notes while I calmed down.

It was totally bizarre. I wondered if this was how all demon catchers through the centuries figured out what worked.

I know this sounds peculiar, but I think the demon kind of enjoyed it. Sometimes I could feel him immediately when I stepped outside, could tell he was waiting somewhere above, ready to test our latest defense.

The demon wasn't the only one hanging out. Relatives kept showing up. Emilio brought us a beautiful picnic lunch from Peck, the amazing deli in the center of town, and sat eating rabbit and roasted onions with Signora Negroponte while I stood outside with a knotted hazel twig in my pocket, seriously considering running back in before I found out whether it worked, in case they decided not to leave me any. Égide stopped in late one afternoon with a loaf of bread, a lovely Crescenza cheese to spread on it, and a bottle of white wine. I could tell that he wasn't sure what he thought of Signora Negroponte, and that he felt loyal to Nonna. In an effort to draw the signora into conversation—polite as always—he brought up the subject of magic from his native country, Rwanda, which she just as politely began to compare to Italian magic, and before they knew it they were pouring a second glass of wine, deep in discussion. Feeling that I could use a break from standing out in the Via Fiori waiting for a monstrous possessing spirit to land on my head, I didn't distract them.

Anna Maria came by with chocolates from Hamburg, where she had been shooting the cover for some German fashion magazine. She touched each of the day's charms with a well-manicured finger while teasing some poor guy on the phone. There was always some poor guy on the phone with her.

While Anna Maria talked, and Signora Negroponte wrote,

and I ate a chocolate very, very slowly, I watched Anna Maria absently line up our experiments in a row: a piece of stone chipped from the threshold of the street door to our apartment; a swatch of velvet cut from the inside hem of a dress Giuliano's mother had worn, braided into one of Signora Negroponte's knots; a hazel twig, also in a knot, which looked kind of heart-shaped; another hazel twig in a knot that looked like a figure eight on drugs; a big splinter of wood from our stairwell; a locket that had belonged to some long-dead relation whose name I had forgotten.

"No, I'm in Milan," said Anna Maria to the poor guy, poking the locket into place. "I can't."

Another day, Uncle Matteo brought a basket with bread, *bresaola,* and a jar of a clear preserve with fruit in it that I thought was some kind of jam, so I spread it all over a piece of bread. Uncle Matteo and Signora Negroponte watched me and didn't say anything while I bit into it.

"Hot mustard!" I yelped.

"A Piedmontese specialty," Signora Negroponte told me, laughing. "You looked like you knew what you were doing."

Uncle Matteo grunted and lit a cigarette. In between puffs, he said to me, "Mustard is good for the spirit. Bolsters you up."

Then he smiled and patted me on the shoulder, and suddenly it struck me how everybody was feeding me and taking care of me, how everybody seemed to know, without saying a word about it directly, that this must be unbelievably hard and frightening for me to walk out each time, to go toward the terrible thing that scared me so much I couldn't even think about it. They were comforting me with food, same as my mom with chicken dumpling soup when I was sick, or hot chocolate when I was wrestling with an essay.

"You've got tears in your eyes," said Signora Negroponte. "We have two more charms to try, but maybe we should stop for the day."

"No—I can do more. I can. I just figured something out, that's all." I realized too late I could have blamed the tears on the mustard.

She smiled her hard smile, that really had so much softness in it, because it faced things as they were. She didn't ask me what I'd figured out, which was kind of nice, because I was still treasuring it. Uncle Matteo just nodded and smoked his cigarette.

That night I woke up with my feet kicking like a person hanging, just as I used to do. I could hear someone growling to a tune, but it took me a minute to realize Gravel was singing a lullaby. When I was able to understand what the words were, they were awful, all about plagues and murders and starvation and prisoners of war. I wondered if I was still dreaming and made myself sit up.

"What in the ethers are you singing?" Pompous asked him.

"A lullaby. She's having trouble sleeping."

I could hear Pompous trying not to laugh. "That's very nice, my dear, but really, I think those verses will just give her nightmares."

Gravel sounded hurt when he replied, "I was just singing about all the things she doesn't suffer from. I thought it would be comforting."

"All this time around humans and you are still a nincompoop," said Pompous.

"I learned from the best," said Gravel.

I took a deep breath.

"Please don't start arguing," I said. "And thank you for the lullaby, Gravel, even if it wasn't exactly something I could fall asleep to."

I knew they would vanish again, and they did, but they left behind such a feeling of kindness that I actually slept through the rest of the night.

SEVENTEEN

The Festa di Sant'Ambrogio

The next day was Friday, the Festa di Sant'Ambrogio. Signora Negroponte worked with me until she went to catch her train to Lucca in the afternoon. Emilio came home early from work and sat with me in the shop, waiting for everyone to gather so we could go to the fair near the Castello Sforzesco, called the *fiera degli Oh-Bej Oh-Bej*, which odd name Signora Negroponte explained to me: *Oh-Bej* was *Oh bella!* in the local dialect of Lombardy. But my mind wasn't on the festival when Emilio came home.

"The trouble with not telling me things the demon might learn," I said to him, "is that I might work them out for myself anyway. You're always telling me to do that. Can't you tell me just a little about the candles or tell me if I've guessed right?"

He gave me an appraising look. "You are feistier than you used to be," he told me. I grinned at him. I loved that word, feisty, *vivace*, even though Lucifero was the first person to use it to describe me. I thought it was a good word for me, even if I still felt scared a lot of the time.

He gestured to the candles, flickering on their shelves like an audience. "Tell me what you've guessed."

"Well, I know you use them to trap demons. That's why you don't want us to blow them out with our breath. And Lucifero and his friend guessed the same thing, which is why they were so interested in them. But then," I added, frowning, "if they imprison demons, is it safe to let the candle go out? And is it safe to leave them right in the store, in the windows?"

He nodded and smiled. "Already thinking like us," he said. "I will answer your first question with two questions of my own: Is it the flame that imprisons the demon? And would it be practical to keep a bunch of eternal flames burning in a wooden-walled shop? I will answer your second question with a saying beloved in our family: the best place to hide things is in plain sight."

That was plenty to chew on, right there. Besides, it occurred to me that if you needed to keep the demon inside the candle and keep the candle burning, you'd need a really big candle. "So why do they light them at all?" I asked him.

"Think about it some more, and tell me what you guess," he said. I picked up an olive pit from my lunch plate and threw it at him.

"Ow!" he cried, laughing, and picked it up and threw it back. At that point, Uncle Matteo and Aunt Brigida arrived, so we didn't get into an all-out olive-pit war.

Pretty much the entire crew gathered to go to the Castello Sforzesco, with me in my usual position in the middle. The fiera turned out to be a huge market full of stalls and street performers, people eating fire and telling fortunes. The air smelled of sugar and fried food. Nonna tucked a wad of euros in my pocket, instructing me to spend them, so I did, buying Christmas presents for my family. People were selling everything: lamps and marzipan and badly spelled English T-shirts and badges with the city coat of arms and wallets and rings and couches and roasted chestnuts. I got small things to send home because I was worried about the postage: for my sister, a badge and a ring with a glass eye in it; for my mom, a really pretty silver bracelet that looked like a band of flowers, which broke about two stalls later; for my dad, a leather wallet, because I couldn't think of anything else to get him from the city his father had left behind.

We were scattered among the stalls, Nonno and Nonna stopping to look at some marzipan saints, Anna Maria and her father arguing good-naturedly about a lamp, and for a moment I thought nobody was near me. The too-familiar feeling of fear started to seep into my gut, but then I felt a hand on my arm.

"Drop this?" asked Emilio.

"Yes—oh," I said, seeing the bracelet had broken apart in its short fall.

"They always sell crap—pretty crap," he said. "I'll show you a better place to get jewelry, a few stalls up. Why do you look so sad?"

"It was for my mom. I couldn't tell . . ."

"Don't be silly. You're new to all this. You should be more patient with yourself," he said firmly.

I felt much better. I was surprised a guy would know where to get good jewelry, but on the other hand, if any guy knew that kind of thing, it would be Emilio. Between the stalls, I saw Francesco talking to someone familiar, and I stopped to look. I didn't know the person, but I knew what she was, now that I knew I had seen one.

"A messenger," I said softly.

"What?" Emilio looked up from a table full of scarves. "Oh, yes."

It was a woman, a messenger like the man who had warned Emilio about the spirit returning to Signora Galeazzo's house, though she looked as unlike him as possible. She was tall and curvy, with a huge mane of red-brown hair and a fierce expression. But now I noticed small things that I had seen with the other one, like the way the shadows on her face fell differently from those on Francesco's face, as if her face couldn't remember exactly where the faint winter sun should be. She seemed angry, pointing and gesturing.

"What are they talking about?"

"I don't know. I've never seen her before. You can recognize them now?"

"I think so," I said, feeling proud.

At last, she gave up and stomped away, her feet making no sound, and vanished among the stalls.

"Uh," grunted Francesco, joining us.

"What was that about?" Emilio asked.

"She doesn't want to do the job."

Emilio shook his head.

"What job?" I asked.

"They don't always like the task that is set them," said Francesco. "They don't have a lot of choices, though."

"What do you mean?"

Emilio spoke, his eyes on the direction she had gone, his voice distant. "They are suicides, Mia."

He swung to face me. "They have to do the tasks appointed them before they can find peace."

"It's a horrible joke, really," said Francesco dispassionately. "They couldn't stand the world, so they took themselves out of it, and now they're stuck here until they can earn their way out."

I stared at them, feeling sick.

"One way is to keep watch and pass messages," said Francesco.

"But why?" I asked. "Why do they have to? Is this like the law of the road and stuff?"

"Something like that, as far as we know," said Francesco. "It just seems to happen."

"How do they know? Who tells them?"

"They seem to just know," said Emilio. "Like we know that things fall downward. When they are done . . . Nonno saw one finish, once."

"What was it like?" I asked.

Emilio reflected. "Nonno said he heard what sounded like hundreds of tiny bells jingling in the open air, and voices calling the messenger's name as if he were an old friend. The messenger smiled and said, 'I suppose I'd better go,' and spread out his hands. Nonno said it was 'as if he were pronouncing a benediction on the whole world.' Then the light on his face changed—you know how they never seem to have the right light on their faces—it changed into the light of this world, and he just faded away, until there was only one last bell ringing, one last voice calling, and then they were gone, too."

For a moment, the three of us stood in a tiny pool of silence in the crowded market. Then the sounds of the fiera around us came back, and Francesco said, "Heavy thoughts for a light day," and Emilio smiled. I felt the same way.

"Hey," I said to Emilio, "can you show me the stall where I can get a better bracelet for my mom?"

He did, and I found a bracelet in the same style, but even more delicate and stronger at the same time, if that were possible: a string of tiny flowers floating on a silver chain, with pale blue stones set in the middle of each flower. It cost four times as much as the bracelet that had broken, but it was worth it.

Then I bought my cousins hot crepes with chocolate, and the rest of the day was good, except for the part where we ran into Alba, shopping with some friends, and she carried Emilio off with her. I felt annoyed with myself for being so happy when he came back to us, smiling and shrugging. "They want to keep shopping, I want to go home and eat Nonna's dinner."

As we walked home, full of crepes and sugar, Emilio explained that Sant'Ambrogio's day was also the opening night of the Teatro alla Scala, a really big deal in Milan. Tickets were insanely expensive, he said, but sometime he wanted to take Nonna. He asked if I liked opera, and I shrugged. My grandparents used to take us, and we had to wear scratchy dresses and sit for hours while a bunch of people sang in a language we didn't understand.

Emilio laughed when I talked about the scratchy dresses; he said he thought I should try it again. He reminded me he was planning to get tickets for La Scala after the holidays, and he would get one for me. But Francesca would need to take me shopping first, he added. That was all right by me.

That very weekend, Francesca organized a Della Torre posse to get us safely to the shops, but fortunately for me it did not include any of the other women of the family—I wouldn't have been too sure of Laura's fashion advice, for one, and I don't think I could have handled Anna Maria at all, let alone her mother. In the end, Francesco and his father took us around, retiring to a nearby café and refusing to get involved any further.

The shop ladies scared me. The one time I had gone inside a clothing store with Aunt Brigida and Anna Maria, the ladies had hovered over me and barked anytime I had tried to touch something. When Francesca and I entered the stores, the women crowded around, scolding Francesca instead.

"How have you let her spend the whole season in these raggedy jeans? And look at that sweater! It's practically a dust rag. No, my grandmother wouldn't even use it as a dust rag. How can you tell what shape she is underneath? *Boh!* She looks like a student from the Brera."

I wasn't sure I minded looking like a student from the Brera, but apparently I wasn't allowed to look like one. Never mind that I was stuck inside most of the time and nobody would see me anyway. I wanted all the dresses that would show what shape I was underneath, but even when I was allowed to try those on ("No, no! Too old for you! I will hang that back up!"), I had to admit that I would never take them out of the closet. I wouldn't have the courage.

The shape I was had changed, as a matter of fact—when they pointed out the raggedy jeans, I realized that not only were there holes everywhere, but that the legs were an inch too short now. All my sleeves were too short, as well, and I needed larger sizes of more embarrassing pieces of clothing. Francesca took me to a surly old woman who measured me in some very intimate places before I could say no and then brought out underwear and bras that my mother would never have approved of, since they were the sort that seemed to be designed for someone else to see. They were very comfortable, though. (What happened to "No! Too old for you!"? I didn't get it.)

I have no idea how much Francesca spent on me. She waved

the little spending money I had away when I offered it. What she really spent on me was time, and in her abrupt kindness I could now read love.

Sitting on my bed after a long day of shopping, footsore and blank, I still found some energy to plan some future outfits. I tried on the dress I liked the best. It hadn't looked like anything when one of the barking shop ladies had brought it forward, but Francesca had nodded at once, delighted. I couldn't see why. It looked brown—what my mother calls "fawn-colored"—and shapeless and dull. It was the last thing I had tried on in the dressing room. When I had put it on I understood much better what Francesca had been trying to explain all day about well-cut clothes. I hadn't recognized myself for a minute. I mean that, I really hadn't. So I waved at myself, and gradually the features I had lived with for sixteen years reemerged from the mirror, along with the thought, *Oh! So that's what I always looked like, underneath!*

I wasn't quite ready to part with my old, tattered jeans, but I had to admit that this was what I was really supposed to look like. I had occasionally allowed myself to suspect that I was pretty, or could be, a little bit, anyway. Now I could see, yes, I was. So, back at home, sitting on the bed, that was the dress I reached for. Looking at myself again, this time in the hall mirror, I saw something else, the second time I put on the dress. I thought of myself as the mousy-haired, dull-featured cousin of these strange, luminous Della Torres, Emilio the Apollo, Francesca with her precise dark hair, Anna Maria with her perfectly straight back. Now I could see the family features in my own face, the high cheekbones, the thick, dark eyebrows with their peculiar arc, and the horizon-seeing eyes.

I thought about what my grandfather would have said to all this. He would have been really angry, I imagined. Now, having spent more than three months with the family he left behind, I thought about what I would say back.

I wore something completely different to talk to Gina on Skype the next day: she could only see the blue shirt, a button-down with a crisp, huge collar and fabulous cuffs made out of smooth, fine cotton with a faint, intricate flower print. But I knew I was wearing some fantastic new jeans that not only went all the way down to my ankles, but seemed to be cut perfectly for me, as well as a pair of black, Italian leather slip-ons that would have made any popular girl back at school die in a fit of envy.

"You look different," said Gina. My parents' computer is old, cheap, and incredibly slow, so she was at her friend Sara's house; Sara had her own laptop and had left Gina alone in her room. I had no privacy on my end, partly because the computer sat on a small desk in the living room, and partly because sound travels way too well in that apartment. At least we both had webcams. It was good to see her face, even if the light in Sara's room made it look like she was underwater.

"I look different?" I asked, hoping this was a compliment. "How?"

"Well . . . your hair seems more stylish."

"Francesca took me to get it cut."

"And you have a new shirt that looks awesome. I love the blue, and the cut."

"Francesca got it for me."

Gina laughed.

"Did Francesca help you lose a tiny bit of weight as well?"

Ouch, I thought, but I laughed. "No, we just eat differently here. Or something. Do I really look thinner?"

Gina shrugged. "You do, which is bizarre, because you're the only one that ever thought you were fat. Me and Mom always felt like you didn't have any weight to spare. Maybe it's that you look—more confident? No, I don't know what it is. There's just something different."

"Whatever it is, it sounds good."

"It is," she said, and smiled. "I miss you."

"I miss you, too," I said, but even as I said it I felt a small tightness in my stomach, because it wasn't entirely true. I realized that, at least this last month, I hadn't really had time to miss her. That first month away had been much harder. We sat still, both trying to figure out what we could say that could be heard by the rest of my relations.

We mostly talked by e-mail, for the privacy. I don't have tons of friends on Facebook and, anyway, I couldn't just post, "Mia Dellatorri is in Italy because she got possessed by a demon, and now she has to learn how to defend herself," or, "I really hate demons today," or anything like that. My family had agreed to tell everyone that our distant relatives had invited me to study abroad, which was more or less true. I guess I had gotten a lot of cool points at school for having gone to live in Italy; it would've been the first time anybody thought I was cool.

"So how are Mom and Dad?" I asked.

"Okay, I guess," she said.

"I never hear from Dad," I said. "He just tells Mom to put something in her e-mail to me."

Gina nodded. "He's still angry. But he grills me, you know? He wants to know everything, what Milan is like, what the family is like. If I even come close to the subject of Grandpa, he acts all fake-uninterested, you know, the way he does when one of us mentions a boy. So I can tell he's dying to know more about his dad and what happened."

I looked around quickly. Nonna was in the kitchen, starting soup for supper; nobody else was home yet.

"I don't know a lot more. It's not the easiest subject to talk about here, either. But I have my suspicions. And Grandpa was raised with Giuliano and Uncle Matteo, who is Giuliano's younger brother. Grandpa's dad died in World War Two, and his mom died of grief right afterward, apparently."

"Of grief?" asked Gina. "People don't do that really, do they?"

"I don't know," I said. "I'm starting to wonder about a lot of things."

"And your suspicions?"

"There was a brother in between Giuliano and Matteo, named Martino. He died around thirteen years after the war, somebody told me."

"That's got to be around when Grandpa left Italy," said Gina, pouncing.

"Yes. Exactly."

I didn't tell her who had told me. I had never gotten around to telling her about Lucifero, either.

"I'll try to find out exactly when he came to America," she said. "I think I can do it without asking Dad."

"Thanks," I said.

At that point, Sara leaned around the door, and Gina said, "We have homework to do. This time difference sucks."

"I know, right?" I said. "Have a good day. I love you."

"I love you, too," she said. "Give my best to everybody."

"Say hi to Mom and Dad from me," I said. One last wave, and we logged off.

The Novena

So those were the middle days of December: streets strung with lights that said *Buon Natale*; thick, freezing industrial fog that left my nostrils black on the inside; the smell of sweet breads baking, and the rustle of paper as I made the acquaintance of dead relations and their fellow dead Milanese, in the books I was able to read faster and faster. Some mornings I still woke up with my feet kicking together like they had when I was first recovering from my possession, but I had no bad dreams, and I hardly thought about my demon. I didn't know how much I would need this peace and quiet, not yet.

I wasn't looking forward to Christmas. Christmas meant tons of presents, a froth of wrapping paper around the tree in the morning, Mom's special coffee cake at breakfast, and a huge roast beef at dinner (I don't know what family tradition that was from, since it didn't seem very Italian to me, from what I knew now).

I have to admit my studies suffered during the holidays, not only the books and the meditations, but the time with Signora Negroponte. The nine days before Christmas, called the Novena, were full of family rituals, Masses, fairs, and parades.

Anna Maria showed up one morning in the most ordinary, worn-out clothes I'd ever seen her in, still looking perfect, of course, and also looking surprised that I was downstairs in the shop. Everybody thought someone else had told me that particular day was special. She chivvied me upstairs and shooed me into my own most worn-out clothes, telling me to come to the kitchen when I was done: when I arrived, I saw every baking bowl and pan out on the counters.

But all the bowls were empty. It took me a second to realize that everyone was waiting for me. Aunt Brigida motioned me to a chair at the kitchen table and passed me a metal bowl. Anna Maria took up a rolling pin and aimed it menacingly at the bowl in front of her.

"One, two, three," counted Nonna, and on "three" they all banged their bowls hard on the table and shouted, *"VAI VIA, VAI VIA, VAI VIA!"*

I nearly jumped out of my skin.

They all grinned at me.

"Mia, want to try it again?" asked Nonna.

"Uh, all right," I said.

We did it again.

"One, two, three . . ."

"VAI VIA, VAI VIA, VAI VIA!" we chanted. It felt good.

"One time for all, much louder!" commanded Nonna.

"VAI VIA, VAI VIA, VAI VIA!" we roared, banging the pots.

"Excellent," she said. "Now we begin."

"What . . . ?" I began when I got my breath back. Nonna shook her head.

"There's time to talk once we get going, *mia piccola interrogatrice,*" Francesca said.

I translated in my head: *little question, maybe?* I stuck out my tongue at her, and she smiled. The recipe looked like it had been written on reused, re-scraped parchment, like some of the notes they'd let me see. Brigida pointed at it with one mauve-polished nail.

"Old family recipe from my great-great-great-grandfather. He was related to the Sforzas. Didn't like the Della Torres. Would have been furious to know that his own children were going to pass this recipe on to them! I think he would have been angrier about the recipe than about my marriage a hundred years later. But then, panettone, it's a very important thing, a special Milanese sweet bread. A nobleman who was in love with a baker's daughter made it for her, that's how the first one was made. Nobody makes it from scratch anymore."

"Except the lunatic Della Torres," Anna Maria put in, not very nicely. The others ignored her, and we set to work, measuring and kneading and mixing. As I said, panettone did seem like a lot of trouble. I couldn't really see the point, but I liked sneaking bits of candied lemon and orange peel. I took my sweater off as the room warmed, smelling of vanilla sugar, orange flowers, and rising bread. I listened while everybody gossiped.

Brigida told about her friend Sandra, who had announced at a family dinner on Sant'Ambrogio's day that: 1) she was leaving her husband; 2) she had never liked his mistress; and finally 3) she was moving in with a university student less than half her age, and her family could just live with it or never talk to her again, she didn't care either way; she was sick of cleaning and cooking for them anyway. She had then gotten up from the table, picked up a suitcase she'd had standing behind the door, and walked out of the apartment. Apparently in the stunned silence that had followed this announcement, her youngest son, who was still in school, had also stood up and said, "And *I'm* gay," and followed her out the door.

While she measured flour, Anna Maria said coolly, "Gay is no big deal," shocking her mother and aunt.

Everyone wanted to know how my family was doing: Had Gina done well in the play, and how was her boyfriend? Had my mother gotten over her cold? Did I think my father would ever come visit?

Francesca dropped a bowl—*bang, bang, bang!*—and I remembered the shouting that had preceded the baking.

"So how come we shout 'out, out, out'?" I asked.

Brigida blinked. "Because we always have," she said.

"Every little bit helps, in this house," Francesca explained.

Everyone had stopped working to look at me.

"It reminds me of New Year's, especially out in the countryside," said Anna Maria. "Out in the villages, people throw all kinds of crap in the streets—old dishes, bottles, even bicycles and bathtubs—and meanwhile it's just like here, all these obnoxious little boys running around throwing firecrackers under your feet."

"Yes," said Nonna. "They do it for the same reasons, too, even if they don't remember."

"*I* don't remember," said Brigida, so plaintively we all laughed.

They never really answered my question, but I had plenty of time to think about it over the next few days while I helped in the kitchen. These women were up to something, I was sure of it. It wasn't just about baking a bread that everyone else buys at the bakery or the grocery store because it's such a pain to make, although that seemed a typically Della Torre thing to do. I was related to a bunch of baking nerds.

At least they warned me about the fast before Christmas Eve, where we didn't eat anything between meals for twenty-four hours. The worst part was cooking all afternoon on Christmas Eve. Once I unthinkingly started to pop a slice of *grana* into my mouth. Nonna slapped my hand hard enough to make me cry. I stomped out of the kitchen for a minute and stood in the hall. When my hand stopped stinging, I went back in. I didn't exactly apologize. Instead I said, keeping my voice steady, "What should I do next?"

I guess that was okay, because she showed me. It wasn't that great an afternoon, because by then I was dizzy with hunger. Emilio showed up with a giant pot of *zuppa di pesce*—fish soup, though it sounds much cooler in Italian. It smelled gorgeous. He said to his grandmother, "It's not my best this year."

I stared at him.

"You cook?" I asked.

He gave me his most condescending look, then turned around, rolled up his sleeves, and took over the tortellini making from Nonna.

Anna Maria arrived with a basket of frozen wild mushrooms from one of her lovesick boyfriends. As usual, she broke an unspoken rule about not complaining by saying, *"Ciao,* Mia! I'm so hungry I could eat an ox, couldn't you?"

"Two," I agreed, grinning.

"Enough, enough," growled Nonna. "You'll get your chance."

Everybody was crabby by then, but at least we could distract ourselves with the arrival of more and more people with more and more food. Giuliano and Matteo appeared, singing loudly and carrying bags of seafood—different fish wrapped in paper, fresh mussels, shrimp, and scallops, all of which went straight into the sink, and then into pans, the scallops to bake with marsala and almonds, the mussels to cook with a bunch of leeks I'd been washing and chopping. Finally Égide arrived in a violently fuchsia silk scarf, carrying a case of wine. Francesco followed him in, singing too, and upset the first bottle to get opened.

"I'll clean it up," said Nonna, cuffing him on the shoulder. "You sit. We all need to eat."

She pressed him into a chair, did something incredibly quick and complex with a towel, and at last, to my relief, we sat down to the feast.

NİNETEEN

All Are Invited

I'm not known for my love of fish. But I think that dinner is the one I'll remember when I'm dying.

"Slowly, slowly," Giuliano laughed; embarrassed, I took his advice. "This is a special goose, an old family tradition. Most Italians just have a lot of fish dishes. Always an odd number, that's important."

We had a lot of fish dishes, too. I used to hate fish when I was little, but I'd gotten over that; I think I would have loved it then if I could have eaten fish like this. Everything tasted heavenly, from Emilio's *zuppa di pesce,* to the fresh mussels Giuliano had brought home, to the risotto with shrimp and champagne that Francesca conjured up at the last minute.

We feasted for hours, finishing with espresso after espresso, because although all anyone wanted to do was lie down and sleep for a day, we still were going to ten o'clock Mass, even Francesca and Égide, who never went to Mass.

By then, I was happy again. We bundled out into the night air, stamping in the chill, and I could hear singing in the streets. We made the short walk to Santa Maria del Carmine and heard the bells swing above us just as we all lined up at the font. That's the only moment I felt truly homesick, smelling the musty water and remembering my grandparents. Again I thought how angry my grandfather would be if he could see me here. I wondered if he had been right, after all, to leave this family and this place.

The whole church was filled with candles, and every altar was decorated with holly and mistletoe, just like every threshold in our apartment. A huge *presepio*, or crèche, full of shepherds and sheep, stood in an alcove. I settled down between Égide and Anna Maria to space out and look at the sculptures and paintings in the shadows. The priest started to drone.

I fixed my eyes on a Madonna in the corner. The sculptor had obviously tried to give her a thoughtful expression, but instead she looked like the Baby Jesus had been giving her a hard time that day. She had the usual starry robe, but I really liked her pedestal: a huge bear cut out of black marble. The bear looked like it could stand there forever without getting tired or, if anybody tried to get fresh with the Virgin, it could drop them with one whack of its huge, long-clawed paw. I couldn't see its eyes under the dark shadow of its brow; I kept trying to make them out and fell into a kind of trance.

"Justice! I want justice!" someone screamed.

We all turned around to stare at the back of the church.

A young woman with dark hair, wearing a gray, cashmere, cowl-necked sweater, was standing and pointing—at us. Her voice dropped to a rolling growl that sounded too much like the voice that had come from Signora Galleazzo, but even more like the voice I had heard inside me. I saw that her eyes were rolled back in her head, and the skin of her face was rippling and moving.

"Justice, justice, justice," she snarled, never lowering her pointing finger.

"It's *him*," I sobbed, knowing it as I said it aloud.

People were staring at us, too.

An acolyte hurried up to her.

"You must come outside with me," he said gently, but as he touched her sleeve, his face went white and he sank to his knees.

"Mother of God," he gasped.

I needed to vomit. I needed to run. It was going to happen here. My feet were going to kick together, my body would rise—

"You're not welcome here," cried the priest, rushing down the aisle toward her. "You are not welcome here!"

She gave a hideous, high laugh that echoed back from the corners and the vaults.

"Your sign says all are welcome, all are welcome!" she shrieked. "I was *invited*!"

Signora Negroponte's rules about houses flashed in my mind, and I understood.

"Justice!" she screamed.

Then she began to rise into the air. I heard her shoes scrape off the marble in the silence.

I screamed, too. People stood up, panicking. The acolyte struggled to his feet and started to steer them to the door. Anna Maria gripped my arm so hard it hurt.

No place was safe, even a church, warded by centuries of law.

"Stay still," hissed Anna Maria. "We have to protect you."

Giuliano, Emilio, and Matteo were up, watching, apparently deciding.

The priest stood in front of the woman, shouting, holding his Bible with both hands: at least he seemed to know exactly what he was looking at. The acolyte was vomiting on the marble floor. The woman spun slowly in the air, twisting her head to keep her eyes on me.

"You," she whispered harshly, and the whisper cut through the cries of the priest. "You are mine. To me you will come in the end. Let all here know it. You are mine!"

My mind froze. Everyone was staring at me, as I stared into the eyes of my enemy.

Then the oddest thing happened. As if they were right under my fingers, I could feel the doorknobs in my parents' house. I could feel myself checking them like I used to do, so many nights. I thought, *How far I have come,* and my mind unfroze. I felt strength descend on me like a mantle.

"Let me go, Anna Maria," I said gently, and to my surprise she did. I stood up and faced my enemy.

I don't know what made me say it.

"Come and get me."

She shrieked in triumph and came at me over the pews, her feet banging against the back of each one.

I thought, *All right, this is it. It was a good life. I hope I don't hurt anyone.*

I felt my family pushed back down the aisle by the force of her attack. I didn't see them push toward me again, once she focused completely on me.

Then she was face-to-face with me, her skin rippling with the power that had taken it over, the mind that rode her mind. Her hair stood on end, her hands bunched like claws, her eyes rolled up to the whites, her jaw worked and chattered, and all around her the terrible, banal gloom of possession dimmed the candles.

I could feel her hot breath on my face. It stank. I've never smelled a corpse, but now I know what one smells like. She raised her claws on either side of my temples and I felt her arms tense to strike. I couldn't seem to do anything about it.

She struck.

All I felt was the rush of air. Her fingers stopped, floating and tight, less than half an inch from my head. She tried again, and again, and again, deafening me with her shrieks. I didn't have time to be afraid.

Sobbing, she groaned, "All were invited," and with one last shiver, she fell, slamming onto the pew in front of me. I looked down, and all I saw was an unconscious girl. *Did I look like that?* I thought.

TWENTY

Il Caso della Famiglia Umberti

Emilio ran to her and knelt, putting a hand to her temple, cupping the curve of her skull. I felt the bite of jealousy in my stomach.

"Nonno," he said, looking up, and Giuliano nodded as if Emilio had said a great deal more. He turned to the priest, saying in a low voice, "Get the rest of them out of here."

"We need to take *her* out of this holy place," the priest growled back. His middle-aged face was wan, and he looked almost too tired to be terrified, but I could see him bracing himself. Behind him, the still figures from the *presepio* looked on.

"No, Father. She's not at fault. This would best be dealt with in this house."

I didn't get that—hadn't he and Emilio thought that taking Lucifero into the Duomo would have been stupid?

"Francesco, Anna Maria, I need you," Giuliano was saying. "Matteo, you, too. Do you have your—?"

At their nods, he added, "Good."

When were they ever without their cases? I wondered. He didn't ask Emilio.

He turned to his wife.

"*Cara*, I need you, Francesca, and Brigida to take Mia home."

I scuttled down the pew toward him.

"*Nonno*, please! I should stay," I found myself saying. I didn't know why, but I knew I was right.

He frowned at me so fiercely I thought he was going to yell at me like he had when he had asked if I was betraying the family. My insides turned cold.

"This is much, much too dangerous," he replied in a low voice that warned me I'd spoken too loudly.

Around us, the acolytes were ushering everyone else from the church. The priest stayed.

I stood up straight and faced Giuliano. I took a deep breath.

"Believe me," I said, low and clear. "I just saw."

He blinked. I think he'd expected me to pitch a fit, or whine, or do something kid-like.

He didn't stop frowning, but rather than answer me he turned to the priest again. I waited. I had a feeling that this was one argument I was going to win.

The priest, on the other hand, didn't see that he was going to lose.

"Father Giacomo," said Emilio gently, "when she wakes, the

unholy being in her will still be there. If we take her into the street, we may not have time to get her to sanctuary before he comes back."

"Who says you're going to work on her, or do whatever it is you do?" the priest replied, his voice rising as the last of his parishioners hurried out the door. "You know I know—you know everybody knows. I protect you, I say nothing to my superiors. But this! This is too much! You should never have let *her* in here, if you knew the danger!"

He pointed at me, and Giuliano abruptly changed his mind.

"*She* is just fine! She's even right—she should stay for the exorcism. You, Father, should stay, too; one of your flock is in the most mortal danger you can conceive of, and I think you are too wise and good a man to refuse her your help." He paused, looking at Father Giacomo. "Aren't you?"

Pretty manipulative; I had started to notice that about Giuliano. The demon, however, was the one who ended the argument, when the girl opened her eyes. She looked up at the ceiling of the church and laughed softly, a sound like sand pouring from the mouths of the dead.

"Father, help her. Let us help her. You know us. You know that we do the best we can—" said Giuliano.

Father Giacomo didn't answer for a moment. He looked at her, lying on the stone floor between the pews. She looked back, insolent, smiling. Then I saw a flicker, as if the girl inside were still there, and her eyes shut again.

The priest said, "Show me."

Emilio and Francesco scooped up the girl and carried her, following the priest into the withdrawing room. Nonna squeezed Giuliano's arm, then turned to go, taking Égide, Francesca, and Aunt Brigida with her. I watched them for a moment, then followed Emilio.

"Better set her on the floor," Emilio warned when the acolyte pulled forward a long, cushioned bench. "She's going to move around a lot."

As they laid her on the floor, Emilio reached into one of her pockets and pulled out her wallet. He flipped it open, ignoring Father Giacomo's protests, and said to Giuliano and Matteo, "Her name is Lisetta Maria Umberti."

Giuliano took the wallet and passed it to the priest.

"Probably one of the Torino Umbertis," Giuliano said. "To judge by the nose. We hardly ever have to deal with them; this isn't one of their kinds of problems."

Uncle Matteo pulled out his case and set it on a nearby table. Emilio struggled to his feet and reached into the breast pocket of his jacket for his own case. This time I could see the dark scar on the underside of it up close.

Emilio bent his head to check the girl's pulse, then said, "Mia, come. You should feel this. If it's safe for her to touch, Nonno?"

"She should know. Risk it. But careful, careful."

He scowled. I knelt across the girl from Emilio, and let him take my fingers and press them against her neck.

"Feel it, if you can."

For a moment, I didn't, first because his hands were so warm and smooth, and I couldn't get past the feeling of touching them, and second because my own pulse was beating so hard I could hardly feel anything. I took a deep breath and waited, and presently I could feel the flutter of the girl's heartbeat tapping insistently at my finger like a plea. Interwoven with it, as if this were a particularly dissonant piece of music, was another pulse, pounding furiously, jolting out three beats for every one of hers.

I kept my fingers on her neck, fascinated, forgetting the pressure of Emilio's hand over mine; then the second, fevered pulse changed. It felt like a finger poking at me from under her skin. I had just begun to get light-headed with terror again when Emilio said, "That's more than enough," and pulled my hand away.

"Did you feel that?" I asked.

"The double pulse?" he replied.

"Yes, and then the way that it—" I tried to find the words.

"Reached for you?"

"Yes," I answered in a low voice.

"Yes," he echoed thoughtfully. He held my eyes. "Do you think there's any chance that you will let him in?"

I stared at him, unable to decide if I was offended.

"Not if I can help it," I said. "No way."

The start of a smile unfolded at the corner of his mouth. He looked relieved.

"Good," he said.

He looked up at his grandfather, then added, "I think we both believe you should stay. But if you sense great danger, or if we tell you to go, you must go. Understand?"

He spoke quickly. We both knew that we had no time to lose, but that the words had better be said.

"Yes," I said.

I looked down at the girl, feeling strange. Just as when I had faced her—really the thing inside her—in the church, I thought about how much had changed. The strangest thing of all was how little fear I felt. I mean, in a situation like that it's a good idea to be afraid, but I didn't feel powerless and paralyzed, the way I had at Signora Galeazzo's, or even the way I used to at night, checking the doors in a time that seemed very long ago.

"What can I do?" I asked, and my voice did not shake.

Emilio smiled briefly: he seemed pleased by my question.

"Three things," he said. "First, you can tell us any instincts you have, any sensations, like when you said 'Majdanek' at Signora Galeazzo's. Second, you can protect yourself. Stay alert. Do not get caught up in what's happening, no matter what. Keep returning to the Madonna in your mind."

"And third," said Giuliano, above us, having finished a low-voiced conversation with Father Giacomo, "you can ring the bell."

Okay, I wasn't feeling so brave after all.

Giuliano helped me up from beside Lisetta, and I followed him over to the table, where he opened his case.

Giuliano's case was tidy and organized. The fine partitions

of aged wood kept every tool secure. Giuliano lifted out his small silver bell, wound around with a design of intertwining birds. I'd seen these same birds other places, I realized, like on the shopping bags that our very few legitimate candle shoppers took away with them, or on the lintel over the door to our apartment. I guess I hadn't really paid attention. He held the bell out to me with such a serious expression that I realized this was an even bigger deal than I had thought.

I turned it over in my hand, and saw that the clapper had a carefully stitched leather cover. I reached to take it off, but he closed his hand over mine.

"Not yet," he said. "I will tell you. Now, when you ring it, terrible things may happen. You understand? You saw how angry the spirit that possessed Signora Galeazzo got. This will be worse. Yet you must ring it. No matter what is happening to the girl, when I ask you to ring, you must ring. Understand?"

Even though I had seen what happened when a bell was rung during an exorcism, I still felt ridiculous nodding to him so seriously while I held this piece of silver that hardly filled the hollow of my palm; what could such a small thing do?

Uncle Matteo already had his case open on the table. He took out a candle that looked like a miniature version of one of the designs in the shop—a Roman milestone in deep gold beeswax—and set it in a candleholder. Father Giacomo brought in a plate with the Host on it: a jug of wine and a silver plate full of communion wafers. I noticed he was wearing a second cross around his neck, this one a heavy rosewood rosary with Jesus in brass, looking very patient—much more patient than the priest, or the acolyte beside him.

The girl on the floor shuddered. Was this what it was always like? Periods of coma punctuated with periods of destructive, supernaturally powerful consciousness?

Anna Maria came back in just then—where had she been?—and saw the bell in my hand. For a moment, I thought she was going to kill me with a look. Then she turned to her grandfather and said, "Did a lot of news management outside. Got rid of some people hanging around."

I could tell she really wanted to be thanked, and for a minute I thought her grandfather wouldn't, but then I saw him glance at the bell in my hand, too.

"Well done," he said. "Anna Maria, we are going to try Mia on bell. Can you help your father with book?"

"Yes," she said. Her face softened. "That actually seems like a good idea," she added generously, earning a sharp glance from her grandfather.

The girl on the floor shuddered again. Anna Maria took her father's arm as he opened his notebook.

"What did you use—last time?" Uncle Matteo asked Giuliano, with a flickering glance at me. Too preoccupied at the time, I didn't think about what he meant until afterward.

"Great-Grandfather's Way," replied Nonno. "But this time, let's start with Gianluca's Entrapment."

Emilio rose from the floor and went to light the candle that his uncle had set up. Francesco joined him. Nonno turned and looked me in the eye. I didn't know what he wanted, so I just looked back, questioning. After a few seconds, he nodded and did the same thing to Uncle Matteo, then Anna Maria, then Francesco, then his grandson, then Father Giacomo and the acolyte waiting in the background. As he did this, the room somehow got quieter and quieter. At last, there was a perfect stillness and a feeling as if we were in a much larger chamber, a great open space, not this close little room. When Nonno was finished, he turned toward me and took my arm.

"Now," he said.

I fumbled with the cover on the clapper. My hands started to shake, but then I got hold of myself and took a deep breath, thinking of the Madonna, wooden folds of blue and star-dappled mantle sliding across my mind. I held my arm out straight and shook the tiny bell over the girl on the floor.

When I heard that sweet sound, like sugar crystals on my tongue, I finally remembered that this was the bell that had rung at my own exorcism.

Below me, the girl's eyes flew open as the force of the demon burst into the silence. Gloom gathered around her, just as it had in the sanctuary, filling the room. I lowered the bell in shock.

"Mine," he growled, and grinned up at me: the rictus of a dead man, the most entrancing smile of the most charming man alive, both played out on a young woman's mouth. I felt like puking and kissing him at the same time, it was that awful.

"N-not yours," I said, and the bell shook, tinkling, in my

hand. He shook his head back and forth as if warding off flies. Nonno moved beside me, and I quickly pinched the clapper between two fingers to still it.

"Good; do the same next time," he murmured.

"What, old man? Come to watch?"

The gravelly voice, emerging from the girl's mouth, started a hideous wave of terror that washed over me.

"No," replied Giuliano calmly. "To send you away again."

The demon shrugged the shoulders of his stolen body.

"This one I can take with me, you know," he said. "Like poor Martino."

I almost dropped the bell, but no one seemed to notice. I felt cold with shock.

"Not if I can help it," said Giuliano, his voice perfectly even, just as if he'd never lost a brother and a son to this monster. "You know."

He touched my arm, and I rang the bell again. The demon snarled and chattered his teeth. The sound carried to the corners of the quiet room.

Giuliano motioned to Uncle Matteo, who began to read in an archaic form of Italian. I could mostly understand it, but I kept my eyes on the body, animating itself on the floor. I realized I was standing close enough for him to grab my ankle and jumped back just as he reached for me.

He cackled like a hyperactive kid when he missed and grinned again. Uncle Matteo droned on.

"We will not wait, we will come, we will reach for you, we will bind you with chains of oaths and exhortations. Render up the body you have infested, the spirit you afflict, release them unharmed, and we will not confine your spirit in the close places, the dusty dark of the ancient underworld, but rather return you to your home. . . ."

"My home? My home?" the demon roared, sounding affronted. "What do you know of my home?" But Uncle Matteo went on.

"We shall neither return you to the Left-Hand Land, but to the place of roaring fires from whence your kind are born, the place of freezing summits, the place of silence and thunder."

Uncle Matteo stopped for breath, and then pointed straight at the girl on the floor. He roared, "Return her to us! Return her unharmed! You shall do as I command!"

The demon rolled his borrowed head upward and chuckled. "Μολὼν λαβέ," he said.

Uncle Matteo didn't even skip a beat.

"Ἀλλ ἄριστ᾽ ἔχει," he replied, and Giuliano touched my arm again. I rang the bell.

It's hard to explain what followed. So much happened all at the same time, but not in the same place, if that makes any sense. I could tell that we weren't just in the room, but also in that open space that Giuliano had something to do with, and inside the girl, and a bunch of other places at once. I could feel movement in the air of each place, too. I think Giuliano must have felt it, known about it all. But I could only see a small part of the picture.

In front of me on the floor, there was the demon, shredding the girl's vocal cords with his roars and laughter. I started to like ringing the bell: every time I did, he jerked and shook like a character in a video game. I loved having the power to piss him off. Giuliano had to keep putting his hand on my arm to stop me; I tried to hold back so he wouldn't make me give it up, but I had a hard time.

I started to get a feel for the rhythm of it. The bell worked like a leash, pulling him back to us each time he jerked away, refusing Uncle Matteo's demands. When Uncle Matteo got hoarse after an hour or two, Anna Maria took over. Francesco spelled Emilio at the candle; I couldn't see exactly what they did because I had to stay on the bell.

That's the thing about fighting evil. There are a lot of boring parts. You have to just keep going and going, keeping your eye on the task in front of you but alert at the same time for sneak attacks. You can't let your mind wander or freak out at the suffering of an innocent person. You have to remember you're there to end their suffering.

That's one of the hardest parts. You've got to keep your head, no matter how much he terrifies you, how many tactics he uses to fill you with fear and horror.

He picked her up at one point, just as he had done with me, and started to throw her at the wall. Francesco and Emilio pulled her back and placed her on the floor again.

At another point, I heard a ripping sound that started softly and got louder and louder; when I looked, making sure I was well back from him, I saw that the fabric of all the seat cushions was ripping as if gashed by invisible claws. He couldn't seem to do that to us, though I noticed that both priests kept out of the way.

As the shock wore off and I got used to the business of the bell, I found I had a lot of questions for the demon. He was right under my hand, so to speak, and I thought now would be a great time to ask them. I whispered this to Giuliano. He did not answer me right away, instead standing so still beside me that I could almost hear him thinking. Presently he answered, "Perhaps now is indeed a good time," and, lifting his head, said during a pause in the chanting, "Matteo. Mia has some questions for the demon. Let us have her ask them."

They all looked at me. I looked down at the writhing figure on the floor, the girl's face misshapen by the peculiar, putty-like nature of possessive control.

I took a deep breath. I shut my eyes for a minute, seeing again the starry blue of the Virgin's mantle, and her calm face. I opened my eyes.

"First of all," I said, "what is your name?"

I heard a snort in the background and saw Francesco and Emilio shrug at each other. The demon laughed. It felt like he was sandpapering my soul.

"My name? Dig for it. Dig for it, and so you will, when you are so desperate to defeat me, you will bloody your fingers digging for it," he replied.

Don't let him get to you, I told myself.

"Okay, fine. Next question," I said, feeling him begin to withdraw again, to roost in whatever distant place he could occupy while still under the girl's skin. I rang the bell before Giuliano even touched my arm.

"Next question," I repeated more firmly. "Why me?"

"Why you? 'Why you' what? Why any one of you puling humans? You all think the world's poles are fixed in your particular ass, don't you? Why don't you all perish, rotting, falling down in your rotten fields!"

Right, so be specific. I tried again.

"Why did you choose me to possess, before? Here are all these powerful people, right around me. Here's Giuliano Della Torre, for goodness' sake. Why an ignorant American teenager an ocean away?"

This got his attention. He rolled his borrowed head toward me, fixing me with a reptilian stare that seemed to go on forever. It came to me that, just like an enraged human, he was working out the meanest, most damaging, most foul words to say.

"Before you start telling me a pile of crap just to freak me out," I said in very fast Italian just as he opened the girl's mouth, "let me say, don't bother. If you're not going to give me the truth, don't bother. If you're going to act like a low-level devil from some second-rate hell, it won't make a difference. We'll just get rid of you, stick you in some candle on the dustiest shelf in our shop. Or if you somehow manage to get away from us this time, we'll watch and we'll wait and, oh, yeah, I'll work out your name. You can talk all the bullshit you want, but you'd be better off telling me the truth. Your truth."

He blew up. He roared until our ears rang.

"My truth?! My truth! You dare ask for my truth, you lying serpent? You wretched excuse for a Della Torre, you widow slut? My truth?! You dare!"

Lying serpent? Widow slut? I had no idea what he was talking about—or who he was talking to. Even so, whether I admitted it or not, his words got under my skin. It's odd. I don't think anyone had ever actually called me names before, except maybe a bully or two at school. I wondered where I'd gotten the wounds they touched, because they felt like old wounds. Maybe it just always sucks the first time someone says words like that to you.

Bad as they felt, my anger felt stronger. Yet I remembered the calm voice of Giuliano at Signora Galeazzo's, and took another deep breath before I answered. I looked at Anna Maria, standing by her father, at Emilio and Francesco by the candle, at Giuliano beside me, all holding still, waiting.

"How dare you, indeed?" I asked calmly. "Do you know, it doesn't matter if you answer my question or not. I'll ask it until I receive an answer. I'll ring the bell until I get what I want. The next time you choose to trouble some poor, innocent person, like this girl, I'll be here."

"Innocent? Innocent? *You* are not innocent! You are guilty, descended from a guilty family! Justice," he shouted as he had in the church. "Justice! Justice!"

His voice dissolved into a thunderous roaring. I thought we would all go deaf. This time, when the girl's body floated upward, Emilio and one of the assistant priests rushed to throw cushions underneath on the floor. Uncle Matteo and Giuliano stepped forward, their expressions identical.

"Switch to Great-Grandfather's Way," called out Giuliano, and Uncle Matteo nodded. *"Le Sue ossa rimarranno!"* they cried out together.

For a moment, I was back in my dark room at home in Center Plains. I remembered those words all too clearly, but this time I needed no rough-voiced translator. The words entered my head cleanly: *Your bones shall remain!* I shivered, feeling the pull of the command. So did the demon—and his victim. When he roared, I heard her scream also. She was back with us, conscious, and imprisoned in the same body with this creature. I thought I would faint. Nonno touched my arm and, when I hesitated, listening to her cries, he gripped it so hard I cried out myself and rang the bell.

"La Sua carne rimarrà!"—Your flesh shall remain!" chanted Uncle Matteo.

The girl cried out louder, her screams reaching high above the demon's roars. I could feel some of what Nonno must be seeing so clearly. First we had brought the demon to the surface, slowly increasing our hold and our connection with him. Now we had to bring her back. It was appalling. I rang the bell again.

"Il Suo spirito rimarrà!"—Your spirit shall remain!"

She screamed, and I could remember fighting, fighting.

"Lisetta!" I found myself crying out. "It's okay! You've got to come back! They can save you! Trust me!"

I didn't know if anyone heard me in the midst of all the noise, but I hoped she did.

With a final convulsion and one last, ear-bursting roar, she fell back on the cushions, and the demon raced up out of her throat. Out of the corner of my eye, I saw Emilio and Francesco by the candle again.

I took a deep breath, then stopped.

"Do you smell that, Nonno?" I whispered.

"Smell what?"

"It's like . . . cinnamon?"

"Your nose is much younger than mine," he said. "I don't smell it. Wait. No, there it is."

He turned to me in the dark that was now only the dark of the room, the candle burning low, and the lights in his eyes flickered. ·

"Like last time," I whispered.

"You remember?"

"Not much. But that, yes."

"Hmm. We must consider this."

He spoke with one eye on the girl, watching her slow breathing. I wondered if she would wake up soon.

He lifted his head, looking a question at Emilio and Francesco. They shook their heads.

"I don't think we've yet made the candle that can hold him," said Giuliano gently. "But we must always try."

TWENTY-ONE

On Guard

Afterward I had time to be creeped out by how much I enjoyed the demon's suffering. I tried to talk myself out of it, telling myself he had tormented me and my family so much that he deserved it, which was almost certainly true, but I still didn't like the way I felt.

I spent the early hours of Christmas morning watching over a girl I didn't even know, in a hospital on the far side of town. At least I didn't have to do it alone. I think everybody figured that wouldn't be safe. What I didn't expect was that everyone would want to stay. The nurses drew the line at more than three people camping out overnight, though, so everybody but Giuliano, Emilio, and me had to leave. Uncle Matteo and Nonna came back to bring us a thermos of coffee and another small feast in a basket.

As we settled down in the hospital room, I looked at Lisetta. She had started to breathe easily again, and when the doctors checked her eyes, they had rolled back into their proper places, but she just wouldn't wake up. I looked at the bruises where she had hit the pew, and thought about what I must have looked like, how my face must have rippled like Lisetta's had.

I guess that was when the shaking started.

Emilio leaned around his grandfather and asked, "Are you all right?" Before I could answer, he said, "But of course, you wouldn't be."

Giuliano put his arm around me.

"I just want it to end," I said.

"I know," he said, and I'm pretty sure he did. He pulled me to him, and I rested on his shoulder. After a while, I stopped shaking.

"Nonno?"

"Yes?"

"What was that thing the demon said? It wasn't in Italian? And Uncle Matteo answered him."

"Μολὼν λαβέ," Nonno said. *"Molon labe."*

He smiled slightly and rubbed his forehead, turning to Emilio, who leaned around him again to explain.

"It's Greek, ancient Greek."

"I didn't know Uncle Matteo spoke ancient Greek," I said.

Emilio smiled, and Nonno said, "My brother and I do, and Emilio and Anna Maria are studying it."

"But not enough," Emilio added apologetically.

His grandfather shrugged. "With more than thirty verb tenses, it takes a while. Don't worry."

"So what did the demon say in ancient Greek?" I pressed.

"You know the Battle of Thermopylae?" asked Emilio.

I shook my head; Milanese history was hard enough, without throwing in some place that sounded like a board game.

"About four thousand desperate Greeks facing twenty thousand Persians, knowing they would have to die to hold the pass just long enough for the Greek lands behind them to organize. King Xerxes of Persia told the Greeks to lay down their weapons, and King Leonidas of Sparta said, *'Molon labe'*—Come and get them."

"Wow," I said. For some reason, probably because it was three in the morning, I could picture a narrow strip of coastline at the foot of a cliff, full of men facing death, some of them looking at the sea for the last time, thinking—what? Probably that they'd rather be fishing.

What a strange thing for the demon to say, to paraphrase the heroic words of some long-dead king. I thought about the immensity of that choice, of being willing to die for the sake of the people and the place you love.

Would I do that? I thought. *Yes,* I answered myself. Not for Center Plains or Milan, no. But for Gina. For Mom and Dad. They would all lay down their lives for me, regardless of how they felt about certain things—regardless of how angry Dad was about my being here. He'd let me go, though, hadn't he? For all three of them, I'd do what I had to. And for my new family? Maybe—yes.

I might have to die, if the demon came back into me and started laying about like he had tonight. To protect others, I might have to die. Had Martino had to make that choice? Or Luciano, Emilio's father? I thought for a moment of that whispered midnight conversation between the two men beside me, that seemed to have taken place centuries ago: "She's not going to survive." I wondered why I didn't feel angry at them; I was probably too tired.

I shook myself out of my thoughts. Coastline, silence, the breathing of the men beside you, waiting: giving up everything. I looked across at Lisetta, breathing softly in the hospital bed.

"The best account, though, is in Herodotus," Emilio went on. "You should read him eventually, once you've got a good grasp of our history here."

I'd at least heard of Herodotus, so I could nod sagely without faking it this time.

"What did Uncle Matteo say back to him, when he said, 'Come and get them'?"

"'Very well then.'" Emilio smiled.

I thought for a minute, frowning.

"What kind of demon quotes from Herodotus?" I asked. Emilio laughed.

"I don't know," he said. "It's a good question, though."

"Definitely one I'm thinking about," said his grandfather. He straightened up, stretching. "But not just now, to be honest."

Nonno pulled out a worn pack of playing cards, shuffling them on a hospital tray.

"Do you know how to play Briscola?" he asked me as he

dealt out to the three of us, discarding a two.

The question made my eyes sting. My grandfather had taught us. That, and the food my grandmother cooked, seemed like the only Italian things that didn't put him in a bad mood.

"A little," I said.

"Good. I'm too tired to teach you."

Emilio chuckled. He took the cards his grandfather dealt him and smiled his one-cornered smile at them. I watched him, thinking about how getting to know him better hadn't helped my crush; in fact, it had made it worse. I decided not to let that stop me from beating him at cards, if I could.

We played until I couldn't keep my eyes open any longer. Sometimes I won, which took my mind off of where we were, and why.

I didn't mean to fall asleep, and for a long time I thought I would be too scared to, but in the end, I only dimly noticed as Nonno gently prized the playing cards from my hand and spread my coat over me.

When I opened my eyes, Giuliano and Emilio were both sleeping, and the girl on the bed was looking at me. She smiled a slow and terrible smile, like a reptile.

When I jolted awake and opened my eyes again, she was still asleep, and Emilio and Giuliano were awake, talking softly. So I'm pretty sure it was a dream.

TWENTY-TWO

La Befana

Somebody must have shuffled me home in a car at some point. I woke up in time to watch the Pope come out on his balcony on TV.

"How is she?" I asked, coming to sit on the couch by Nonna and Nonno, cradling my usual bowl of morning coffee in my hands.

"She? The Pope's a he. Mind your pronouns," Nonna corrected absently.

"No, I mean Lisetta, in the hospital."

"Ah!" She gave me an approving look.

"Good that that was the first question you asked," said Giuliano. "Matteo and Francesco are there. They will call us when she wakes up. She will wake up; she was looking better before we left."

"What did you tell her parents?"

"Father Giacomo and I agreed that it would be best to say she had a fit. He's coming over this afternoon," he added to his wife.

"Of course he is," she said, looking fixedly at the TV.

"I don't think we have to worry," Nonno said.

"Wait and see," she replied expressionlessly.

There was a whole panettone on the coffee table, plates beside it. I cut myself a slice. Nonna smiled at me and said, "You helped make it taste so good." I smiled shyly back and said, "It probably tastes good in spite of me. . . . Oh! I mean, thank you, Nonna." I had already tried a slice of a store-bought one that a new neighbor had brought by the shop. Giuliano had eaten his share out of politeness, content to let someone else in the neighborhood explain why this was a faux pas; it certainly hadn't seemed very special to me, kind of like cardboard with currants and citrus peel in it. Dipping it in coffee had helped, but not enough to make me see why our family would go to the trouble of actually *making* the stuff.

I took a bite. Nonna watched.

"Better than that neighbor's?" asked Giuliano.

To my surprise, it was: sweeter, softer, richer, far more flavorful—even the currants and lemon peel made sense—a much more fitting gift from a nobleman. I could imagine that Renaissance lover and his baker girl much more easily now. I didn't answer Giuliano, just nodded vigorously, my mouth full of sweet bread.

Bit by bit, the house filled up again. Nobody seemed to want to talk too much about what happened the night before. They would drop their bit of news into the conversation and go into the kitchen to get something to drink. On normal days, Nonna was the one who got glasses for everyone. It looked to me like Christmas Day was her day off. I was suddenly filled with love for them, coupled with annoyance that that was probably her only day off.

We gradually moved into the kitchen, everyone adding their dishes to our Christmas Day lunch: Matteo and Brigida brought a roast turkey stuffed with chestnuts; Emilio finished up the tortellini from the night before and tossed them into chicken broth; Anna Maria brought a horrible stuffed pig's leg, which she assured me was delicious; and Francesca and Égide rounded off the meal with breads and salads.

"Nobody at the butcher's remembers," said Francesco. "I dropped off a panettone for Signora Strachetti, after we came back from the hospital. Lisetta is doing as well as can be expected," he added, looking at me.

"Thank you," I said.

"Good, good," said Emilio. "Signora Strachetti was in one of the back pews, so that's good news too. Beppo doesn't remember, either." He quickly changed the subject. "Tell us about Christmas in America, Mia."

So I did. I told them how mall Santa Clauses kind of creeped me out, how my mother baked the best coffee cake in the world, how hard it was to wait until after breakfast to open presents.

"Some people open presents on Christmas Day here," said Égide. "But most people wait until January sixth. It's mostly for children, of course."

"Yes, and Santa Claus doesn't bring them," said Emilio. "*La Befana* does."

He gave me a quick grin and added, "She's an old witch all dressed in black. The three kings asked her to come with them to Bethlehem, but she didn't think it was a big deal, so she waited, and then tried to follow them later, but it was too late. So she flies around the world and leaves gifts at every house that has a child in it, just in case it's the Christ Child."

"I think she mostly flies around Italy," Francesca amended mildly.

For some reason, I pictured *La Befana* as Signora Negroponte. But I didn't think Signora Negroponte would be that dumb. She would have worked out that all these kids weren't Christ.

"That explains the witches hanging in shop windows," I said. "I couldn't figure it out. You don't really have Halloween."

I felt a knot of disappointment in my stomach, although of course it could have been just too much food. I hadn't known what to do about presents for everybody, but I had gotten something small for each of them, sneak-purchasing gifts while out on errands with various relations, saving money that they gave me, getting Nonna or Égide to pass by one shop or another on our way to somewhere else.

I'd gone to some trouble, and the gifts were wrapped and waiting in my room. I hadn't been sure where to put them.

Now maybe I would embarrass everyone because nobody gave gifts? I knew that a few small packages were sitting out on a pyramid-shaped shelf that had only come out the day we had hung up holly and mistletoe. But there was no tree, no pile of presents. That's when I really missed home.

When we all retired to the living room with coffee and a few last sweets, I made a decision.

"I'll be right back," I said.

I went to my room and brought back all my packages, pressed to my chest.

"I know it's not really tradition and maybe you want to wait for *La Befana*, but where I come from we do give gifts on Christmas Day. So, uh, here. You can wait till January sixth to open them if you want."

I started passing them out while my relatives stared at me. I wondered if it had been a bad idea, but it felt right, and I have never liked the feel of gifts that sit ungiven.

For Francesca and Égide, I'd gotten beautiful bottles of ink from the shop down the street. They were handblown glass, with real corks sealed in wax, and the ink was supposed to be really high quality. For Nonna, a bracelet like the one I had gotten my mom, only with green stones in the flowers. For Nonno, a brass bookmark with a cloisonné design of a candle on it. For Uncle Matteo, a pot of the Piedmontese mustard that disguises itself as jelly. (He laughed for a long time when he opened it.) For Aunt Brigida, a simple silver bracelet, really elegant, I thought. (I couldn't tell if she liked it.) For Francesco, an

American mystery novel translated into Italian with big serious block letters on the front. (I'd seen him reading them.)

Anna Maria had been really hard to choose for, because nothing would be cool enough, and every time I thought I saw something she would just die for and that would finally prove how cool *I* was, it was way, way too expensive. So I handed her her package, which was a lot bigger than the others, and said, "This might seem kind of strange, but I just had a feeling, and I hope I'm right," while she blinked at me. I swallowed hard, hoping she'd at least get the joke, even if she didn't like it. She started opening it right then and all around the room I could hear the sound of rustling paper, which I hadn't known until then was the sound I was missing. Nobody was waiting for January sixth. Anna Maria was the last to pull off all the wrapping paper, from the lamest thing I think I've ever bought: a stuffed Snoopy doll.

She stared at it for a full minute, then burst into tears and stood up and hugged me really hard.

"Who told you? Who told you?" she demanded.

"Wow, I'd forgotten," Francesco said behind us.

"Nobody told me anything," I said. "It's okay? You like it?"

"I love it," she said. "Really, nobody told you?"

She looked around the room accusingly, but everybody shrugged. She turned to me.

"Thank you so much. I have to go fix my eyes," she said, and with another tiny sob she grabbed her purse and ran to the bathroom.

I watched her go.

Francesco repeated, "I'd completely forgotten. Ah. It's not a pretty episode in my history."

"Ah, yes, Noopo," said Uncle Matteo thoughtfully. "Now I remember."

"You were such a bad boy," said Aunt Brigida. "She cried for days."

"I know, I know!" said Francesco, and to me, "She kept reading my comics without asking, so I stole her Snoopy doll and put it on the roof. She had one almost exactly like that. She called it Noopo. Anyway, I put it up on the roof, and then I forgot about it. She couldn't find it, she looked everywhere, she cried and cried, and I remembered—but it had rained in the night, and Noopo had gotten washed off. We never found him. She was six. I didn't think she'd remember, let alone get so emotional about it."

Anna Maria came back in just as he was saying that, walked over and punched him in the shoulder. He yelped.

"Idiot," she said to him. And to me, "*Buon Natale*, Mia. I have something for you, but I was waiting for *La Befana*."

I thought she might be lying to be nice, and immediately felt guilty for thinking that when she picked up her purse again and said, "In fact, I'll go get it. Wait here," she added as if I were about to rush off somewhere.

Emilio stared after her. He smiled at me.

"Who knew?" he asked.

Then there was Emilio's present. His had been the hardest of all. I gave it to him, and he laughed, shaking it to tease me. "It's not a stuffed animal, anyway," he said, and then he opened it.

It was a very fine, light blue cashmere-and-silk scarf. I'd seen one on a guy with his coloring, and after days of agonizing about what to get him, I had decided on that. I had spent way too much time thinking about how it would look on him, how it would bring out the darker blue of his eyes.

But he wasn't looking at the scarf. He was looking at the red box it came in, with the shop logo on it.

Nonna made a soft sound, her eyes on him.

He stared out the window, a long time. Égide came over to thank me for the ink; Francesca teasingly congratulated me on making Anna Maria cry. I kept waiting, worrying about Emilio. Was he angry at me? I didn't think I'd ever seen him so still and grave.

"No one could have told her that, either," said Nonna, resting a hand on his shoulder.

He looked down at the box in his hand, then up at her. He coughed.

"Do you want me to explain?" she asked very quietly.

"No, thank you, Nonna. I should. It's right. Mia," he said.

I came over.

He made himself smile. I could tell it was hard work.

"You seem to be quite a psychic gift-giver today," he said with painful wryness. "Thank you very much. This scarf is from a shop that is special to me. Our mother used to take us there every year for my father's gift. He was always losing scarves," he said, and paused. I had never heard his voice so rough. "Thank you. *Buon Natale*, Mia."

"*Buon Natale*, Emilio," I said when I could speak. I wasn't sure I was ever going to dare buy Christmas presents for any of them ever again, but it was a good day anyway.

Someone buzzed the door, so it couldn't be Anna Maria returning. Indeed, it was not; it was Father Giacomo, who wished us *Buon Natale* with an effort. Giuliano took him into the kitchen and made him a coffee, but we were Della Torres, so of course somebody had to eavesdrop; Emilio stood in the hall doorway and listened. We watched his face. The news wasn't good.

After a while, Francesco traded places with him, and Emilio said, "He feels he's put up with us long enough. It's no secret in the neighborhood, but everybody protects us. Last night was too much. She wasn't one of his parishioners—a student at the Brera who was staying in town and got lonely for Christmas Eve Mass. He says he doesn't know what we are playing at, but it can't happen in his church."

Nonna sat up very straight at that. For such a tiny woman, she looked awfully tall.

"He is forbidding us to go to Mass?" she asked.

"I don't know," said Emilio.

She stood up and marched into the kitchen like a general. Aunt Brigida joined her son at his post, and the rest of us gave up trying to make small talk and leaned in to listen.

"Is she asking him?" I whispered to Francesco. He and his mother shook their heads.

We could hear the calm buzz of Nonna's voice for quite a

long time. When Father Giacomo came out, he didn't look at any of us, but murmured his farewells. When his footsteps died away on the stairwell, Emilio started to laugh.

"Defeated by panettone, I think," he said.

"And the fact that the family has been in this neighborhood longer than the church," said Aunt Brigida.

I knew from my studies (and my relatives) that the first Santa Maria del Carmine had been built in 1268, and of course we'd been around; after all, only nine years later the Visconti had taken the rule of the city from us.

Anna Maria opened the front door and said, "I passed Father Giacomo looking like he wanted to violate all Ten Commandments. What happened?"

"Nonna happened," said Francesco. Nonna and Nonno were still in the kitchen talking.

"Ah," Anna Maria said in a satisfied tone of voice.

"Still, we'll have to tread carefully there for a while," Uncle Matteo pointed out.

Aunt Brigida rolled her eyes. "Tread carefully! We always have to tread carefully with the Church. Sometimes I wish the Tiber would rise up and swallow the Vatican."

"Ah, well, the Church is an outdated opiate that doesn't even seem to work on the masses anymore," Anna Maria said.

"Don't let Nonna hear you say that," said Francesco.

"Don't let *me* hear you say that," snapped their mother. Anna Maria stuck out her chin. But it was Emilio who stopped them from turning Christmas Day into a fight.

"Tell me," he asked gently, "Anna Maria. Why is it that you believe so easily in demons, but cannot imagine the presence of saints?"

I thought it was a good question. It certainly stumped me. She opened her mouth to answer, frowning, then shut it again. She walked over and touched her mother on the arm.

"I'm sorry, Mama."

Her mother touched her fingertips and said, "I know."

But under cover of Nonna and Nonno's return, Anna Maria said to Emilio and me, "It's not the saints that bother me, Cousin. It's the institution."

He mimicked his aunt's tone, saying, "I know."

She added, spreading her fingers on her purse as she sat down between us, "I don't know what I believe, but I do know what I see. I've seen more demons than saints."

He laughed and clasped her shoulder.

"Maybe you should look harder. Certainly today there have been miracles." He looked at me and smiled. I didn't want to blush; in fact, I wanted it less than anything else in the world at that moment. But I did anyway.

She followed his eyes and said, "Oh, yes! I almost forgot. Here you are, Mia. I hope you like it."

I unwrapped her gift. It was beautiful. It was beyond beautiful, and it must have been about ten thousand times more expensive than Noopo II had been. It was a worked leather purse, beaded and fringed and studded until the purse itself was almost completely hidden, but somehow the whole thing worked out to pure gorgeousness. It was also about a zillion times more stylish than anything else I owned, 110 percent up-to-the-minute Milan *moda*.

"Every girl should have one," she said, smiling at my expression.

Maybe she wrapped one of hers—I still don't know. I wanted to believe she had gotten it for me. I gave her a big hug.

I stayed up late, sitting with everyone, so strangely filled with joy. Sometimes a memory of the possessed Lisetta, floating in front of my face, reaching out to strike me, would jolt me— but at the same time I would remember ringing the bell, and the way I had stood still. Every now and then, all day, someone from my family would touch my shoulder and say, "Well done last night, Mia."

The whole family gave me another gift before I went to bed: an hour alone in the living room, talking with Mom, Dad, and Gina on Skype. The first thing I saw on the screen was a giant, dim eye. I squealed until I realized that Gina was holding up the ring I had sent her and laughing hysterically. Everybody wanted to talk at once, and all that English ran together and made no sense. They finally settled down to taking turns, Mom first.

It was so good to see her face. Now that I had been in Italy for almost four months, I could really see how she looked so much like people I saw in the street here. When I had time, I would research where her family came from. I knew they had gone to America much earlier than Dad's side of the family. While Grandpa Roberto had never wanted to talk about Italy, my relatives on Mom's side just didn't seem to remember or care all that much, unless Italy was doing well in the Olympics. All I really knew was that they weren't Milanese. But that was okay, I guess.

"Thank you so much for the bracelet," she said, modeling it for me on her slender, brown wrist.

"You're welcome. It looks great." I smiled.

"You look great, too. Looks like they're feeding you really well," said Mom approvingly.

"Thanks," I said.

"You look different," she added. "There isn't a . . . a boy in your life, is there?"

"Mom!" I groaned. "Please. And, anyway, since when do you care about that stuff?"

She smiled, caught in the act. "I know. I was just trying to figure out what's changed."

"Just my entire life," I said, rolling my eyes, but then I smiled to soften my words. "My entire life except for the boy thing, that is. You know me, Mom."

Dad didn't ask about boys directly. He just said, like always, "You being good?"

"Trying my best, actually," I replied, looking him seriously in the eye. He looked startled.

"All right then," he said. "They taking care of you? You think you're going to be able to see this thing through?"

These were all questions he'd asked before, mostly through Gina and Mom, but I didn't mind answering him yet again, facing him on the screen.

"Yes, Dad. They are. And I do. I really do."

"Something's happened," he stated.

"Yeah," I said. "But I can't really explain it right now. There is something you can do for me, though."

When I said that, he lit up.

"Sure! What is it, honey?"

I felt bad, because all I really wanted was an answer to a question I'd been meaning to ask. He looked like he wanted a dragon to slay or something.

"I need to know when Grandpa left Italy. It'll help me figure some stuff out."

He knit his dark eyebrows together, just like his father—and just like his cousins.

"Is that all? Okay. Well, let's see. He married Mom seven years after he got off the boat, he always said that. Although actually I think he might have taken a plane, to tell the truth. And they got married in sixty-five, because it took them three years after they got married to make me. There were a couple of miscarriages."

"Poor Grandma," I said. "She never said anything."

"She only told me about it once, after your mom almost lost you. She said, 'Well, when you want 'em, you want 'em.'"

I had forgotten that I'd nearly been lost. I was quiet for a minute, thinking about how we come into this world on a slim chance, and stick around on an even slimmer one. Dad, on the other hand, was busy doing math.

"So that makes it 1958. Dad left Italy in 1958. That help?"

You might ask him about a young brother of his, named Mar-tino, who died about thirteen years after the war.

"Yeah, Dad," I said when I found my voice. "That helps a lot."

I wanted to tell Gina about this next piece of the puzzle, but Mom and Dad were still in the room and, anyway, she wanted to tell me all about Luke, who was the most important person in the universe right now. She was petitioning to be allowed out with him on New Year's Eve. Neither of us was sure how that was going to go. It was hard to say good-bye to them, but I kept yawning, so Mom got back on and told me to go to bed.

The last person I talked to that night wasn't a person at all. I was tucking myself into bed when I heard Pompous speak.

"We heard," she said, and it took me a moment to realize she was speaking to me. "Well done, Mia." She had never used my name before, either.

"Yes, well done," added Gravel.

"Thank you," I said, when I stopped feeling shocked. "And *Buon Natale.*"

TWENTY-THREE

A Soldier

The next day started badly, so it was just as well that Christmas had been so nice. Emilio shook me awake.

"Get dressed, quick as you can," he said.

"Uh?" I sat up, dazed.

"Signorina Umberti is worse," he said. "We have to go."

"Oh! Lisetta. I'm coming."

He slipped out.

I rolled out of bed, landing on my feet, and took a wide step to the dresser. As I was pulling on my jeans, I heard Pompous speak overhead.

"Mia?" she asked.

I stopped dead.

"Yes, uh . . ." I almost called her Pompous but caught myself. "Signora—?"

"Signora Gianna," she supplied helpfully.

So! That was her name. I filed it away to remember; I was pretty sure I had seen it somewhere in the apartment.

"Yes, Signora Gianna," I said.

"Be prepared, my dear. I must be frank with you. Many do not make it, after such a possession. Do you understand? Be as kind as you can, to her—and to yourself."

I stared upward, trying to guess where her voice came from. "Thank you," I said. "Thank you."

She was right. Lisetta didn't make it.

Her family was there when we got there: parents, a sister and brother, some aunts, uncles, and little cousins. She was awake, her face gray. Now I know what that means; I'd never seen anyone look so drained before, even in hospital shows on TV.

She didn't exactly remember us, at first. Her mother thanked us for finding her and rescuing her. I didn't know if they'd been told anything about what really happened, so I just said, "It was nothing," like everyone else. I had never seen anyone fade like this, slipping out of the world so fast; but then, I'd never seen anyone die before, and it took me the whole of our few minutes in the room to realize that it was truly happening.

"I don't think there's much time," said the doctor apologetically, turning to ask us to do what we were already doing, which was leaving so that the Umbertis could have a moment alone. But as we went, Signora Umberti called out to me.

"Signorina Della Torre!"

I turned back.

She pointed to the bed. Her daughter's eyes were rolled toward me.

I ran over and stood beside her, then bent down. Her eyes were hard to read. I thought she would be full of questions about why she was here, what had happened to her; I thought she would be as dazed as I had been.

She spoke very softly in my ear.

"Get him," she said, her voice still hoarse from the night before last. I shivered at the ferocious determination in her voice. I was wrong. She knew exactly what had happened.

"I will," I whispered back.

She heaved in a breath.

"Good."

She paused, then added, "He wants revenge. Find. Out. What. For."

She shut her eyes in exhaustion.

"I will," I whispered. "You'll be avenged, too."

I wanted to say something more, but her family was right there, needing those last minutes with her. I straightened up, said, "Thank you," and walked quickly out of the room.

I didn't see the others right away. Apparently I couldn't walk anymore, because I found myself leaning up against the wall, and finally, finally, the tears came.

I don't think I'd ever expected to find such a good friend in such a stranger, so briefly met. While I stood there, I thought of Emilio on Christmas Eve, and the Battle of Thermopylae. Lisetta, stranger, had spent part of her last breath on me, soldier to soldier. I owed her; I owed her big-time, and I was determined to pay her back, for the sake of her memory, at least.

Nobody tried to make it better; nobody tried to hold me; they just let me cry. I wanted more than that, but after a while I understood this was the best thing they could do for me.

I don't remember much from the next few days; what I do recall are strange, inconsequential moments. I remember apologizing to Signora Gianna for never thinking to ask her name before. I wondered what Gravel's real name was, but I couldn't get up the energy to ask.

We did have one last duty to Signorina Lisetta Maria Umberti. The day after she died, we paid our respects to her in the hospital's *obitorio*, because we would not be attending the funeral (in Turin, after all). I don't remember anything except Lisetta's face, as deserted as a boarded-up building. I'd like to say she looked peaceful, but really how she looked was—just not there.

I know this is going to sound strange, but I was glad they had an open casket. I needed to see her one more time, even if it wasn't really her. I made myself look down into her empty face. I had only seen her body full of life, her life, once, when she was dying. I wondered why she hadn't hated me; after all, I had called her back, asked her to trust us, and we hadn't saved her after all, had we? She was still dead as dead.

I couldn't stop picturing myself in the coffin.

We didn't stay to talk to her family again. Emilio came up

beside me, breathing frost, as we walked back to the car. He didn't say anything, just walked close beside me, and opened the door for me when we got there. I looked up at him as I got in, just one look of thanks. He gave the faintest, kindest blink of both eyes in reply.

We came back to Milan late, pulling slowly up the Via Fiori Oscuri while a bunch of small boys threw firecrackers under the car. Older neighbors greeted us with cries of *"Auguri, auguri!"* rising up to the lights strung across our street that spelled it out in twinkling letters: *AUGURI*, good fortune. I wasn't sure that the New Year would bring me any. I looked up at the glittering word and thought about the eyes that were darkened and would never see those lights again. I made up my mind.

TWENTY-FOUR

The Case

The next day, the sun got up and so did I, somehow.

"I still don't understand what protected me," I mused over coffee with Nonna. I was thinking about Christmas Eve. I still felt certain about my decision, but I needed my caffé Nonna for courage. "Now that it's over I can feel him waiting outside again. Thank goodness, Signora Negroponte is coming back."

She shrugged. "It may well have been the Madonna by the altar."

"The one where there's a bear holding her up?" I asked.

"Yes, that one. We gave that to the church, you know, a long time ago."

When I had first arrived in Italy, I would have assumed she

meant that she and Giuliano had given the Madonna to the church. Now I thought differently; I assumed some distant ancestor gave it, centuries ago.

"She has useful protections worked into her," Nonna went on. "Nobody pays attention to the little things, but they should."

She swirled her coffee. "Speaking of little things," she went on, "Francesco tells me he saw that worthless man, that Lucifero, the other day. He said he still looks pretty sick, but he was out on the street. Francesco doesn't think Lucifero saw him. Be careful, Mia."

She held my eyes until I nodded.

When she stood up to start her day, I stood up, too. I made sure she didn't need my help, which was a relief, because I needed to act before my courage failed me. I walked down the wooden stairs to the shop, my feet feeling like lead, my stomach churning with anger.

I found Giuliano in the shop, along with Emilio, who was just picking up his briefcase to go as I came in.

"Good morning," he said, and this time I heard all the unasked questions in his voice: How are you doing? How are you managing after yesterday? What do you feel?

"Good morning," I said. "Um, before you go, Emilio. I have something to ask both of you."

They waited in the dim shop, eyes of different shades of stormy blue glinting, looking at me. I smelled the old wood around us, the beeswax, the sulfurous ghosts of matches and, as always, the scent of the candle flames themselves. I took a deep breath.

"Teach me," I said. My voice shook. I tried to fill it with all the frustration and rage I felt about everything that had happened: Lisetta's death, the world's worst first date, the suffering of the woman of Signora Galeazzo's house, my claustrophobic life in the apartment, the miserable words I had overheard, the secrets I had guessed—everything the demon was responsible for, some stuff he wasn't, and a few things that were their fault, too.

"Teach me everything you can. Please: teach me."

Nonno and Emilio looked at each other for a long time. I saw then that there had been more than one midnight conversation about me, many more than one. I wonder if perhaps at that moment I realized, truly, for the first time, that the world was not a stage that sprang to life only when I walked onto it.

"It's not enough to protect me," I went on. "You know that now. It's not enough to show me just part of it. You can see that I am . . . that I can feel things, that I know things. You know that I'm really a Della Torre." I paused, because that was so scary to say. "At first, I thought that figuring out Majdanek was an accident. But we all know now that it wasn't. And I"—my voice broke—"I have to avenge Lisetta, I have to. You must understand. I know you understand," I said, looking into the eyes of Martino's brother, Luciano's father. "I survived; I have to avenge them all. And I have to fight for myself. I have to."

Nonno held up his hand.

"Steady, steady," he said. "One impossible thing at a time." Emilio twitched the corner of his mouth, eyes narrowing.

Nonno frowned for a century or so, looking out the window,

over the candle flames. Then he nodded, partly to his grandson and partly to himself, before walking back to the office. Emilio only looked at me. I couldn't tell what he was thinking, but I didn't see any haughtiness, any condescension in his eyes. Nonno came back, holding something close to his side where I could not see it.

"There are books to study, histories to learn," he said. "But we have been doing this a long time, our family, since before we wrote things down. So we begin, always, with our hands, with our tools. We begin with *doing*. So, we start with this," he finished, placing the thing he held into my hands.

I looked down. I caught my breath.

It was the last thing I expected, the only thing I really coveted, the strangest thing I could imagine holding in my hands and calling my own: a demon catcher's case.

"I—" I tried again. "I haven't even started to earn this yet, Nonno, have I?"

I met his eyes.

"No," he answered gently. "That's why I've given you this particular case. You should get used to handling it, taking care of it, restocking it. When the time comes, you will replace it with another, finer case."

As I looked down at it, I saw that it wasn't slender like the other cases; it was bulky and kind of clunky, actually. The fittings were battered, and the leather covering the wood had been improperly stretched, so that it was too thin on one side and too loose on the other.

Yet I had worried that they would give me a new case. I had wondered whether they had run out of old ones. After all, didn't the cases sometimes fall apart, or get destroyed—my mind faltered as I thought about how they might be destroyed—or get married off into other families with their owners? This case, however, was very old. I could tell because the gilded letters proclaiming the name of its first owner looked much like those on Emilio's case. I ran my hands over the tops of them, spelling them out under my fingers:

G. DELLA TORRE

I had seen the gilded name before, in ghost letters long since peeled away in the window of the shop and on the spines of books. The founder of the candle shop, Francesca had said. Had he looked like Giuliano, gazing through the glass, sheeted by the reflections of the buildings across the street, watching the light change, waiting for a grandson perhaps?

"Thank you, Nonno. Oh, thank you."

He smiled the widest and purest smile I had ever seen on his face and closed his worn hands over mine where they held the case.

"Mind you, this is only one of nine he used at one time or another, and the most cantankerous."

"What do you mean?"

"Well, everybody has small preferences, you know? Anna Maria uses a Tibetan bell instead of a local brass one. Emilio had his case refitted so he could use a Waterman pen and some fancy leather notebook. Francesco is always losing nails, so he had a box built in. Sometimes the case is too large for your tools, or too small, or falling apart, anyway. When he made this case, he was trying out all kinds of things. Nine cases, all different sizes, different fittings, different covers. I've had three in my lifetime. Emilio will probably always keep the one he has. He's such a sentimentalist," he said, looking up at his grandson, who smiled.

"This one, our ancestor was experimenting with a new imported wood—mahogany—and different fixtures. The candle always falls out, and the notebook too. The wood itself is very hard to rework. But it's a start.

"Begin by familiarizing yourself with the case. Also, Signora Negroponte returns today," said Nonno. "Find that ward you need, to be safe in the street for a time."

I clutched the case.

"Thank you," I said. "Thank you, Nonno."

He smiled sadly.

"Thank me when you realize what you have asked," he said. I saw Emilio start out of the corner of my eye, as if to say, "She already knows, Nonno." He came forward.

"I believe it is well done," he said gravely. He leaned across and kissed me on the cheek. "I'm late for work," he said. "It is well done. Good luck with Signora Negroponte."

"Thank you," I repeated. "We'll need it."

He smiled and slipped out the door, bells jingling.

I watched him go, his pinesap smell hanging in the air behind him. I heard him speak to someone in the street; then the bells jangled again and Signora Negroponte walked in.

She sniffed the air, then raised her eyebrows and looked at Nonno and me.

"What's changed?" she asked.

"Long story," Nonno said.

"Ah," she said, shrugging. "You Della Torres."

TWENTY-FIVE

The Bell

In the end, I was the one who found the right talisman to protect me. It was an odd choice, I suppose.

"What's that?" Signora Negroponte asked when Nonno had gone to get us coffees. I looked down at my new case. I didn't want to show it, not yet.

"A case, I see," she answered herself. "He has given you one? Well. I think that is good. Are you ready to start?"

"Yes," I replied, and she raised her chin at the fierceness in my voice. "Very ready."

She smiled grimly.

We did the usual drill, but the first time I stepped outside, I didn't feel the same slow panic I'd felt before. I'd faced my demon up close since then. I knew exactly what, or who, I was afraid of; I knew what he felt like from the outside now. I'd rung a bell over him. Besides, I was mad now, too. Signora Negroponte had to make me take breaks. I went in and out all morning, carting a new assortment of twigs, family heirlooms, and increasingly random objects from around the house.

By noon, even Signora Negroponte was starting to look a little rattled, and she didn't rattle easily. I was standing by the doorway, fiddling with a knot in my pocket to take my mind off the fear and anger that wore me out each time I stepped outside. Signora Negroponte was massaging her hand, having taken notes all morning. I felt like I could fall asleep right there, leaning against the door frame. Signora Negroponte took up her pen again and made a few final notes, while I absently opened the door and swung it back and forth, jingling the shop bells.

"Don't do that," she said without looking up. "It'll ruin the next trial."

As I banged the door shut, I heard the church bells toll just as the shop bells chimed. The shop bells are a chain of sweet-sounding brass bells that hang from inside the door. I'd never really looked at them before. Now I walked over and lifted the chain.

They were tiny and fine. The artist who had made them had carefully tapped a design into them some time after they were cast, I thought, not surprised to see the same bird as that I had seen on Giuliano's bell, on the shopping bags, on the stone lintel above the shop door. The clappers looked like raindrops cast in bronze. I loved the sound of them.

"Hey," I said, "what about one of these?" and lifted the strand to show Signora Negroponte.

She frowned, making herself look like a frog.

"It would be odd, considering," she said.

"Considering what?" I said, dropping them and coming to sit at the table.

"Considering that in your family's profession, bells are used to *summon* demons," she answered shortly.

"Oh, yeah. I'd forgotten." I really had, though how, I don't know, after all the bell-ringing I had done recently.

She snorted. "However," she added, "why not? We can at least try it."

As we were prying open the small brass ring that held our chosen bell to the chain, I asked, "Do you think they'll mind, Giuliano especially?"

"I think they will be much happier to know that we have solved the problem, if this is the solution. Otherwise, we just put the bell back and don't say anything. Right?"

She gave me a bad grin. I could see her much younger, giving her parents all kinds of trouble. I said so. She laughed loud and hard. "Oh, I did."

We put the small, brass bell on a leather thong that had held any number of hazel knots and bits of jewelry that day, and I stood before the door, taking a deep breath. I looked back at Signora Negroponte.

"I think this is the one that's going to work," I said, surprised at my confidence. I felt the solid wood floor beneath my feet, and I was not afraid.

I stepped outside, into the street full of weak January sun, and nothing happened. Finally after ten minutes of wandering around in view of the shop, counting cobblestones, and looking at the beautiful, totally useless fancy journals in the window of the gift shop a few doors over, I saw Signora Negroponte come out and join me. She put her hand on my shoulder.

"Nothing," I said. "Just open space. And somewhere out there—but he can't get in."

She smiled. "It is well done," she said. "I think this calls for a coffee and a bite of something sweet, don't you? What about that little place in the Via dell'Orso, the Brera something?"

"The Caffè Vecchia Brera," I said, translating in my head: *the Old Brera Café, in the Street of the Bear.* "They do great crepes, but there's better coffee at the Cafè Fiori Oscuri if that's what you want—I mean it's still good, just not the best."

"Crepes would be just the thing," she said, looking happier than I had ever seen her. "Just the thing."

We both ran back inside for jackets, scarves, and purses. We left the notes on the table and didn't even tell anybody the shop was unattended. We walked quickly up the street, my tiny shop bell jingling under my coat—and my case in my coat pocket, because no demon catcher ever travels without one.

When we were full of crepes and coffee, Signora Negroponte said, "Off back to the shop?" as if she knew what my answer would be. I looked out the door of the café.

"No," she said, and smiled her hard smile. "You want to run around Milan alone, eh? What would your family say?"

"I don't know," I replied. "I think I'll be okay. Will they be mad at you if you let me go?"

She shrugged. "Let them be, if they are. But I think they'll understand. I'll go back and look after the shop."

"Thank you," I said, and kissed her on the cheek. She hugged me like family, and said, "You might come to me to study some time, when your task is finished."

I couldn't tell whether it was a statement or a question. I said I would like that, which made her smile, and then I got it: she had given me a huge compliment. I smiled back. We parted in the street. I watched her walk up the Via dell'Orso. She didn't look back.

Then Milan and I had a date, and I have to say it beat the heck out of my last one. For about the first ten minutes, I missed having some random relation beside me, especially when guys started to catcall, but frankly after what I'd been through they just didn't get to me that much, and I began to revel in being alone. Even with the maps I had memorized during months of confinement, I got lost three times. I walked through the Castello Sforzesco and rambled in the leafless, brown gardens, watching the Milanese walk their dogs. I took myself to Peck for an early dinner (you save a lot of money when you aren't allowed out alone), where one of the cute deli guys took me under his wing and chose me a "perfect winter menu": tiny, stuffed onions for an antipasto; buckwheat polenta with butter (tastes way better than it sounds); *polpette* (special Milanese meatballs); braised winter greens; roasted chestnuts; a glass of good, red wine; polenta and elderflower cake with Vin Santo for dessert.

I took my tray to a table in the back, pulling a chair up next to me, so that I could finally take a look at my case in peace and relative quiet, since the family next to me had gotten into one of those conversations in which one joke tops another, and everyone keeps laughing harder and harder. They were loud, but I didn't mind; it made good cover.

The column of gilded names on the lid started with G. DELLA TORRE and ended with STEFANO MARTINO D. T. Was that Martino, Giuliano's brother? I thought Martino was his first name. In any case, the lettering looked like it came from much earlier than the 1950s. When I opened it, I got a better idea of when the case was last used, because the yellowed box of matches inside proudly advertised the miracle of sulfur—no more flint and tinder! There was also an old dipping pen and a dried-up bottle of ink, as well as eleven very tarnished silver nails. I guess when you got an old case you also got to clean out your dead relation's junk. Or did you do something special with it all? I thought I should ask. The straps for the notebook and mirror were empty. Tucked away in the top corner, beside the ink bottle, was a little brass bell with a pale green patina. I took it out and turned it over. A tiny bird was chased on the side. I pulled out the bell around my neck for comparison; they were identical. I laughed to myself for a long minute, wondering about this Stefano. He and I had shared a thought, maybe a century apart—and I had thought I was the first one to use one of those bells for anything but the shop door.

I ate my food slowly, touching each object in turn, the bell from the case more than once. The big family got even louder. Then one of the sons at the table turned around, leaned across his chair, and began reciting poetry to me. I thought it was a joke at first, that he was drunk or he thought I was cute. But it wasn't love poetry. At least my Italian was fast enough now to translate.

No, brothers, when I die I will not feel
cool coins on my eyes, nor the Trojan bronze
that pulled my breath with it when it withdrew—
but brothers, by Hera I beg of you:
no soldier's songs when the gluttonous fires
lick at my corpse on our sandy pyre,
no "he died for our cause," no show of spears—
for I will feel those lies, those words that praise
this waste of men and boys and harvest days.

Better for me if this vast field of spears
had been spears of wheat in my Sparta's fields,
and far better for us to outlive our fame,
for mouths are not fed by a hero's name—
better my firm sword arm should only wield
my cup—let it shake as I gray and die,
at peace with men—with gods—with soil and sky.

268

I thought it was beautiful and sad and the weirdest thing that anybody had ever said to me (besides being the first piece of poetry anybody had ever recited to me, that I could remember).

Everybody at their table had fallen silent while he spoke.

Only when he was finished, did I hear my tiny bell ringing. I looked down.

"Molon labe," I whispered. "Come and get them."

That's when I realized I'd said nearly the same thing as the demon, when the possessed body of Lisetta floated towards me in the church. I'd said, "Come and get me." Did anyone else remember? Did anyone else know?

I was born for this, I thought.

Then the boy blinked and shook himself. He looked at me and then down at himself, and he turned in his seat. "What . . . ?" he said.

His family was already forgetting; I could see that in their eyes—all but one little girl, who looked at him thoughtfully. I've noticed more and more that most people don't seem to notice the things that don't fit into their world, at least when it comes to the supernatural bizarreness that happens around us Della Torres.

I put my hand on top of my new case.

"Not tonight," I whispered. "You'll have to wait. But I'm coming. Believe me, I'm coming."

I got home well before anyone else, even after roaming the streets for so long. I went to my room, sat down at my desk, and pulled out my case from my coat pocket again. I ran my fingers carefully over the list of names embossed in the leather.

I thought of the woman of Signora Galeazzo's house. I thought of the vast plain of bodies: had I seen something real, or had it been a vision alone? I kept my fingers on the case while I let my mind dwell for a moment on the horror of it all. I remembered the hours we had spent at Signora Galeazzo's house, watching as Giuliano patiently helped the woman find her way. Had she ever come to the end of her grief and rage? Had anyone ever, the survivors and the ghosts alike?

I didn't want to do this job only to avenge Lisetta or save myself. I wanted to do it for the others, like the woman of Signora Galeazzo's house—and Signora Galeazzo, too. I wanted to help both the quick and the dead. I wasn't quite so afraid of either anymore.

I stepped out on the balcony, hugging myself in the chill air, and looked down into the courtyard, still thinking. The two guys who lived across from us and fixed cars were down on the cobbles again; one of them—as usual—only visible as a pair of legs sticking out from under his tiny, battered Festiva, calling out what he was seeing to the other, who smoked a cigarette steadily and responded to each new remark with, "*Sì*," or, "I thought so."

I leaned against the railing, and the movement caught his eye; he looked up and grinned.

"*Ciao, bella!*" he called. (Was he really saying "Hey, gorgeous" to me?) "How's your grandma? Tell her thanks for the panettone!"

I almost stepped back from the railing and didn't say anything, but then I thought, really, what was there to be scared of? I had just been rejoicing that I wasn't so frightened of people anymore, and boys were people, weren't they? Mostly, anyway?

"I'll tell her," I said. "I helped make it, actually."

He widened his eyes theatrically.

"Did you? Good job!"

"Hey! Stop talking to the women!" shouted his friend from under the car, and he laughed, waved his cigarette at me, and went to squat beside his friend's legs.

I went inside and put my case back in my coat. Then I took it out and moved it to the top drawer of my desk. After that, I decided I should put it in my fabulous Anna Maria purse; then I tried under my pillow, on the shelf above the desk, hidden behind some of the bad romance novels on the bookshelves, in a shoe box under the bed—before returning it to my coat pocket. I decided to ask the others where they kept theirs, then changed my mind and decided to watch and find out for myself.

"Signora Gianna?" I said to the ceiling. She didn't reply. They were probably out doing whatever incorporeal house spirits do; I knew they'd be back. I went into the living room to e-mail Gina the news. I'd mentioned the cases before. I wondered if she would understand what it meant to me. So much had happened, so much she hadn't shared.

I heard the front door to the apartment slam, and Francesca's voice: "I'm home!"

Exactly, I thought.

Acknowledgments

When I was a kid in Palo Alto, most parents believed that without a billion hours of piano lessons, German, and so forth, their children wouldn't get into Harvard. My parents, Ann and Karl Beyer, felt such a crowded childhood would not be healthy for me and my brother. I suspected this, too, so when I was nine, I asked my parents for an hour of solitude after school. They gave it to me, and the stories I made up during that time lie at the root of the stories you read from me now. My parents also took us to Italy for the first time, when I was fourteen.

Sure enough, I didn't go to Harvard. I went to the University of St. Andrews, Scotland, and I would like to thank my professors in the Department of Medieval History, who taught me how to dig deep into the past, and to take time to go to the pub afterwards. In particular, Dr. Crawford, Dr. Magdalino, Dr. Hudson, Dr. MacDougall, thank you.

I would also like to thank my friends Gay Bordin and Michele Konrad, who introduced me properly to Italy, through the dinner table, the family—and the snowboard, naturally.

My brother, Jon, has listened to, and read, my stories from

the beginning. My stepdaughter, Rain, kept me in touch with my readership. Jed Hartman sent me to WisCon to learn my trade. Sarah Prineas and Jenn Reese demanded to know when I would finish the rewrite; Sarah helped steer me down the tricky road to publication with advice and faith. Millard Knepper taught me truths about heroism while caring for my dying mother.

Nancy Flowers taught me to write. The members of Smoky Wizard Bacon—Brendan Day, Carrie Ferguson, David Englestad, David Gallay, and Kelly Janda—tore the manuscript apart and put it back together again. Because of the trouble these doughty writers took, what you read is far better (and far scarier). Karen Meisner and I shared a couch through a long winter, working on our novels and comparing socks. Her firm belief in me propelled me forward. Robert Kent has always known I could do it. Folks who attended my WisCon readings listened to bits of the book *four times* before it was sold, and laughed every time, bless you all.

The women of Art Chocolate, Cathy Couture, Jane Washburn, Kim Long-Ewing, Stacie Arellano, Rhea Ewing, and Rio Mayoleth, and the Dobrá Goddesses, Beth Hoover, Lisa Fiala, Adrien and Hilary Joyner, Laura O'Hadley Allen, and Maggie McKeown Jakubczak, carried me through many ups and downs, offering their support and chocolate (sometimes the same thing). Caitlin Blasdell helped me prepare the manuscript for submission, and then ran off with it to New York, watching over it during the difficult journey books make, until at last she put it in the hands of Ruth Katcher. *She* made the book even better, with the help of the magnificent team at Egmont, including Bonnie Cutler, managing editor, and copy editor Susan Jeffers and proofreader Joan Giurdanella, from whom no error was safe. Caitlin also made sure that my mother got to hold an advance copy of this book in her hands before she died, for which I will always be grateful.

Professor Richard Martin from the Classics Department at Stanford University made sure that the demon and Uncle Matteo spouted the correct Greek; Margo Keeley lent a helping hand.

My husband, Wolfgang Lochner, always reminded me that when I put my work first, everything else falls into place— including time together. Thanks, pardner.

All of this began with my mother and father, who gave me life, pen and paper, and *time*.

Finally, dear reader, thank you for opening this book; as you turn its pages, take a moment to thank those who helped bring it about.

Kat Beyer

March 13, 2012
Deer Island, Oregon

Author's Note

My knowledge of Italy and Milan is only the knowledge of a foreigner and a historian. I have learned that a person needs years
to scratch the surface of a culture, yet, as many would agree,
there's something about Italy. Each time I go there, I seem to
find my senses opened, so that I absorb detail after detail. I
also took a degree in medieval history, so I relish reading Italy's
ancient chronicles as much as her modern newspapers. I have
tried to give a faithful, if very individual, portrait of a city, a
people, and the history of both. I suppose I could pretend any
mistakes are Mia's, but—no, they are my own.

There is a candle shop in the neighborhood where my Della
Torres live. It's called Candele Mum, and I recommend a visit.
I'm pretty sure you can breathe on the candles there, though
the proprietors might ask you what you're doing. There is also
a thriving *Famiglia Della Torre*, with a website and everything.
Don't bug them about demons or my errant, imaginary cadet
branch, please.

Regarding the fate of the Milanese Jews in World War II: I
do not know if any of the several hundred Jews deported from

Milan, starting in 1943, were sent to Lublin/Majdanek. The timing is right, as are the nationalities in the camp population. Since many people are so familiar with the name *Auschwitz* that it has lost some of its power to appall, I thought I should remind my readers that there were other camps, with equally horrific conditions. Besides, not everyone knows that Italian Jews were taken away, along with so many others.

In my research I also came across stories I was not taught in high school, about the Jewish resistance in the camps. I think we are wrong when we focus only on human suffering, and treat human triumph as the story of one or two rare individuals. Whole groups resisted in the camps, just as whole groups of Italian Gentiles resisted the deportation of their Jewish neighbors.

Having said that, I chose to leave the story of the woman of Signora Galeazzo's house sad and unresolved for a reason: we *must not* forget.

He pulled an old, leather-bound book out of a pile on the shop table. It wasn't a notebook, but a printed tome with thick pages and detailed engravings. I was still thinking about Bernardo, but as he paged through it, I found myself trying to make out the illustrations.

"Everywhere you walk around the city, you can see signs in shops that look like ours," he said, pointing to the shopwindow, where the gilded letters read CANDELERIA DELLA TORRE, DAL 1733.

"Now, in our case, we have been on this spot, in this shop, since 1733. Sometimes we've closed our doors for a while, because of a plague or an invasion or some other nuisance, but we've always had a shop here. On the other hand, some restaurants, they claim to be far older than they are. Even universities do that! But the point is, all those centuries seem to matter to people. They want to feel connected to the past, and older things just seem holier, stronger. Maybe that's why we learn to respect our elders.

"A man came to me a while back wanting to study with me," Giuliano continued. "He called himself a witch and claimed he came from a long line of Italian witches.

"Now, there are some who really do come from such a family. You have met one."

He waited, and after a moment, I heard a voice saying in my head, "I untie knots, and I tie them." I thought of a woman's stern face, and of stepping outside the candle shop, over and over, with some object in my hand, as she and I struggled to find a way to protect me from my demon.

I said, "Signora Negroponte."

"Yes."

"And you, yourself, come from such a family, with a long tradition in a dangerous, occult profession. But this young man, he didn't come from any such tradition, and he wanted the ancient ways to be his own.

"I am rambling like this for a reason, *carina*. The funny part about that young man, who said he came from a long line of witches? *He had power.* He had a real gift. He didn't need fifty ancestors who'd done the same thing over and over to be good at what he was doing.

"You have plenty of ancestors who have been doing the same thing over and over, and that's good; we've had a chance to get rid of some of the things that don't work. We need the notes we take, we need the centuries behind us. It's a good thing. What I am trying to say is that it is not the only thing, do you understand?"

I nodded, and he went on. "The ritual we use to open the Second Door is a newer ritual. Do you remember what G. Della Torre called it?"

I'd written it down; I could see it in my handwriting, on the page.

"The song of something," I hazarded. "The song of the gate of . . ."

"Yes. *Il canto della porta d'Orchoë*—the song of the gate of Uruk. It uses words from a much more ancient text. I do not know where G. found it, because it has only recently been found on some clay tablets and translated. He died long before those books were published."

I knew when he said "recently" he could mean anytime in the last couple hundred years; I'd even started to think that way myself.

"The text he uses is a song sung by a goddess, a great goddess, while she stands at the gates of the Land of the Dead.

"Signora Negroponte spoke to you of the gods of place, the laws of the house, and the laws of the road," he said. I couldn't tell if it was a question.

"Yes," I said. "Everyone can use the roads, no matter if they are good or evil, demon or saint or angel. . . ."

I didn't mean to wax poetic, but Giuliano smiled with approval.

"Yes," he prompted.

"But to enter a house," I went on, "you must be invited in. And you are under the protection of the roof, even if it is a roof where you are giving silver for food, or a bed, or for anything, really. You are under the wings of your host."

"Yes."

He waited. I'd gotten used to this over the last few months. Neither he nor his grandson ever liked to do my thinking for me. I suppose I should have been grateful, but it always made a place behind my eyebrows ache.

"So . . . we have to be invited into the Strozzi house."

He nodded.

"But haven't they already given their permission, because Signora Strozzi said it was okay to build the balcony?"

He nodded again.

"So . . . we have to ask someone else?"

Another nod.

"A spirit," I said, more to myself now, thinking hard, no longer looking at him to see if he agreed. "A spirit. Not the demon we are after, I am guessing. Someone else who lives there. A member of the family? Probably."

I looked up at him. He was smiling.

"Do we know who we have to ask for permission?"

He shook his head.

"Oh," I said, meeting his eyes. "That makes it complicated," I said.

He nodded, grinning like a boy up to no good.

You love *this job!* I thought, suddenly enlightened. *You love it with all your heart. The study, the danger, helping others, all of it.*

I grinned back.

"So," Nonno went on. "We are using very ancient words, which people once believed were spoken to, and by, a powerful goddess. We know it has worked once before, because G. succeeded in subduing the demon of the palace. But the song of the gate is just the first part: it is a song of descent into the underworld. We are going outside of our ordinary time and place. It is the only way to reach this demon of place."

"We go to another place to reach the demon of place? No

offense, but this is getting weird," I told him.

Giuliano laughed.

"It always does," he said. "That's the way it is."

I thought of the smell of stagnant water in my mind the night Tommaso Strozzi had dropped by, the night I had seen the candle go out. I shivered suddenly, thinking about Lisetta Maria Umberti's face, so still in death. Was the underworld where she had gone?

I shivered. As much as I wanted to learn this job, I felt afraid down to my bones.

"Nonno," I said.

"Yes?" he asked.

"I'm glad I got to help with the Second Door. But I'm too young for this. I'm not ready to go with you."

Nonno laughed.

"Don't be ridiculous," he said brusquely. "In any other age, you would already be a wife and mother—or you would have taken the veil—or you would have already stood your vigil for a witch."

He looked hard at me.

"Of course, you cannot conduct the ritual. Of course, it's a risk to bring you. You might make a mistake. But too young . . . ? No, that is no excuse."

I was still thinking about Nonno's words when I climbed into bed that night. A wife and mother? At sixteen? A witch, a nun? It was so hard to imagine.

"He's quite right," Signora Gianna agreed, speaking over

my head in the dark.

"You are certainly old enough," said Gravel. (I still had no idea what his real name was.)

"Not that you know anything about it," Signora Gianna told him.

"Oh, don't I?" Gravel riposted. I started laughing.

"You guys know I have a big day tomorrow, right?" I asked.

"You do, don't you?" said Gravel, speaking to me directly for the first time.

"Yes," I answered, fascinated, sitting up in bed.

"Opening a Second Door, I hear," he continued, in his deep, rough voice.

"Yes," I said again.

"They're going about it the right way," said Signora Gianna with what sounded like professional interest. "Research, precedents."

"Thank you," I said. "We're not missing anything, are we?"

Signora Gianna and Gravel both laughed.

"There's always something missing," said Signora Gianna. "You do the best you can with what you know."

"But you would tell us, if you knew something, right?" I asked, suddenly full of hope. "You would mention it to me?"

"I would, if I remembered to," she said kindly.

"Which wouldn't be very likely," Gravel put in, less kindly.

"Hush," snapped Signora Gianna. "You are ridiculous. My memory is not what it once was, true," she went on. "And I cannot see all I would want to see, with the case you are working on. There's a great deal that I have no way of finding out."

"I hoped . . ." I began.

"I know," she said. "But you will have to do it without my help," she finished wryly. "Go to sleep, young one." I did, which would have surprised me if I'd been awake to notice.

The next night, we gathered for a rather solemn dinner, with what I was starting to think of as the usual crew for a big job: Nonno Giuliano, of course; Uncle Matteo, Emilio, Francesco, and Anna Maria.

Nonna Laura made *trofie al pesto*, a dish from the Ligurian coast that reminded me somewhat of gnocchi. She roasted chicken and pigeons, and served fresh fava beans in olive oil for a *contorno,* followed by a salad of baby greens, then cheese and fruit.

"A simple meal, before a big job," she explained. "It will sustain you, but it shouldn't be too hard on your stomachs."

"Yes, none of this should taste too bad coming back up," Francesco told me cheerfully.

I looked down at my plate, then back up at him.

"Really?" I asked faintly.

"Behave yourself," Nonna told him sharply. But she did not look at him when she said it, and both she and Francesca seemed unusually quiet. Égide squeezed Francesca's hand where it rested on the table.

At the end of the meal, Égide said, "Why don't I make the coffee, Nonna? Go sit."

She accepted his offer gratefully. Francesca stayed behind

to do the dishes; her brother stood beside her at the sink, drying and teasing her, snapping his towel at her. I wiped down the table and watched them, thinking what they must have been like as kids together. It seemed like Emilio was trying to comfort her.

I ferried the coffee to the *soggiorno*, handing the first cups to Nonna and Nonno, sitting beside each other on the couch, holding hands, fingers tightly interlaced. Nonno kept her hand in his even when he opened a notebook. Emilio came in and sat down on the arm of the couch, cupping his coffee in both hands; I heard Francesca and Égide finishing up in the kitchen.

"We will be using an invocation called the *canto della porta d'Orchoë*," Giuliano said, nodding at me. "This is the same entry spell that G. Della Torre used in the account Anna Maria and Mia found. I will also bring Nonno Francesco's spell in case the *canto* does not work, but I believe it will. It's a straightforward enough recital, and then we fit the key in the lock. We may not be welcomed in, precisely, but we should be allowed to enter. Emilio will wait with his candle ready in case anyone comes out at us right away."

He paused and met his grandson's eye, then looked around at the rest of us.

"Once inside, we do not know what we will find. Keep together. Keep to the patterns of exorcism you know. Keep your senses wide open. We may have to wait to do an exorcism; we must see what we find. Is it understood?"

My cousins nodded, and so did I. Uncle Matteo got up with

a grunt and went out on the balcony to light a cigarillo. Emilio moved to a chair and leaned back, running a hand through his curls. Anna Maria asked, "Can I see what's on?" and got a nod from Nonna.

She settled on a Roberto Benigni film that was halfway through. I wasn't the only one who kept glancing at the clock. The second hand ticked round and round, but the minute and hour hands seemed to stay in the same place. Then, somehow, they moved, and it was midnight.

The doorbell rang and Anna Maria jumped up. Nobody else seemed surprised that we might be having visitors. Then Anna Maria opened the door, smiled, and said, *"Buona sera,"* letting in an older man who seemed familiar, and a younger man who looked very much like him: Bernardo.

He glanced down at me once, smiling slightly. At least this time, he got to see me dressed entirely in black. I looked good, I thought, though not as stunning as Emilio and Anna Maria.

The older man kissed Nonno and Uncle Matteo on both cheeks, and I understood that he was Rinaldo Tedesco, Bernardo's father.

Bernardo and his father were dressed in ordinary clothes. Bernardo wore a dark shirt and a smooth chocolate-brown leather jacket. Standing calmly beside his father, listening to the small talk of the older men, he looked even more beautiful than I remembered.

Then we were all rising, and I was touching my shaking fingers to my breast pocket to make sure I had my case, and following Anna Maria down into the courtyard, where we crowded into her father's Fiat. Everyone else was riding a *motorino* tonight: even Giuliano had one. He took Emilio on his; Bernardo took Francesco; Signore Tedesco rode alone, talking on a cell phone, his tight scarf unfurling over his shoulder as we followed him out under the archway and into the Via Fiori Oscuri. The drive to the Via Vincenzo Monti didn't take long. I watched the streetlights flash over Signore Tedesco's back as he leaned and dodged from street to street.

"Why is everyone but us on *motorini*?" I asked Uncle Matteo and Anna Maria.

Uncle Matteo grunted, eyes on the road.

Anna Maria said, "So we can scatter faster if we have to. Papa is bringing us like this because we get to stay behind and do a bit of—information management—if anything happens."

"Oh," I said, worried I would be expected to help out with that. I was afraid all I could do was stand there if the police showed up. It hadn't even occurred to me that they might. Or was that what she meant by "if anything happens"?

We parked in the courtyard belonging to the Intesa Sanpaolo. All the BMWs had gone home to wherever BMWs live; there was only a lone Mercedes, grand and forlorn, close to the door of the bank. The Strozzi apartment building rose up before us in the dark. The balcony and the door were faintly lit by the streetlights. No lamp shone in the windows of the Strozzi apartment.

Nonno had decided earlier we would leave the scaffolding

up for an easier climb tonight. Francesco started up first. Emilio stood apart, speaking in a low voice with Uncle Matteo while Bernardo and his father waited. Then I saw Bernardo head out to the street. Uncle Matteo faded into the shadow of the courtyard with Signore Tedesco.

"Mia," whispered Francesco, and I saw him gesturing to me. I started climbing, looking over my shoulder one more time. I saw Bernardo standing near the bank, looking back at me.

I felt my body freeze with embarrassment. It didn't matter that he'd seen me climb this a hundred times. My foot slipped and I felt a firm hand on my calf.

"Take it slowly," said Giuliano. "But go."

I remembered myself and pulled myself off the scaffolding and onto the balcony, feeling it creak under my weight.

Nonno took his time, and Anna Maria came last. Emilio remained on the ground, looking up.

"I believe this is the lock our ancestor used for the door to the palace," Giuliano whispered solemnly.

"Er, no—it isn't," I whispered back, before I could stop myself. Three pairs of eyes widened toward me in the dark. "I went ahead in the notes. It got blown to bits by another demon, a couple of years later."

Giuliano blinked. I heard a smothered snort, probably from Anna Maria.

"Oh! Oh, well. It's got strong wards, anyway," he said, and chuckled.

He took the key from his pocket. It was so small it would

have slipped through the floorboards if he had dropped it. Thankfully, he didn't.

I hadn't thought about it when Emilio had fitted the lock, but I found that now I wanted a big, ponderous lock, with a large, clanking piece of iron for a key. I wanted a lock that would keep in the dead.

I wanted it even more when Nonno began to recite the transliterated Akkadian poem, the words soft, then crunchy, then sonorous by turns: the chant of a goddess as she stood before the portals of the Land of the Dead. Earlier, I'd seen the translation.

> *Gatekeeper, ho, open thy gate!*
> *Open thy gate that I may enter!*
> *If thou openest not the gate to let me enter,*
> *I will break the door, I will wrench the lock,*
> *I will smash the doorposts, I will force the doors.*
> *I will bring up the dead to eat the living.*
> *And the dead will outnumber the living.*

I shivered, staring at the plain wooden door with its iron fittings and silver nails, the tiny silver lock beneath a battered brass knob, and just for a moment I felt farther from home than I ever had in my life. Then Giuliano reached forward, fitting the key in the lock while he went on reciting the commands of the ancient Queen of Heaven.

He turned the key, put his hand to the doorknob, and opened the Second Door.